ETERNAL

In the dark, Glen seemed even more familiar to Fia. The gait of his walk. The rhythm of his breathing. When they passed a red maple tree growing against the side of the walk, his hand brushed the sleeve of her jacket.

She tried to breathe slowly, deeply, as she walked beside him. She'd only had the one pint, but now that she was on her feet, outside, she felt a little off-kilter. Overly warm. Slightly disoriented. It made no sense to desire him, but she knew the sensation entirely too well and it was dangerous. Dangerous for her. More dangerous for him.

He smelled like her Ian . . .

His hand brushed her arm again and this time she knew he had done it on purpose. He was feeling it, too.

Against her will, that familiar tease curled low in her groin. Tendrils of desire. Her blood quickened. *Blood . . .*

Books by V.K. Forrest

ETERNAL

UNDYING

IMMORTAL

Published by Kensington Publishing Corporation

ETERNAL

V.K. FORREST

ZEBRA BOOKS
Kensington Publishing Corp.
http://www.kensingtonbooks.com

ZEBRA BOOKS are published by

Kensington Publishing Corp.
119 West 40th Street
New York, NY 10018

All Kensington titles, imprints, and distributed lines are available at special quantity discounts for bulk purchases for sales promotion, premiums, fund-raising, educational, or institutional use.

Special book excerpts or customized printings can also be created to fit specific needs. For details, write or phone the office of the Kensington Special Sales Manager: Attn.: Special Sales Department. Kensington Publishing Corp., 119 West 40th Street, New York, NY 10018. Phone: 1-800-221-2647.

Zebra and the Z logo Reg. U.S. Pat. & TM Off.

ISBN-13: 978-0-8217-8099-2
ISBN-10: 0-8217-8099-9

First Kensington Books Trade Paperback Printing: December 2007
First Zebra Books Mass-Market Paperback Printing: September 2009

10 9 8 7 6 5 4 3 2 1

Printed in the United States of America

Chapter 1

They walked in single file, heads bowed in the silent, velvety darkness. Twelve hooded figures, one purpose. Down the long, narrow hallway and into the gathering room they proceeded, the magnitude of their responsibility as heavy on each man and woman's cloaked shoulders as the ancient daggers they carried.

At times, she felt an aching separation that could not be breached between her and the others, but on this special night, she was one of them. Tonight, all acknowledged that she was a member of this sept . . . this clan that had existed since the beginning. Fifteen hundred years they had walked the earth side by side, apart from mortals and more powerful. Knowledge and immortality that, she knew, came at a terrible price.

As the twelve judges entered the room, candles hissed in a black oak chandelier and then ignited abruptly, casting light across the deeply scarred table that had come centuries ago from the green land that mortals called Eire. Macabre shadows of the tall hooded figures fell against the recesses of the four wainscoted walls. Near the door, the ship's bell clanged hollowly, sounding of its own accord, and she felt an inner thrill remembering how, long ago, the illusions had seemed so wondrous and magical.

As she moved to her appointed place at the judgment table, she felt a slight breeze off the bay. No matter that there were no windows in this sealed room, her senses were so keen that, even half a mile from the inlet, she smelled the tang of the salt air. She heard the sand fleas' endless digging and a hermit crab's footfalls in his moonlight stroll. And there was the scent of blood carried on the wind. Always, always the scent of blood.

The hooded council members gathered around the table, and she looked down at its marred surface, each scar as familiar as those she bore on her own immortal flesh. Instinctively, she tightened her hand on the hilt of the silver dagger tucked inside the sleeve of her cloak.

"*Caraidean*, we gather tonight in solemn accordance with the laws established by this sept . . ."

The chieftain uttered the words of the sacred ritual. As always, he spoke in the old tongue, their native Gaelic, his gravelly voice crackling in the night air. With each ancient word, the circle seemed to grow smaller, the lives of those who gathered more tightly woven, until the energy in the room crackled and a faint blue light arced between them.

He chronicled, by rote, the establishment of the sept in the fifth century of recorded time. Those were the days when Rome was in decay and the great tribes of Ireland and Scotland struggled with old and new ways, battling for their faith. Christianity was on the ascent, but not without violence. It was a time when the sept developed a taste for power and for blood.

Then came the *mallachd*.

They were all damned by God for their refusal to reject their pagan gods, for their refusal to accept St. Patrick's message of the new faith. They were cursed for the blood of mankind they spilled.

With all the skill of a trained Shakespearean actor, the chieftain continued his time-honored speech. He reminded the council members of the vow taken only a short time ago. Only three centuries ago, a blink in the past. He warned of the nearly unbearable weight of the decision the High Council would make tonight.

She listened carefully as a human name was formally brought to the table of judgment, the sole reason for the gathering. Another voice quietly spoke. Specific details of the charges against the accused were given.

Stark. Cruel. Gruesome.

There was no doubt in her mind this human was a pestilence beyond redemption, one known as a serial killer to this generation, but she listened to every word. Carefully, she processed the information, refusing to allow her emotions to rule. There was a time for questions, but few were asked. Those around the table already knew of this man's heinous crimes. They had read the humans' newspapers. Watched CNN. The accused was clever, very, very clever and had evaded arrest for years, but it was his own private thoughts that had betrayed him to the sept.

Despite the evidence, the conclusion was not foregone; the pendulum could yet swing either way. Here in this place, there could be no measure of doubt. These who had been judged most severely by God Himself held compassion in their hearts that humans could not fathom. They possessed the bleak understanding that suffering did not end with death, and so they decided his fate slowly, deliberately, almost sadly.

The chieftain called for the *aonta*.

One by one, each member voted. Blade down, flat against the table was a nay—not enough proof to convict. Point down, knife tip thrust into wood was a yea. Guilty. Death to the forenamed.

She watched as an unearthly calm settled over the shadowed chamber and, one by one, the hooded figures cast their ballots. To her surprise, there was dissension. One member was not convinced of the human's guilt.

She was last to vote, the youngest and newest of the council, but she did not hesitate. She grasped the hilt of the sacred dagger entrusted to her for this life cycle, and thrust it, point down.

The decision was final. The human would die.

She was the first to throw back the black hood of her cloak, the white gold of her Milesian signet ring sparkling in the candlelight. A rich, guttural cry erupted from deep inside her throat as she bared her canines. . . .

The cell phone on the nightstand beside Fia's bed rang, startling her. She blinked as she lifted her head from the pillow and glanced at the digital clock, the numerals silky red in the stygian darkness.

Her last hours were hazy in her mind. She must have fallen asleep.

She sat up, throwing her feet over the side of the bed; one stiletto heel caught the sheet.

She hadn't even taken off her boots?

Out of habit, she wiped her mouth with the back of her hand before flipping open the phone and bringing it to her ear. "Special Agent Kahill."

"Christ-a-mighty, Kahill, don't you ever sleep? Just once I'd like to hear that husky voice, a little disoriented, drowsy, maybe. All playful. Sexy."

She pressed the palm of her hand to her forehead, feeling hungover, even though she'd not imbibed alcohol. "What do you want, Sedowski?"

"What does any man want? True love, of course. That's all I'm looking for."

"And your teeth? Will you be looking for them when I knock them out and they're spread all over the conference room?" Her tone was a warning, laced with just enough humor to keep the exchange light between them.

The night-shift supervisor chuckled. "Just sweet nuthins to me, Kahill." Then his voice changed and he was the old-school FBI agent she had admired since joining the Philadelphia Field Office nine years before. "Listen, I'd love to talk dirty with you, but I got a homicide needs your attention. Over in Lansdowne."

"Lansdowne?" She walked into the bathroom and turned on the cold water at the sink. She didn't need a light to know she looked like crap. "What? Some guy catch his wife cheating on him and strangle her with her pantyhose?"

"Got no details, Kahill. Only that the vic had her throat slashed, and an address."

"Give it to me."

Sedowski knew better than to bite on that one. Unlike some of the men in her office, he knew where the line was between light banter and sexual harassment. Besides, he was married to a pleasingly plump woman named Ann, who made him potato dumplings on Sunday afternoons and still adored him, despite his protruding abdomen and receding hairline. Fia admired the intimacy Sedowski shared with his wife; maybe she was even jealous of it.

He read the address to her and she committed it to memory. Tossing the phone onto her bed, she splashed water on her face and walked back into the bedroom.

She glanced at the clock again. She hadn't been home long. Couldn't have been asleep more than half an hour.

She perched on the edge of a chair in the corner and grasped the heel of one knee-high black boot. She gave it a hard tug. With a groan, it released and the supple leather slid off her foot. She yanked on the other boot and dropped it on the floor. Next came the black thigh highs. Not fishnet; she was classier than that. Sheer black argyle.

She rolled them off and tossed them into the clothes hamper, then wiggled out of the black leather skirt and bustier and walked naked into the bathroom, still in the dark. She made sure there was steam rolling over the glass shower stall door before she stepped in.

A few minutes later, wrapped in a towel, Fia folded the skirt and bustier and crammed them into the back of her closet behind her suits. She rarely invited anyone into her apartment, and never into her bedroom, but these were trappings best concealed from the light of day.

Trying not to think about where she had been tonight, what she had done, Fia chose a dark navy suit from a dry-cleaning bag. She grabbed a blue sleeveless shell, donning the clothes quickly over a black bra and panties.

She was out of her apartment by 4:45 A.M. Too bad she didn't drink coffee. She probably could have used a cup.

Less than an hour later she was at the scene in the suburb of Philadelphia, red and blue flashing lights marking the location of the crime. She displayed her credentials, *X Files* style, the way she and her brothers used to, playing cops and robbers under the eaves of their attic.

"Special Agent Kahill," she told a uniformed cop. He was nice looking. Young. A little scared. She wondered if this was his first messy homicide.

He glanced up at her and even in the bleak light of the flood lamps, running on noisy generators, she could tell he found her attractive. She was used to it. She saw that gleam of lust in most men's eyes. What she also saw was intimidation. People tended to become uncomfortable pretty quickly when confronted with a six-foot-tall redhead with no-nonsense eyes. It used to bother her, but over the years she'd resigned herself to it. Besides, it was handy with thugs. Or men, in general.

"Your investigating officer?" she asked as she glanced away, already taking in the scene.

The narrow, normally unlit alley was framed by the brick walls of two buildings. It looked like any other in Philly, or any city in the United States: a dumpster, some trash, a few used condoms, and some broken bottles. She smelled cat piss, and three-day-old potato skins. Typical and yet not typical. This alley also had a young blond woman, sprawled dead not fifteen feet from the street.

Fia felt, at once, as if she'd been here before. As

if she had seen these very same walls, these same shadows, and the body, unnaturally twisted on the damp pavement.

Caught off guard, she tried to inhale through her mouth, exhaling through her nose, blocking out the smells, reining in her thoughts. Her job was not about weird flashes of déjà vu or uncanny feelings. It was about facts and evidence, and she needed to focus and get to work. The ME's van was here and the police would want the body out of the alley before citizens hit the streets, headed for work. Early-morning joggers were already out, gawking on the other side of the street.

"Lieutenant Sutton's in charge, ma'am." Flustered, the uniform stepped back and pointed to a trench-coat hunkered down over the body.

Fia brushed by him. She had her "FBI Special Agent" game face on, practiced for years in the mirror. It kept her safe. Kept the men around her safe. Usually . . .

"Lieutenant Sutton? Special Agent Kahill, FBI." The badge in its leather case again. Fia squatted beside the suit in the shadows over the lifeless body.

The victim was half nude, her black miniskirt pushed up around her waist, her silver metallic tank top ripped down the middle to expose small, round breasts. No bra. High heels were missing from her bare feet, but nearby. There was a halo of blood. A lot of blood.

It wasn't just a murder; it was a sexual assault, too. The front of her thong panties had been shoved aside and Fia could still detect the pungent scent of semen. She could *smell* the terror of the last moments of life on the victim's absent breath.

"I'm from the Philadelphia Field Office. I'm go-

ing to need my own photos, if you don't mind," Fia
told the officer in charge, without looking at him.

"Special Agent Kahill, thank you for coming."
The lieutenant glanced over to meet Fia's gaze,
still squatting.

He was a *she.* Forty, maybe, honey hair, shoulder–
length bob.

"Time of death?" Fia glanced down again at the
victim. She appeared to be in her late twenties. Nice
clothes, good haircut, no roots showing in her plat-
inum blond hair. Expensive lingerie. She was edu-
cated, a professional; a CPA, attorney, maybe.

"ME just took a liver temp, but he can only give
a range until he gets her into the morgue." The
lieutenant continued to study the body. "Happened
between one and two this morning. A barback called
it in at three-fifteen. He was tossing out trash, closing up for the night. We've got bars on both sides
here, upscale. She was in one or the other, I'm sure.
We'll have to wait until tonight to ask around, see
if the regulars saw her.

Fia shifted her weight, inching to the left, taking
care not to step in the blood, already dark and con-
gealing. She tried to keep breathing through her
mouth, tried to ignore the fresh, heady scent.
"Throat's obviously been slashed. I don't suppose
he left the weapon behind?"

"My guys are walking the block, digging through
the garbage, but you know he took it with him.
Makes a nice souvenir, *the bastard.*"

Lieutenant Sutton stood and Fia did the same.
Both women sighed.

The crime was certainly hideous. Shocking. But
this type of homicide took place in cities all over
the United States every night of the week. The FBI

wasn't called in by local police forces for random killings. There was a reason why Sutton had called them and down deep in the pit of her stomach, Fia knew why. She cleared her throat. "So, what's unusual about this one, Lieutenant? What can the FBI do for the Lansdowne police?"

The cop had to look up to meet Fia's gaze. "This homicide appears to be overly brutal. Blood everywhere; on the ground, splattered on the walls. Bruising on her arms suggests she was beaten before she was raped. This guy either hated this woman, or hates every woman."

Fia nodded, focusing on Sutton's words, trying to ignore the weird tingling in her fingertips. She *had* been here before. There was something hauntingly familiar about the crime. No, about the man who had committed it? . . .

"But see, the thing is"—the lieutenant looked down at the pavement, scuffing one sensible brown loafer, and then she looked up again—"I think he's done this before."

Again, the creepy vibes washed over Fia. They made her slightly sick to her stomach, but again she suppressed them. "Where? When?" She kept her tone professional.

"A couple blocks from here, if I recall correctly. I was still driving a squad car. I wasn't called to the scene, but I remember the guys talking about it later. It had to have been fifteen, maybe sixteen years ago. We never made an arrest."

The year flashed in neon in Fia's head. She'd been a student at Temple. Barhopped most nights of the week. Prowled this same street. Maybe that was why it seemed so familiar.

"Let me have a quick look here before your ME

gets her out. Can you put together a jacket for me?" Fia said. "I'll read it, present the information to my boss and get back to you once I know if we can help out."

"That's all I'm asking for, Agent Kahill."

At that moment, a city paramedic walked past them. "Excuse me," Fia asked. "Could I get a pair of disposables?"

"Sure." He tugged a pair of blue gloves from his back pocket. "No problem."

As Fia reached out, the white gold of her signet ring picked up the light from a spot lamp and the reflection from the precious metal caught the young man directly in the eye.

The paramedic blinked, startled, stepped back, and then walked away.

Smart move, Fia thought as she slipped her hand into a glove.

"What is this? The Special Agent Kahill all-request hot line?"

"Sir?" Fia was barely in Ed Jarrell's office before he was grumbling at her.

Jarrell was the Philadelphia Field Office ASAC, assistant special agent in charge. He had held one of the two ASAC positions as long as Fia had been at the Philadelphia office on Arch Street. He'd been in that chair at least five years before then, maybe longer. For all Fia knew, the office had been built around him.

Jarrell was an okay guy. Most of the agents didn't think he had much of a sense of humor, but Fia thought he was pretty funny. Usually when he wasn't trying to be, like now. He wasn't a bad boss.

She'd seen men and women better suited to be a
supervisor, but she'd certainly seen worse. The thing
that annoyed her most about him was that he always seemed irritated when a new case came in, as
if the violent crimes and dope sales taking place
on the streets around them were somehow getting
in the way of his paperwork.

"Door." He pointed.

Fia lifted her polished black Cole Haan boot and
pushed the door shut behind her with her heel.

"I just got a call from Senator Malley's office in
D.C. You know Malley? Ways and Means. Senator
Big Fish from the little Delaware pond."

Fia slid her hands into her pants pockets, having absolutely no clue where this conversation was
going, but it was often that way with Jarrell until the
very last second. "Yes, sir. I grew up in Delaware,"
she said carefully. "I think he was first elected in the
early seventies." She saw no reason to tell him they
were related.

Jarrell glanced over the top edge of his black,
military-style horn-rimmed glasses. "There's been a
homicide in Kent County and the senator has specifically requested that you be assigned to the case."

Fia's first impulse was to say "Me?" and tap her
chest like some teenaged dope, but she managed
to keep her hands securely in her pockets. "Delaware
is in Baltimore's jurisdiction. Sometimes they get
touchy about this sort of thing."

"Well, duh," he intoned. "Tell me about it."

Fia tried hard not to smile as she thought about
the office joke that ASAC stood for Asshole Special
Agent in Charge.

Jarrell reached for a blue file under two red ones.
He had some kind of system with the colored files

known only to him, his secretary, and God. "I have a call in to Baltimore, but the Senator's office tells us jump, we all ask how high."

"Yes, sir."

"Stay a few nights if you need to. Get a pay chit."

"Yes, sir." Fia pressed her lips together. "I've got some prelims on that case I was sent on this morning in Lansdowne—"

"Let it sit or pass it on to someone else." He opened the blue file and then glanced across his desk, in search of something. Spotting a small note pad, he ripped the top page off and offered it to her. He was already looking at the file again.

Fia accepted the sheet of paper and read the address. A chill rippled through her as she read it again, thinking her eyes were playing tricks on her. She had, after all, been up all night.

"This . . . this says the homicide took place in the post office in Clare Point."

"Yup." He scribbled something in the file, not really paying attention.

"I . . . I grew up in Clare Point, sir."

"Yup."

She started to speak again, but stopped when he frowned at her. "Look, Kahill. I don't like it any better than you do, but when Senator Malley's office calls—"

"I know," she interrupted. "How high?" She pulled open the door and walked out of the office. Bobby McCathal dead?

It was impossible.

Literally.

Chapter 2

The cell phone on the car seat beside her rang, but Fia didn't pick it up. The little screen identified the caller as *máthair*. It was the fifth call from her mother in the last two hours. One of her brothers had also called, as had her uncle. She hadn't even known Uncle Sean *had* her number; he probably hadn't, until her mother *gave* it to him.

The phone stopped ringing, was quiet for a moment, then chirped accusingly, signaling that *yet another* message had been left. The screen flashed. Seven messages. "Fine," she muttered. "Perfect."

Fia downshifted hard, engine-braking the BMW down the exit ramp off Route 1 before stomping on the gas pedal out of the curve. She had decided it would be better that she not speak to her mother, *or* her uncle, or anyone from Clare Point until she saw the crime scene. Her first loyalty had to be to the Bureau. She knew some family members wouldn't understand, but if she was going to find out what happened to Bobby McCathal, she had to be an FBI agent first, Kahill sept member second. She had to follow investigative protocol, and that meant not allowing her mother to cloud her thinking with any doomsday proclamations, or her uncle with his arm-chair Discovery Channel police procedures.

As Fia left the interstate behind, the terrain changed quickly from soy beans, corn, and sorghum to pine and hardwood forest. The road surface morphed from pale cement to shiny blacktop, then crumbling blacktop as the woods crept closer until it surrounded her. She flew past a state sign marking the west boundary of the Clare Point Wildlife Preserve. The needle on the speedometer slipped up over eighty-five. Littering in the preserve was a three-hundred-dollar fine. Speeding was practically a Kahill birthright.

Fia turned up the air-conditioning in the car and pushed her sunglasses back up her nose. Shadows from the trees fell across her windshield; patterns of light and dark danced on the glass. It was the last week of August. Central Delaware was still hot as hell, but at least the humidity was not ungodly high. The tourist season was *almost* over. Most of the students had gone back to college or school or begun sports training so there would be few visitors on a Wednesday. The fewer the better.

She followed the winding road, wondering what could have happened to Bobby McCathal. She needed to get to the bottom of this quickly, but absolutely nothing was coming to her. Possibilities flitted through her mind, but she was having a difficult time focusing as she fought that familiar feeling of inadequacy that was always part of returning home.

What was wrong with her? She was thirty-five years old, well respected in her field, and yet she allowed these people to make her feel like a child. As if she wasn't good enough, as if nothing she did would quite meet their approval. "Sweet Mary," she breathed softly.

The woods opened up, the road widened, and Fia passed the hand-carved wooden sign, embellished with a shamrock and a cattail, welcoming visitors to Clare Point. The state road fed directly onto Main Street, which ran west to east, straight down to the bay. Both sides of the street were lined with Victorian houses, pink—*Sorry, Aunt Leah, salmon*—baby blue, pale yellow, their gingerbread molding painted in contrasting pastels of peach, teal, and lavender. The colors were silly, like a bag of Jelly Bellys spilled on carpet. But the tourists, especially the blue-haired ladies, marveled at the authentic turn-of-the century houses. The hometown atmosphere they helped to create brought in ninety-five percent of the town's annual income in three short months.

There were no parking meters in front of the Clare Point post office; it was a friendly town that welcomed visitors . . . well, at least from Memorial Day to Labor Day. The post office was the only stone building on the street. Built in the thirties, with gray sandstone slabs hauled south in pickup trucks from Pennsylvania, it had originally been a bank. It was an auspicious building, solid, formidable, secure. From its WPA "historical building" cornerstone, to its ever-present American flag flying overhead, it had always seemed like a safe place to Fia. As an old woman, she had even spent a night here during Hurricane Hazel.

Where had that protection been last night when Bobby needed it?

Uncle Sean's blue police cruiser was the only vehicle parked in front of the building. She pulled the parking brake, grabbed her cell phone and digital camera, and climbed out of the car, tucking the items into her suit jacket pockets. Yellow crime-scene tape danced in the bay breeze, blocking the stone steps leading to the double doors. She wondered where the tape had come from. They hadn't needed crime-scene tape in Clare Point since its invention.

Glancing up, Fia saw Anna Ross and her sister, Peigi, both in their mid-sixties, at the far end of the sidewalk, talking quietly. She turned away quickly, not wanting to catch their eye. When they spotted Fia, they hurried toward her, calling her name, but she ducked under the tape and made it up the steps ahead of them. Inside the post office, she swung around, closing and locking the doors behind her. She pulled down the old-fashioned shade.

"How long it take to drive here?" Sean Kahill still had a slight Irish brogue, even after all these centuries.

Fia turned around. The question caught her off guard. It just seemed, well . . . bizarre, under the circumstances. But her Uncle Sean had always been that way. He'd never been very good at focusing.

"I'm sorry it took me so long." Less than five minutes in town and she was already apologizing. "I had to stop by my place. Grab some clothes and get someone to feed my cat." She pulled off her dark sunglasses and tucked them into her breast pocket. As she walked toward him, the heels of her boots clicked crisply against the polished stone floor, and echoed off the walls of the lobby.

She could smell the blood in the building. *Taste* it.

And smoke was there too, with a putrid, undeniable undercurrent. She swallowed hard. Of course, she had known. But still . . . she hadn't been prepared. How *did* one prepare for the stench of burnt flesh?

She met her uncle's gaze. Sean Kahill was a tall man, like all the other Kahills, probably six–five in his prime, now with a slight paunch. In his early sixties, he had salt-and-pepper hair he kept cut short, military style. His dark blue uniform, with short sleeves and a shiny gold badge, was slightly rumpled.

"Tell me what the hell happened here, Uncle Sean." Fia already had had enough small talk. "And let's keep this strictly business. Strictly police protocol."

There were no signs of a fire in the lobby. No sign of any disturbance whatsoever. The center island, with its REGISTERED, RETURN RECEIPT REQUESTED stickers and HOLD MY MAIL slips, was neat and orderly. All the cheap black plastic pens attached to their metal chains were in their appropriate holders and free priority-rate envelopes of different sizes were stacked neatly on the counter. "How could this have happened?" she murmured. "How could Bobby—"

Fee, ye musn't—

It took her a second to register that she had heard him telepathically, rather than audibly. Nonetheless, his tone made the hair on her forearms bristle.

There was a sound of male footsteps. Someone else was in the building. One of her uncle's patrolmen?

Her uncle cut his eyes to his right. Fia breathed deep. She could smell him. A *human*! A stranger.

She saw him walk through the door from the back of the lobby. She rapidly made eye contact with her uncle again. *Who?*

Her mental telepathy was rusty. She rarely used it, even when she was in town. It just didn't seem . . . *appropriate* in the twenty-first century.

"Special Agent Duncan," Sean Kahill announced in a strained tone. "This is my niece I told ye about, so I did."

It was the face more than the name that knocked Fia mentally off-balance. She felt, for a moment, as if she were free-falling.

He had classic good looks: high cheekbones, a patrician nose, and sensual lips. His sandy blond hair was no longer shoulder length, yet it was a color she had not forgotten. Could not. But it was those green eyes of his that pierced her heart. Her mind. And every bit of hatred she could muster.

Even in the charcoal gray tailored suit, he could have walked right out of the sixteenth-century Highlands.

Fia mentally caught herself in her downward spiral and yanked herself upward. She struggled to make herself heard in her uncle's head. Centuries of survival instinct kicked in. In a situation like this, appearance was everything. *Special Agent Duncan? Uncle Sean, what are you talking about? Who is this? Why does he look so much like—*

"Some . . . mix-up, I think. Something about jurisdiction," Sean said in an odd, vaguely official-sounding voice. *Ah, now, I'm sorry, my colleen. Don't know why he looks so much like him. But I tried to warn ye he was here. Called the number yer mother gave me.*

"Special Agent Kahill, Philadelphia Field Office." Trying to rapidly process on multiple levels, Fia offered her hand to the stranger. She couldn't tear her gaze from his face. Couldn't quite catch her breath.

Ian, she thought, a sob of emotion rising in her throat.

No, of course not. She choked it down. *That was ridiculous. Ian had been dead for centuries.*

She regrouped, refocused. *Uncle Sean, this isn't safe. This man can't be here. He puts us all at risk.*

"Special Agent Kahill." The one who also called himself Duncan shook her hand firmly. "Chief Kahill was just telling me that you were coming." He released her hand, bristling. His tone was curt, challenging. "I'm sorry you had to drive so far for nothing. I understand your concern due to your relationship to the deceased, and to the chief here, but Baltimore's jurisdiction—"

She cut in. "I was sent by the Philadelphia Field Office to investigate this crime scene, Special Agent Duncan." Her tone was even crisper than his. She needed to send him on his way as quickly as possible.

"*Baltimore* has jurisdiction." He repeated it as if he thought she was too stupid to understand the first time.

It was Ian's voice, and yet not quite his voice. The Highland burr was gone. In its place was an authoritative American antagonism.

"I'm pretty clear on the jurisdictional lines," she responded. She was back on her game now, knew she could think her way through this.

Did you call the wrong phone number, Uncle Sean? Does Uncle Bill know this ass is here? Uncle Bill's office called my office and spoke with my boss directly. "The mistake must have been made in your office." Fia never broke eye contact with the agent. She gave him her best condescending smile. "I guess you better call in, see where the snafu in _your_ office was. Arrangements were made before I left Philadelphia. I believe it was a special request through Senator Malley's office."

Ah, now, I didn't know what to do. Who to call. Her uncle's thoughts were shaky. Emotional. _Gair said it couldn't be handled from inside. Not with Bobby dead in the post office. A federal building and all. Gair said we'd have to take our chances._ Sean pressed the heel of his hand to his barrel chest. _Jezus, I got heartburn._

Special Agent Duncan hadn't moved. He just stood there, frowning. She didn't blame him for being PO'd. Had the tables been turned, she'd have been as mad as hell to have him walking in on _her_ crime scene. But no one was getting any slack from her, not today, not ever.

She turned her full attention to her uncle, making an event of removing a small notepad and pen from her pocket. The other agent flipped open his cell and walked away.

"Let's start at the beginning, Chief Kahill," Fia said. _Just answer the questions I say aloud, with verbal responses, Uncle Sean._ "Who found the body?"

I . . . I'll try. "One of my officers. His . . . Bobby's wife called in 'bout six this morning. Said Bobby called her around seven last night saying he was going to work late. But he never arrived home." _You know Bobby. He likes to diddle Mary Dill, Tuesday nights. They have a regular arrangement. Only he never made it there, either. I called and checked._ "So I sent Patrolman Mahon Kahill over."

"After the call came in at the station at 6 A.M.,

you sent Patrolman Kahill directly to the post office?"

"To check on Bobby, that I did." *Had no idea. Thought maybe the fool had gotten drunk, just fallen asleep or some nonsense. Missed his date with Mary.*

Again, Fia heard the emotion in her uncle's thoughts.

Had . . . had I known, I'd never have sent the kid. I didn't know what to do, I didn't. Where to even start looking for the head.

Looking for the head?

She gripped her pen. She could hear the Baltimore agent talking on his cell, his voice sharp. But he was still close enough to monitor her and Uncle Sean's conversation if he wanted to and she had to be careful.

Looking for the head? She couldn't shake the thought.

She'd forgotten how challenging it could be to have a conversation with or for the benefit of a human, while carrying on a mental conversation with another vampire.

"And . . . and what did Patrolman Kahill tell you he discovered when he came looking for the deceased? I assume he radioed in," she said. *Of course, Bobby had to have been decapitated. It was the only way to kill a vampire. But his head was* missing? *How had that information not been conveyed through her office? And where was Bobby's head?*

"Ye want to see where it happened, do ye?" Sean pointed beyond the lobby, toward the back. *I didn't know what else to do, Fee. Didn't even know where to start. His wife was so upset. Mary, too. Hardest visits I've had to make in four hundred years.*

"We can go have a look," Fia agreed. "But I'll still need your full statement. I can get it later, though, back at the station." She glanced in the direction of the open door. "In the back room?"

"Right through here. Back door into the alley was unlocked, it was, so anyone could have gotten in. Not that locks—"

Be careful what you say, Uncle Sean. The human is listening, Fia warned.

". . . Not that locks mean much. Not these days, they don't," Sean bumbled.

"You're not serious," the Baltimore agent barked into his phone.

Fia glanced over her shoulder at the Ian imposter as she followed her uncle into the large, open mail-sorting room. She halted as all at once the smell of burnt human flesh filled her nostrils and the meaning hit her again. Bobby was *really* dead. Her stomach did a somersault. *Oh, Bobby . . .*

There was a large charred spot on the floor. Blackened goo still puddled haphazardly, blood, tendons, sinew, muscle, and ligaments melted, burnt, and gluey. A gelatin of what had probably been paunch fat had bubbled on the floor and pooled into a translucent smudge.

"We didn't know whether we should clean that up, we didn't," her uncle apologized.

Fia patted his arm, thinking old men shouldn't have to deal with this. She let her gaze drift over the scattered ashes that had obviously been paper. Envelopes. Newspapers. Mail . . . She could smell the accelerant, gasoline probably.

You're sure the head isn't here somewhere? She moved a piece of charred paper with the toe of her boot.

I'm sure. Not the head or the feet.

She stared at him. "His feet are missing? Sweet God—" The words were out of her mouth before she realized she was speaking out loud in response to something Sean had said silently. Glancing over her shoulder in the direction of Agent Duncan's voice, she just hoped he wasn't paying too close attention. She pulled her camera out of her pocket and flipped the power switch on.

I understand the head, Uncle Sean, but why the feet?

I can't say, Fee.

"So the body was discovered by Patrolman Kahill minus the head and feet, with no sign of either in the vicinity," she said aloud, again refocusing.

"I got all my available men out looking for the body parts or any blood trail. Pictures, I have, back at the station. Knew ye'd want to see just what things looked like before Bobby . . . before we removed the body," Sean said.

Mahon's got one those fancy digital cameras, he does. Shows the pictures right on the computer. Didn't think they should go to the drugstore. I never liked how those pictures came out of that machine anyway. Our faces are always kind of hazy. Why do ye think that is, Fee? Imprints of a man's soul?

I don't know why, Uncle Sean!

She didn't mean to snap at him, but the hurt look on his face shamed her. *I'm sorry*, she thought. *I'm as upset as you are. Let's just get through this, OK, Uncle Sean?* "I'd still like to take some of my own photographs, if you don't mind," she said aloud.

She turned slowly, surveying the entire room. It was only twenty-five by thirty feet. Eight-foot tiled ceiling and pale government-green walls that appeared to have been painted recently. Everything as neat as a pin, just as in the lobby . . . except for the obvious.

Fia heard Duncan snap his cell phone shut out front and footsteps followed as he approached, their echo booming in her head. She clicked the shutter, barely bothering to look at the viewing screen on the camera.

Click, click, click. She took photographs of the charred, gory spot on the floor. The ashes of the mail. Other than an overturned mail cart, and a stool Bobby could have been sitting on, very little else looked disturbed.

She looked up and, spotting a few drops of blood spray on the ceiling tile, she pointed the camera lens and clicked again. She expected more blood. *Remembered more . . .*

"Looks like we're stuck with each other, Special Agent Kahill." Duncan walked through the doorway, sounding as if he was trying to speak through clenched teeth. "My SAC talked to your SAC and decided this would be a *bipartisan* investigation."

Great, Fia thought. She'd been afraid of that. *Uncle Bill's office was probably able to request her without riling any suspicions, but she guessed the senator wasn't willing to put up a fight when the Baltimore office screamed "No fair!" He had his own causes to protect.* She continued to take photos, not looking at Duncan.

"The accelerant was probably gasoline. Easy to obtain without suspicion. Easy to carry. Mail was used to build the fire." He walked over to stand beside her, sliding his hands into his pants pockets. He sounded as if he was narrating one of her uncle's favorite police-procedural TV shows. "An amateur. The fire wasn't hot enough to burn much more than the skin and some fat. You want to completely burn up a body, the fire's got to be a hell of a lot hotter than this one was." He glanced overhead, then at Sean. "Fire alarm go off, Chief?"

Sean shook his head. "Battery's probably dead, it is. Bobby didn't get up on ladders, lest he absolutely had to, bein' the big man that he was."

Duncan frowned. "We'll check for fingerprints on the smoke detector, see if the batteries were taken out."

"Uh, have to get some more print powder before we lift any more prints. We're out."

"You've got to be kidding me." Duncan looked at Fia, but she didn't respond.

"We don't lift many fingerprints around here, Agent Duncan."

He exhaled. "And I don't suppose there was a burglar-alarm system?"

"Never needed one," Sean answered.

Fia pressed her lips together. Everything Duncan had said, a rookie just out of the academy would have been able to deduce. So far, she wasn't impressed. "No gas can found?" she asked her uncle. "Not in here, not in the alley?"

He shook his head, reaching for his handkerchief in his back pocket. *No, but I once saw this case on that* Cold Case Files *where this guy—*

She snapped another photo. *Please, Uncle Sean . . .*

"Perp brought it with him; he meant to start a fire," she intoned, silencing the camera. She tried to take in the entire scene, attempting to concentrate on the crime and not her uncle's rambling and not the man standing beside her, who was as close to a ghost as she had ever seen.

"Maybe there was something here the killer

wanted, or didn't want to leave in the post office,"
she continued, nodding in the direction of the canvas mail cart lying on its side. "Perp wasn't expecting the postmaster to be working late. Came in,
surprised him. Maybe Bobby was sitting on that stool,
back to the rear door. Perp figured he had to kill
Bobby so there'd be no witness."

"Maybe. Of course, the cash is missing, too, bank
bag and all," Duncan one-upped her.

Fia glanced up at her uncle. They hadn't gotten
that far in her questioning, but she didn't like surprises. Not this guy springing them on her. "Could
be motive," she agreed. "But *decapitation*? Setting
the body on fire? Talk about overkill to steal a bank
bag that couldn't have had more than a couple
hundred dollars in it. And why take the head and
the feet? And how the hell did he cut them off?"
Her last words were as much for her own benefit as
his.

"Perp was probably strung out on PCP. I've worked
some pretty gruesome murders where—"

"I have, too, Special Agent Duncan." She looked
him in the eye. "But this is my first with *stolen body
parts*. Yours?"

He seemed unable to tear his gaze from hers for
a second, then looked away. "Yeah."

She'd gotten him on that one.

He freed his hands from his pockets, walking
around to the other side of the black, bloody soot
ring that marked where Bobby's body had lain.
"There's no point in speculating why the body parts
were taken. Not until we have all the evidence."

It was easy for him to say. He didn't understand
what the decapitation meant to one of them.

"You say you have photographs at the station,

Chief?" Fia looked up at her uncle, who was beginning to pace now. "I imagine Special Agent Duncan would like to see them."

"Actually, I was able to get here in time to see
the body before it was removed."

Fia glared at Sean who was wiping his forehead
with his handkerchief. It was her turn to grit her
teeth. *You've got to tell me these things, Uncle Sean. I
feel like I'm coming in way behind.*

"I see." It sounded so lame. She cleared her throat.
"Then why don't we go to the station, so *I* can have
a look at the photos." She looked to Duncan. "It's
going to take us a full day to process this scene the
way we're going to want it processed, and we are
going to need that print powder. The chief can put
in an order as soon as we get to the station." She
looked to Sean. "The back door is locked now, cor-
rect?"

"'Course, Fee, what kind of fool do ye think—"
Sean cut off the last of his sentence, tucking the
handkerchief back into his pocket.

She shifted her gaze to Duncan, slipping her
camera into her pocket. What a mess. How was she
going to do this? Investigate Bobby's murder and
keep Special Agent Duncan out of the town's business? She couldn't believe Uncle Bill had let the
Baltimore office send an agent. But maybe Gair
was right. Maybe because this was a federal building, they wouldn't be able to keep the murder under
wraps.

Fia looked to her new so-called partner. "Care
to go back to the station with me, Special Agent
Duncan?"

"We drove over in my car." Sean gestured in the
direction of the front door.

He drove two and half blocks? Fia almost laughed aloud, though it really wasn't that funny. Sean didn't like to expend any more energy than absolutely necessary, except when it came to lifting a pint of ale.

"He left his in the station parking lot," Sean continued to ramble. *Drives an unmarked Crown Vic. Nice car. V8 engine. How come you don't get a Bureau car, Fee? Came in your own, didn't you? I could hear the Beemer engine. Runnin' a little rough, she is?"*

Fia turned away from her uncle, blinking to block his thoughts. If she wasn't careful, she'd find herself wrapped up in a mental conversation involving maintenance schedules of BMWs built before 1998. Something he'd learned on the Speed Channel.

"I think I'll walk," Duncan said. "Care to join me, Special Agent Kahill?" He waited.

Apparently, he wasn't going to give her a chance to speak with her uncle alone. Not yet, at least. She exhaled and started for the front lobby. "Meet you there, Chief."

Sean followed them outside, locking the front doors behind them. At the bottom of the steps, Fia ducked under the yellow tape and turned right on the sidewalk. A car passed. A cousin waved. She didn't wave back.

"Pretty weird. So many of you related in this town." Duncan glanced in the direction of the passing car as he caught up with her. "Lot of Kahills to keep track of."

She stepped off the curb and started across the street without looking either way. She didn't have to look. She could easily hear the cars two blocks over. "My family's been here for a long time, Special

Agent Duncan. We have a big family." She shrugged. "So a lot of us have the same name."

The redhead made it somehow seem simpler than Glen sensed it was. Not that he was fortunate enough to be one of those agents with a sixth sense. But something was a little odd here; he just couldn't put his finger on it.

Maybe it was merely his imagination. His irritation. When he called his SAC back in Baltimore, Krackhow had made no bones about the fact that Special Agent Kahill would not be removed from the case. It was out of his hands, he had brusquely told Glen. The order came as a result of a request out of Senator Malley's office. Case closed. If Glen wanted out, Krackhow would send over another agent.

Of course Glen didn't want out. A decapitation in a federal building? Missing body parts? It was the kind of case most agents dreamed of their entire careers. Certainly more exciting than the identity-theft unit he'd been working in. But it still pissed him off that the redhead would be assigned to the case, out of her jurisdiction, just because somebody knew someone who knew someone else in Senator Buttinksky's office. The Bureau his father had grown up in had been that way, àla J. Edgar, but this one wasn't supposed to be. Things were supposed to have changed. Like bureaucracy ever really changed. . . .

He had to hurry to keep up with her. Those long legs of hers covered a lot of real estate with each step. He couldn't deny that she was one of the most strikingly beautiful women he had ever seen. She sure didn't look like most G-men. Besides having a bombshell figure, she had that dark red hair that no way came out of a bottle. Her skin was pale, like many redheads, but so flawless it was like porcelain, with the tiniest sprinkling of freckles across the bridge of her perfectly upturned nose. Her full lips seemed naturally red, but her eyes were what really drew him. They were the strangest color, pale blue with flecks of indigo. Eyes a man could lose himself in . . . *if the woman wasn't such a hard-ass*, he reminded himself.

Special Agent Kahill was everything Glen despised in a female FBI agent, in any woman trying too hard to do a job society still saw as a man's. Glen didn't have a problem with female FBI agents, or cops, or even Navy SEALS, for that matter. He knew women who were better shots on the firing range than he was. Women with sharper intellects. What he had a problem with was the chip on the shoulder they always seemed to come with. It wasn't enough for a woman like Fia Kahill to just do her job. She wanted to do it better than he did it, and she wanted to throw it in every man's face. She didn't want to be one of the boys; she wanted to be better than them.

He glanced at her, her face set with determination as she strode down the sidewalk. If they were stuck together on the case, he had to make the best of it.

He slid his hands into his pockets. "When I arrived, the body was just being removed. Chief Kahill said you had a local morgue."

"Uh-huh."

"Said the autopsy would be done here rather than in the state medical examiner's office in Wilmington?"

"If that's what Chief Kahill says." She didn't look at him.

It didn't matter. The minute they'd stepped into the bright August sunlight, she covered those amazing blue eyes of hers with a pair of dark wraparound sunglasses.

"That just seems odd, doesn't it? I would think an autopsy of this nature would go to the state medical examiner."

"I can assure you Dr. Caldwell is fully qualified and licensed to perform the autopsy, Special Agent Duncan."

She was using that curt tone with him again. It was really beginning to annoy him that she didn't look at him when she spoke. "I'm not questioning the doctor's credentials, *Special Agent Kahill.* I'm questioning procedure on a federal case."

They had turned off the main street in town and were now approaching the police station. There were only two cars pulled up in front, his unmarked, and the chief's old cruiser. All the other officers were, no doubt, out combing the streets for a head and a pair of feet right now.

She strode up the steps leading to the front door of the hometown police station that greeted "visitors" with a welcome sign. *How many visitors did a police station get,* he wondered.

"So call the state medical examiner's office and verify it." She pulled open the heavy door as if it was weightless.

Glen had to hold it as it swung back hard. All he could think about as he hurried to catch up with Fia Kahill was how thankful he would be to find this killer, and get the hell away from her and her weird little town.

Chapter 3

"Fia?"

She sat in the worn, gray, government-issue office chair in the rear of the police station. Every police station in America had a bull pen just like this one—wanted posters, a Heimlich maneuver instruction chart, a photo of the officers at last year's annual Punkin' Chunkin', grinning and only slightly drunk, hung crookedly on the wall. There were a couple of desks, some file cabinets, an old copier on a microwave cart, and a coatrack that had seen better days.

She leaned forward, her chin resting on her closed hands, and stared at the eight-by-ten photographs, spread across the ancient gunmetal gray desk.

Hours had passed since she arrived in Clare Point. It seemed like years. Police officers had come and gone in the station, reporting to Sean in subdued voices. Before the shift change, a couple of the men and the lone female patrolman had ventured over to say hello. Everyone had the same information to offer. There was no sign of a severed head or feet, or suspicious persons or activity in the town.

Her gaze moved from one photo to the next. They

were gruesome even to a seasoned agent, but she couldn't stop studying them. She kept shifting her gaze, looking for something certain, something to help her, some sign. She told Duncan she was searching for clues. Told herself the same lie, but really, she was still staring at them out of disbelief.

The heat of the fire had made Bobby's tendons tighten, pulling his arms and legs up into his body. Twisted, on his side, the once big man appeared infantile. Helpless. She shuddered when she saw in her mind an innocent child sleeping, sleeping in flames.

The Kahill sept had come to the New World in search of sanctuary, to escape from those who had committed these outrages against their people. No humans were aware of their presence in Clare Point. Everyone in the town knew that all of their lives depended on keeping the secret of their identity, and so it had been for centuries. No one knew but the family. But what if someone did?

Fee . . .

Sean's voice inside her head startled her. She straightened up in the squeaky office chair, letting her arms fall to her sides. She glanced up. Both Sean and Duncan were standing in front of the desk, looking at her.

"I'm sorry, I was concentrating. What did you say?"

"I sent the midnight and day shifts home; no more overtime today. Most of 'em have been at it twelve hours or more, and the mid-watch has got to be back in four hours."

"Good call," she responded. "Tired cop's as bad as a drunk one. We don't want anything missed."

From the rear of the bull pen came the crackle of the radio, and the evening dispatcher, in her small office, responded to a transmission. From behind the large glass window, neither the officer's words nor the dispatcher's could be heard. Just static and indistinct, disembodied voices.

Sean wiped his forehead with his handkerchief. "I told my boys to keep looking, fer sure, but every dumpster's been picked through. Every alley walked. Mahon even drove out to the old feckin' city dump. He said no one could have been there any time recently, he did. Weeds were too high."

"No sign of the head," she said softly, her gaze falling on the photo directly in front of her again. From the side, where you couldn't see his hands grotesquely bent back towards his forearms, Bobby looked as if he was praying. His legs were all wrong, chubby thighs narrowing down to the knees, then coming to a charred point at the ankles. *What the hell was up with taking his feet?*

"No blood in the alley behind the building, I suppose?" she asked.

"Nope. No blood anywhere. No tire tracks, neither." He glanced at the other agent, who was just standing there. "We were thinking, Glen and I. It's after eight. Maybe go grab a wee bite at the pub?"

So Special Agent Duncan and Uncle Sean were buddies now, were they, on a first name basis? And his name was Glen. "What about fingerprints you collected so far in the post office?"

"Didn't get much. A lot of people go in and out of that post office, they do, Fee."

"But not in and out the back door."

Sean shook his head, folding up his handkerchief. "Couldn't recover any but Bobby's." He hesitated. "So what ye say, eh? Let this go until morning. Get an early start? Go get a bite, now?"

She stood and began to shuffle the photos together. She couldn't imagine eating, but she knew it wasn't food her uncle was thinking of. It was his evening pint. "I didn't know if you just wanted to grab something to go, Special Agent Duncan," she said without looking up. "Go to the hotel. Maybe review a few things. Peggy, the station's administrator, made us reservations at the Lighthouse before she took off for the day."

"I don't know." Glen shrugged. "I could use something to eat. Maybe a beer. Been a hell of a day."

He pulled his suit jacket off the back of a chair and slipped into it. It was warm in the station, even with the air conditioners in the windows running full blast. Fia had taken her jacket off earlier, but she suddenly felt self-conscious. She grabbed her jacket and pulled it on over her thin silk T-shirt. Glen was watching her. She couldn't tell what he was looking at, maybe her boobs, but she didn't think so.

He met her gaze across the desk. "Maybe talk to a few people," he went on. "See if anyone saw anything. Heard anything."

His eyes were green. Of course they were.

This was going to be tricky, trying to solve Bobby's murder with a human hanging around, breathing down her neck, especially one as sharp as he was.

She looked down at the photos in her hand and reached for the manila envelope they had come from. It *was* smart to go to the pub tonight. See what the locals were saying. Under ordinary circumstances, it would have been good investigative work.

Of course, there was no way for him to know that Kahills didn't talk to strangers. Oh, sure, they would give him the appearance of being open and cooperative, just as Sean and his patrolmen were doing. But she knew from past experience that the town would dance a merry jig around him when it came to giving up anything of any real consequence. The federal government might have sent someone to work the case, but the citizens of Clare Point would solve the murder on their own.

"All right," she said slowly, tucking the photos and a growing pile of notes into a file folder. "Easiest thing is to just leave the cars at the hotel and walk over to the pub. Not a lot of parking. It's faster to walk most places in town, anyway." She strode toward the front door, the evidence under her arm. "We'll see you at the Hill, Chief?"

Sean was headed toward the back where his small office was located next to the dispatcher's. He gave a wave over his head as he walked away.

"He's pretty shook up," Glen observed, holding the door open for her. Because she was as tall as he was, he had to reach around her and his sleeve brushed her shoulder.

It took all she had not to flinch. Like most Kahills, she was more sensitive than a human. Her sense of smell, her hearing, her eyesight, even her sense of touch was keener. Some said vampires felt more deeply than humans. More pleasure. More pain.

Fia chastised herself for not beating Glen to the door. She didn't like any special treatment from men, especially other agents. Especially men who looked like her Ian. *The lying, murdering bastard.*

"Clare Point has never had a murder, not since

the town's founding," she said, keeping her voice
flat, unemotional, matter-of-fact. "This place isn't
Baltimore and it sure isn't Philly."

He halted at the bottom of the steps, raising both
hands as if in surrender. "Hey, you're not telling
me anything I don't already know."

It was almost dark and the security lamp, mounted
high on a corner of the building, was just beginning
to glow, casting a yellow, vaporous light over the
sidewalk and the now-gray grass. In the fading light,
the familiar objects in front of the station—the lilac
bushes, the flag pole, the tiger lilies blooming in
the flower bed next to the steps—seemed somehow altered, almost surreal. Maybe it was just the
sight of Ian standing there in a Brooks Brothers suit
in twenty-first century America, or maybe Clare Point
really had been changed forever with Bobby's murder.

Fia kept walking, heading up the sidewalk toward Main Street.

"You want a ride to your car?"

"Nah," she threw back.

"Special Agent Kahill?"

She couldn't ignore him, though she considered
pretending she didn't hear him.

"Agent Kahill," he repeated.

She halted, half turning to look at him.

"You weren't intending on going into the post
office again tonight, were you?" He didn't wait for
her to answer. "Because I don't think *we* should. *We*
need to go back together tomorrow. Have a fresh
look at the scene. Together."

"I'll see you at the hotel in ten," she called, crossing the street.

Damn, she thought, jingling the post office key in her pocket that she'd snitched. *He's good.*

She just hoped not too good.

By the time they walked into the pub together, Uncle Sean was already at the bar and on his second pint. At least. A small chalkboard inside the door informed patrons that the bar mistress was serving her Houndstooth Stout tonight. It was an excellent, heavy brown ale. Fia knew it well. Uncle Sean liked his stout.

Music played from an old jukebox in the far corner of the public room; a rollicking tune from the seventies. An image of Tom Cruise sliding across hardwood floors in his tighty-whities flashed through her head.

The Hill, as it was known in town, was the second oldest continuously operated bar in the United States, right after the White Horse up in Newport. If it hadn't been for the eighteenth-century hurricanes, it would have been the oldest. Originally built down near the water on top of a sand dune by one of Fia's aunts, they had finally surrendered to the elements and rebuilt inland on higher ground. The town had sprung up helter-skelter around the pub, and year round, the public room was the heart of the Kahill sept. No one fought, no one made love, no one bought a new or used truck without word going around inside the Hill.

There wasn't a sign outside announcing the pub's presence on the street and the interior of the Hill wasn't much to look at. Tavia kept it that way to discourage tourists from visiting. There was a proper

Disney World-style pub on the other side of town
called O'Cahall's that had been built just for them.
Still, there were a few humans here tonight. Two
couples, and a middle-aged widower who came, each
year, with his grown children, all of whom spent
August in the town and liked to fool themselves into
thinking they were locals.

The walls of the pub were dark wood wainscoting,
stained by years of spilled ale and smoke. The floor
was planked hardwood, once washed regularly with
sand and seawater, now with some pine product that
always smelled just slightly like toilet bowl cleaner
to Fia. There were heavy wooden booths along two
walls, and a few scattered tables and chairs in the
middle. The bar that ran the length of one wall was
built of wood from the ship that had carried the
Kahills to Clare Point. Stained by salt water, scarred
by years of abuse, and with more than a few worm-
holes, the bar was as much a part of the sept as its
individual members. The long, etched and gilded
mirror reflected the faces of those Fia had known
for centuries. Some she loved, some she hated, but
she was absolutely loyal to every one of them.

"Why don't we grab a table, Special Agent Duncan," she suggested, steering him away from the bar
and her Uncle Sean and his brother Mungo.

She could feel Sean trying to speak to her, but
she ignored him, turning him off in her head.

Duncan followed her toward a table. "This is silly.
Call me Ian."

As the words sank in, she stopped abruptly, spinning around. "What did you say?"

Confusion showed on his face. "I said, this is
silly. Call me Glen."

"Oh." *Where the hell did that come from? God, she was tired.*

Luckily, Shannon bounced up to them at that instant, all boobs and lashes and Pam Anderson hair. In her mid-twenties, she worked nights for Tavia when the tourist season petered out. In the summer, she cooked and served at a large B and B down the street. She wasn't as tall as most women in the town, but was every bit as beautiful, almost in an exotic way. She always wore tight, low-cut T-shirts and blue jeans that looked painted on. Like all vampire women, she exuded a sensuality that even human men could smell in the air.

Shannon ignored Fia, lifting a feathery eyebrow with interest in Duncan. She already knew perfectly well who he was. Shannon was just expressing her pleasure at having gotten a look at his handsome face.

Shannon hadn't known Ian. Had no idea of the resemblance between the two men. But it was just like Shannon to get under Fia's skin, right off the bat. It was the relationship they'd been sharing for years.

Bring us two pints and quit your ogling, Fia shot in Shannon's direction. As an afterthought, realizing she'd not spoken aloud, she showed two fingers.

Both of Shannon's brows shot up this time. *Look at us. Talking like a proper Kahill tonight,* she taunted, tucking an empty tray under her arm.

Fia glared. The girl wasn't as old as most of the others in the sept, but her mental telepathy was good, better than Fia's. She always came through loud and clear. Fia figured Shannon had plenty of time to practice since all she had ever done was bake soda bread, cook lamb stews, wash dishes, and fornicate for the last two hundred and sixty years or so. Shannon sashayed off to the bar.

Glen beat Fia to the table and pulled out a chair for her.

She sat down reluctantly, arms crossed over her chest as she surveyed the room. "It's Fia."

"I know. Pretty name. Unusual."

He'd left his suit jacket behind at the hotel and rolled up the sleeves of his pressed white button-down oxford.

She was still wearing her suit jacket. He looked relaxed, approachable. She looked uptight.

"I ordered you a pint of stout. Around here, we drink whatever Tavia's tapped. She brews on site," Fia said, looking across the table at Glen. "I hope you like heavy brown ale because that's all we have here. You have to go up to O'Cahall's if you want Coors Light."

"I like stout." He looked around the table. "Any menus?"

She pointed to another black chalkboard, this one larger than the brew board and hanging on a chain from a wooden peg on the far end of the bar. *Lamb Stew* had been handwritten and crossed off. Below it read *Fish & Chips* with a small cartoon of a fish drawn beside it, its eye an X. Shannon's idea of being cute, no doubt. "Guess I'll have the fish and chips," he said with a half smile.

She leaned back in her chair, not returning the smile. "Guess you will."

When she had first walked in, she'd purposely put up a mental wall to prevent all the jumbled thoughts of the pub's patrons from slipping into her head. Really, it was more of a curtain than a

wall. Even without listening, she'd been able to
hear the low and high rumbles of the voices the
minute she walked through the door. Seeing no
need to chitchat with the man across the table from
her, she now eased back the curtain. At once, she
felt as if she were being bombarded by heavy ar-
tillery. Everyone in the room except for Shannon
and the sour old Englishman, Victor, was thinking
in Gaelic, but because it had been her first language, she didn't have to translate the words. The
problem was that everyone's thoughts hit her like
storm waves, approaching from a thousand directions.

Poor Bobby.

Poor Mary.

Poor, dear Mary.

Both his wife and his current lover were called
Mary, so Fia didn't know who was thinking of which
woman.

How did this happen, eh?

I knew this was bound to happen.

What are we going to do?

What are we going to do?

What are we going to do?

And then there was an undercurrent of conversation concerning Special Agent Duncan. Everyone in the room except for the tourists, Shannon,
and Victor had known Ian Duncan. For many, he
remained the very icon of evil.

How is it possible, he looks so much like him?

It can't be a good sign.

Why has herself brought him here?

What are we going to do?

What are we going to do?

What are we going to do?

Overwhelmed by the bombardment, Fia had to fight the urge to cover her ears with her hands. Telepathy carried not just words, but the depth of the emotion behind the words. She didn't so much hear them as feel them, and the intensity was overwhelming. She was already tired, and the anger, the confusion, and the very real fear were exhausting her. They were all so afraid . . .

And frightened Kahills were doubly dangerous Kahills.

"Here you go, Sugar."

Shannon drew Fia's attention and the voices faded in her head until they were again a low rumble.

Shannon set Fia's glass on the table, just out of reach. Glen's, however, was personally delivered into his hand with a sway of shapely hips, and pursed red lips. "Dining with us, are you *Special Agent* Duncan?"

If Glen was surprised the chippie knew his name, he didn't act like it. Closing his hand around the bock pint glass, he smiled up at her. "I'm thinking the fish and chips." His voice was teasing, with the slightest hint of flirtation.

Glen Duncan could be charming when he wanted to be, Fia would give him that. But Ian had been the same way.

She had been such a loodar fool.

Fia leaned forward and grabbed her glass. One couldn't help but admire the cream-colored head on the ale. "Married man, Shannon. Move along." *And human. You know better.*

Shannon smiled, not in the least bit dispirited. "Fish and chips, comin' right up." She smiled at him again and sidled away.

"I'm not, you know." Glen raised the glass, almost in toast, and then drank. "Damned decent."

Fia sipped the dark ale, breathing in the heady scent. Tavia's ales didn't smell so much like traditional beer as sweet oak. She'd only have one. She only drank ale, and usually only in this room. "You're not what?" she asked.

"Married."

"No? You?" She set the glass down and slid it forward on the scarred table. Rather than look at him, she watched foam slosh up the sides of her glass. "I just assumed . . ." She lifted one shoulder.

"She's cute. What's her name?"

"Shannon. Shannon Trouble. You want no part of that."

He chuckled. "I'm not interested. Not my type." He took another sip. "And . . . I'm engaged."

She nodded, but didn't respond. She really didn't want him sharing his life with her. She certainly had no intentions of telling him anything personal about herself.

Glad you came, I am, Fee. Uncle Sean's thoughts drifted across the room. *We need ye. The family needs ye.*

Of course I came, she thought.

Sorry about him. *Double sorry, I am. What are the chances the FBI could have sent a man who looked so much like—*

Uncle Sean, don't worry about it. We'll talk tomorrow. Try to enjoy your pint.

Enjoy his pint? How can anyone enjoy a pint after something like this? It was Sean's brother, Mungo, sitting on the barstool next to him.

Ordinarily, it was considered rude to listen in

on thoughts not directed toward you, but in these circumstances it was understandable. From Mungo, she caught a flash of memory of the bloody scene that night back in Ireland. The screams of the horses, the terror of the women as they scattered into dark fields outside the village. The blood and flames that stained the grass black.

"Her name is Stacy. She's a dental hygienist."

Fia was jerked back into the present. "I'm sorry?" She glanced up at Glen and then back at her pint as she reached for it.

"My fiancée." He sipped his beer, watching her carefully. "You?"

She shook her head. Against her better judgment, half smiling. "No. Never been married." *Fifteen hundred years. An old maid by any standard.*

"Two fish and chips," Shannon declared cheerfully, swaying in the direction of their table, both hands high in the air, balancing two small plastic trays. "For you." She plopped a tray down in front of Fia so hard that it rattled. "And you, Sugar."

Each tray held a cone-shaped roll of old-fashioned checkerboard butcher paper, overflowing with battered whitefish and finger-sized russet potatoes deep-fried to a golden brown. Glen smiled up at her as she slid his tray squarely in front of him, brushing her bare forearm against his. "Malt vinegar," Shannon sang as she plucked a bottle from her tiny apron. "Another Houndstooth?"

"Please."

She glanced disdainfully at Fia and turned on the balls of her feet. She knew better than to ask. Fia never drank more than one a night. "Be right back."

"Don't bother asking for ketchup, cocktail sauce or tartar sauce. You can have it 'old style'—plain— or 'new style'—with vinegar," Fia instructed.

Glen shrugged, dribbled vinegar over everything. He slid the bottle towards her, but she shook her head. "You want to talk about the case?" he asked. Just then, his phone, attached to his belt, vibrated. He unclipped it, looked at the screen, and set it on the table, face down.

She stuffed a chip in her mouth. Tavia always made them herself, from real potatoes, never served the frozen kind from a plastic bag. They were the best she'd ever eaten, anywhere, any time. "Maybe we should let the details stew. Not discuss anything until tomorrow."

He nodded, chewing thoughtfully, and a silence fell between them. Fia wasn't particularly hungry, but she ate anyway, knowing she should. Shannon brought Glen another beer, flirted for a minute beside the table, and then headed off to the kitchen from where Tavia's impatient voice could be heard, beckoning her.

The two ate in silence. Glen was halfway through the second pint before he looked up at her across the table. "Look, I don't like this any better than you do. You think it's your case. I know it's mine"—he didn't pause long enough for her to answer—"but my SAC says we're in it together. We might as well make the best of it."

He was right. She knew he was right. Her little silent temper tantrum was unprofessional. It wasn't his fault he looked like Ian. Wasn't his fault the FBI had drawn these particular jurisdictional lines. She needed to be civil, at least until she could figure out how to get him out of Clare Point and off the case. She was already planning on making a call to Malley's office in the morning.

He was still waiting.

She sighed and sat back in her chair. He was offering a truce, and it was up to her to accept it.

"I don't mean to seem bitchy. I'm just preoccupied. Bobby McCathal—"

"You don't need to apologize. I've never investigated the murder of someone I knew, but I can imagine it would be difficult."

His phone vibrated again. Again, he looked at it and then laid it screen down. She guessed it was the fiancée again. The woman was persistent. Twice in half an hour.

"Frankly," he said, pushing his empty tray away, "I suppose that was why I was surprised when the chief said you'd been called in. Guess you know someone in Senator Malley's office, or someone knows you."

She didn't answer that. Instead, she asked him how long he'd been at the Baltimore Field Office, why he was an FBI agent, where he went to college. Fortunately, he picked up the ball and began to tell her about how he'd come to be sitting in this pub with her, investigating a murder on just another Wednesday night.

She smiled inside. He didn't realize how high the alcohol content was in the stout, and she sure wasn't going to tell him. Alcohol always made humans talk. Fia thought about saying something, but decided against it. It wasn't her problem if he had a headache in the morning.

The pub began to fill up with those who had eaten at home and were just coming in for a pint and to see what news there was of Bobby. Shannon brought Glen a third pint. All around her, the voices seemed to swell, growing louder in Fia's head, then quiet, then building, then quiet, again and again, almost in a rhythm. Some people were angry she'd brought the FBI agent into the family pub. Everyone wanted to know how he'd ended up in Clare Point and the explanation, apparently supplied by the chief of police, had to be repeated over and over, until everyone was in the know.

When Glen finished his stout, he rose, excusing himself to go to the men's room. While he was gone, Fia took the opportunity to ask if anyone had seen Dr. Caldwell tonight, but no one had. She was wondering if he had started the autopsy. She almost regretted asking, as she set off a new tangent for all of them to follow. Unfortunately, she couldn't communicate with Dr. Caldwell directly. Although there were a couple of people in the sept who could "talk" over great distances, she didn't have that gift. Even the walls of a room stopped her short.

The small pub had gotten crowded and noisy. It was time to get back to the hotel. She was looking for Shannon and the check when Fia's father walked in. "Fia, your mother was wondering where you were, she was," he said, approaching the table stiffly, his hands stuffed in his pants pockets. He reeked of cigarette smoke. "You should have come by."

She nodded, looking up. He was never stern with her, not even when he was well in his cups, but ever since Ian, he had seemed emotionally distant from her. Even during her teen-year cycles, when she became his child again. She knew she had deeply disappointed him, though he had never actually come out and said it. "I was planning on coming by tomorrow, sometime. I have to be careful." She glanced up to be sure Glen hadn't returned. "I guess you heard I got stuck babysitting this other agent."

"Your mother has extra rooms open now that they've gone home." In her father's world, the tourists were simply *them* or *they*. "You should have come to the house."

He was a big, stocky man with inky dark hair and hooded eyes. He made her feel small. She nodded.

He was quiet for a second and then tapped the table, turning away, sticking his hand back in his pocket. "You should come tomorrow."

She watched him walk through the crowd, wondering how long it had been since they'd had a conversation that didn't involve him telling her something she should or shouldn't be doing. Sighing, she glanced around again, looking for Glen, wondering where he was.

During their meal, he had mentioned how surprised he was that not a single person had approached their table. They wouldn't officially begin their interviews until the following morning, but he had been hoping people would be talking freely to him. The poor soul had no idea. . . .

Still not seeing him, Fia rose. She caught Tavia's eye. The room was getting louder. *Check—I better get him out of here before things get rowdy,* she told Tavia.

I don't know where that worthless colleen is now. Just pay up before you leave town. Better yet, find out who did this to Bobby and your fish and chips are on me. Tavia gave a wave of the bar towel that always seemed to be in her hand and pushed through the kitchen door.

Glen's cell phone vibrated, humming and hopping across the tabletop. Unable to resist, Fia picked it up. The front screen said "Stacy." She didn't answer it, but she took it with her as she got up from the table.

Several people stopped Fia on her way toward the restrooms. Everyone had the same questions concerning Bobby's death. *How was this possible? Who could have done this?* She, of course, had no answers yet and her job kept her from speculating aloud.

As she turned down the dark, narrow hall, she spotted Glen. Shannon had him backed up against the wall near the pay phone, breasts thrust up and forward, practically touching his chin.

"There you are," Fia called. "Your fiancée called again." She waggled the phone.

He looked guilty at once, which had been her intention, though now she didn't know why. Why did she care if he cheated on his fiancée? Of course, if he was going to cheat on Stacy the hygienist, Shannon was not the person to do it with.

"Shannon, Tavia's looking for you," she said lightly, passing them. *You know better. Leave the human alone.*

Shannon didn't move.

"She wants you *now*, Shannon." Fia pushed open the ladies' room door. *Council members are watching,* she warned. "We better head back, Glen," she continued aloud. "I already took care of the check."

When she came out of the bathroom, Glen was still standing next to the phone. As she approached him down the long hall, it struck her how handsome he was. No wonder Shannon was attracted to him.

"You call her back?" She walked past him and he followed.

"Uh, no." Glen glanced down at the phone in

his hand. He didn't know why, but right now Stacy was the furthest thing from his mind. "I'll, uh, call later."

As they wove their way around the tables, through the noisy barroom, Glen got the impression they were being watched. But he knew that was to be expected. Small town. Big city FBI agents. He followed Fia out the door, into the warm, muggy, August air and took a deep breath.

"Wow," he said, drawing his hand across his forehead. Out on the not-quite-level brick sidewalk, he realized just how off-balance he was, though he wasn't entirely sure it was the beer. "Pretty strong brew." He certainly didn't feel drunk, but he didn't sound stone-cold sober either.

Fia surprised him with a laugh. One that was deep. Sensual.

"Tavia's a talented brewer."

He glanced at Fia Kahill as they turned the corner, walking closely side by side on the sidewalk. The moon had risen, but still hung low on the horizon, bathing the treetops on the street in strange yellow light. He knew very well he hadn't had *that* much to drink, but he felt odd. Slightly off.

Fia was as beautiful a woman as he had ever seen. He'd always liked redheads, but there was something different about her. Something tantalizing, that suggested she might be just a little bit dangerous. He hadn't been interested in the brazen waitress beyond listening long enough to see if she had anything to say about Bobby McCathal's death, but this Fia, she was in a completely different league. As much as he might like to deny it, he *was* attracted to her and his attraction was growing by the second. It was the damnedest thing. He'd never reacted to a woman like this, especially not one who irked him the way she did. He liked his women uncomplicated. But there was no denying the tightness in his chest and in his groin.

In the dark, Glen seemed even more familiar to Fia. The gait of his walk. The rhythm of his breathing. When they passed a red maple tree growing against the side of the walk, his hand brushed the sleeve of her jacket.

She tried to breathe slowly, deeply, as she walked beside him. She'd only had the one pint, but now that she was on her feet, outside, she felt a little off-kilter. Overly warm. Slightly disoriented. It made no sense to desire him, but she knew the sensation entirely too well and it was dangerous. Dangerous for her. More dangerous for him.

He smelled like her Ian. . . .

His hand brushed her arm again and this time she knew he had done it on purpose. He was feeling it, too.

Against her will, that familiar tease curled low in her groin. Tendrils of desire. Her blood quickened.

Blood . . .

Chapter 4

They followed the sidewalk up to the 1950s-style motel and Fia muttered something nearly incoherent about getting an early start in the morning. She fumbled for her key in her pocket as she halted at room 104. She knew she needed to get inside quickly. Didn't trust herself with Ian.

Glen.

She jabbed at the doorknob with the key, missed, tried again.

She felt his warm hand close over hers. "I'll get it." His tone was light, mocking.

Ian mocking her from the grave. *Not Ian.*

Despite the three pints of ale he'd consumed, Special Agent Glen Duncan, unlike Fia, had no trouble sliding the key into the lock and turning the doorknob.

Her pulse throbbed, her breath tight in her chest. It had been a long time since a man had made her feel like this.

She reached for the key, moving toward the open door, inadvertently toward him.

The same height as Fia, all he had to do was turn his head slightly, and then his lips were on hers.

She couldn't tell if he had done it of his own will, or had been lured by the age-old spell of the vampire.

His mouth tasted of stout, of the excitement of the unfamiliar, and at the same time, of the smoky past. She felt surrounded, overwhelmed by the scent of his skin and the warmth of his lips.

It took every fiber of self-control for Fia not to grab him by the shoulders, push him into the room and onto the bed.

"Agent Duncan," she heard herself say against his mouth.

It seemed to snap him out of his fugue.

"Agent Kahill." He seemed as surprised by his behavior as she was. He cleared his throat, stepped back and made a beeline for the next door down.

She heard the rattle of his key as she closed her door and set the dead bolt. She leaned against the doorframe. Her blood rushed in her ears as she breathed heavily, her thoughts darting in opposite directions, one after another.

All she would have to do was knock on his door. She knew he would let her in.

She couldn't do it. Wouldn't. Too much at stake.

She tried to think fast.

Pulling her cell phone from her pocket, she made a call she hadn't made in some time. He answered on the second ring. A moment later, she was out of her room, walking down the dark street again. She put one foot in front of the other, putting more distance between herself and the FBI agent with every stride.

Perspiring heavily, she removed her jacket, carrying it over her arm.

She couldn't believe she'd let him kiss her. *Almost* kiss her . . . their mouths had barely touched. *Was she out of her mind?*

The path of the yellow moon led her four blocks through town, directly to Arlan's door. He was waiting for her on his back porch, a four-foot-long creature with a curling tail and slanted gold eyes one moment, a lanky six-foot-tall man the next.

"Heard you were in town," he said lazily, leaning on the bowed porch rail. It needed paint.

"I didn't come to talk." She hurried up the steps.

His arm shot out, grabbed her.

She gave a little grunt of surprise. Her jacket fell as he spun her around, pushing her up against the corner post. The back of her head hit the post, smarting. She took his mouth hungrily. "Just tonight," she warned between kisses.

He bit down gently on her lower lip, then harder. "Just tonight."

"Don't want to talk." She ran her hands over his bare, muscular chest. He was barefoot, just in jeans. He must have jumped in the shower right before she called. He smelled fresh. Comfortable. Safe.

"No talking," he repeated, forcing his knee between her legs.

She moaned, grabbing a handful of his shaggy, dark hair. Nipped at his ear lobe, then his neck . . . just lightly. No blood.

He slid his hand up over her breast and squeezed. She moaned again. He pulled at the high neckline of her blouse. When the silk fabric wouldn't give way, he jerked downward and it tore down the middle, exposing her breasts in a lacy bra.

"Ass," she muttered. "It was a Ralph Laurén."

He grasped one of her legs, above her knee, and

lifted it to wrap around his waist. She pressed her groin to his, grinding against the hard bulge in his jeans. All Kahill males were well-endowed.

He grasped the lacy edge of her bra and pulled back the cup to expose her breast to the humid night air. Her pale nipple hardened at once and she guided his head downward, encouraging him to take it in his mouth.

Arlan had been her lover on and off for hundreds of years. He knew her as well as she knew herself, and knew her body better, perhaps. He'd always had a thing for her, even before Ian; she had never been able to reciprocate those feelings. For that reason, the guilt occasionally got to her and she'd stay away from him for awhile. Sometimes as long as a life cycle. But she always came back to Arlan and he was always waiting for her.

He pushed her bra strap down, covering her breast with his warm hand, massaging her nipple with his thumb. "Inside or here?" he panted in her ear.

She nipped his neck a little deeper this time, feeling his pulse against her lips. He would offer her his blood. He didn't always, but tonight, he would. "Inside," she whispered.

The following morning, Fia met Glen at the breakfast buffet inside the lobby of the Lighthouse Motel. He was already at a table, drinking coffee, eating scrambled eggs and sausage links, when she walked in. She made herself a cup of hot herbal tea, grabbed a plain bagel and sat in the chair across from him.

An elderly couple stood at the breakfast bar arguing over the fat content of a blueberry muffin; the other tables were empty.

"Morning," she said.

He didn't look up over the edge of the newspaper he was reading. "Morning," he said cheerfully.

Cheerful enough that she wondered why she was feeling so awkward and he wasn't. Had he really tried to kiss her last night or had that been a figment of Fia's overactive imagination, spurred by the fact that she couldn't get over how much he looked like Ian?

Or had it happened and he didn't remember? Maybe he didn't hold his liquor well and he really was drunk last night. Or maybe he was just embarrassed and good at covering for himself.

For whatever reason, it didn't appear they were going to have one of those clumsy morning-after conversations, for which she would be eternally grateful. She dunked her teabag in the hot water in the Styrofoam cup in front of her and nibbled on the uncut, untoasted bagel.

Glen finished reading whatever had been holding his attention and folded the newspaper and set it aside. "Sleep okay, Agent Kahill?"

There was something in the tone of his voice now that made her think he *had* tried to kiss her last night, and he remembered it all too well.

"Fine. You, Agent Duncan?"

"Like a baby." He scooped up one last forkful of scrambled eggs and pushed it into his mouth. He wasn't exactly avoiding eye contact, but he wasn't looking at her, either. "You have a plan for this morning?"

"Of course, but you go first." She pulled the teabag out of the water, wrapping it around a spoon.

"No, no. Your hometown, Agent Kahill. Your connections with the senator's office. Go ahead."

She dropped the bagel onto her napkin, instantly annoyed. *Fine. They'd do it her way. Her way was usually better in most situations, anyway.* "While we're waiting on the autopsy report—"

"Which should be interesting," he interjected.

"We take another look at the crime scene, get some additional photos, clear it so the federal building can be reopened, and then we start interviewing anyone who saw the victim the evening of his death and work backwards from there."

He took a drink of coffee from the white mug. "We order a background check on the vic. Have a look at his bank accounts, credit cards, nose around in his personal life."

She worked her jaw, raising her cup to her lips. He'd have to know about Mary . . . Mary his girlfriend, not his wife. Of course, his wife had a steady thing with Joey Hill. Tuesday nights. Had for twenty-five years, at least.

Men and women of the sept remained with their own spouses or partners life cycle after life cycle, but were free to have sex with whomever they pleased . . . so long as he or she was not human. It was the way they had been doing it for centuries and it made everyone's lives less problematic.

This investigation in Clare Point was going to get complicated. It wasn't going to fit into any neat FBI investigative-techniques box. She really needed to get Glen Duncan out of here before he got hurt.

She took another sip of tea, the taste of Arlan's blood still cool and metallic in her mouth.

She had to resist the urge to pat her lips with the napkin.

Arlan had come through when she needed him. No questions asked. Multiple orgasms included. His arms had felt good around her. He was good for her. He thought so. Everyone in the town thought so. So why had it been Ian's face she had seen last night when she closed her eyes?

Or had it been Glen's?

She suppressed a groan. "My plan work for you, Agent Duncan?" She rose from her chair, balling the uneaten bagel up in the napkin. She'd take the tea with her.

They stopped at the waste can at the end of the buffet bar to leave their trash. He was watching her. No . . . staring.

"You okay?" He touched his luscious neck with his fingertip. "Looks like you've got a spot of blood there."

She turned away, headed for the door, resisting the temptation to rub at the mark. She had *told* Arlan to be careful. "Cut myself shaving."

By three o'clock, Fia knew this wasn't going to be an open-and-shut case. By three the following day, the prospects for solving Bobby McCathal's murder within the week were looking dismal. No one had seen or heard anything at the post office that night, and there was still no sign of the decapitated head or severed feet.

Fia and Duncan completed their photographs, and Paddy's Cleaning Service of Clare Point was called in to remove the bloodstains from the floor at the crime scene. Sixty-one-year-old Catherine Kahill, one of two mail carriers in town, agreed to run the post office as soon as it was cleared by the FBI and reopened by the postal service. The two agents then began their interviews.

For the most part, Glen and Fia just stayed out of each other's way, which was fine with her. She did, however, manage to convince him to hold the interviews inside the post office lobby, rather than going door-to-door. She suggested that the police station was too small, too crowded, and they wanted to keep their investigation as separate from local law enforcement as possible. Fia didn't tell Glen that part of her reasoning involved keeping her Uncle Sean out of the fray. He didn't know that the police chief was too loose a cannon for her to trust entirely. The bonus that came with not operating out of the police station was that she didn't have to deal with any of Uncle Sean's armchair *COPS* advice.

The tricky thing was that she didn't want Glen in Kahill family members' houses, either. Everyone was used to behaving in a certain manner in public places; it was the way they had been coexisting with humans since their arrival in the colonies. But inside their homes . . . Fia wasn't so certain they would keep their guards up as well. Besides, with her and Glen both interviewing in the post office lobby, she could keep an eye on him.

Fia's gaze strayed from Anna Ross, whom she was interviewing, to her notepad, where she had made no notes in the last twenty minutes. Anna was going on about how Bobby's dog had barked in the yard. She had not seen Bobby the day of the murder and knew nothing about it, but Fia couldn't get her to budge out of the chair no matter how many times she thanked her for taking time out of her busy day of watching game shows and soaps on her new big-screen TV.

"Some kind of mixed breed," Anna continued. "A dumb mutt, not smart enough to . . ."

Fia glanced at her wristwatch and then her gaze strayed across the room to where Glen was interviewing Anna's sister Peigi. Fia could tell by the look on his face that he was having a difficult time ridding himself of his interviewee as well.

Just as she looked down at her notebook again, out of the corner of her eye, she saw Glen abruptly rise from his chair. Fia got up, looking in the direction he was looking. The back room.

Both sisters, oblivious to the fact that their respective agents were out of their chairs, continued to chatter.

"Agent Duncan?" Fia called out from across the room. He was closer to the rear entrance than she was.

He held up his finger. He was still watching something or someone in the rear of the building.

Suddenly, he took off across the lobby. "Stop, FBI!"

Fia sprinted after him.

There was a crash in the mail room. Something fell. An unidentified object slid across the freshly mopped and sanitized marble floor. By the time Fia made it through the archway, Glen was going out the back door into the alley.

"You! Stop. FBI!" he hollered.

Fia leaped over a box of spilled envelopes. "Agent Duncan, wait!" She burst out the back door, down the steps, through the fluttering strips of freshly acquired yellow police tape the local police had used to block off the building. Glen ran ahead of her, down the alley, toward the street that ran behind the post office. He was chasing a pigtailed teenager.

Fia immediately recognized the girl from the back of her head. *This is getting better by the second.* This young lady was *not* someone in Clare Point the human needed to meet. She was an important woman in the sept, but in a vulnerable place right now, which made them all vulnerable. "Kaleigh," she called. "It's Fia. Stop."

The teen flew around the corner and down the block.

Fia pushed to catch up with Glen, but he had almost half a block start on her. "Duncan," she called. "Slow down. I know her."

He continued at an all-out run.

They crossed the street and Kaleigh zigzagged, cutting through another alley, down the next block. Dogs barked. Pat Hill stopped his pickup in the middle of the street to watch the two FBI agents in suits chase down the teenager in shorts and a tank top. They had picked up a yellow lab, that ran behind them, barking excitedly.

"Duncan, for Pete's sake," Fia hollered. She was fit and a good runner, but she had not packed her running shoes and she was going to be pissed if she broke the heel on her new loafers. "I know where she lives!"

He slowed and Fia caught up. He was panting pretty hard. Fit, but not as fit as Fia. Most humans weren't.

"She was in the post office. In the back," Glen panted, jogging beside her. "I don't know what she was doing, but she took off the minute she realized I saw her."

Fia looked up ahead, shooting thoughts in the

girl's direction. *What are you doing in the post office? What are you doing, running from a federal law enforcement agent?*

If the teen heard Fia, she didn't respond. Kaleigh leaped a line of waist-high azalea bushes, cutting across Victor Simpson's scraggly lawn.

"Damn it, Kaleigh!" Fia called out, skirting two garbage cans turned over on the sidewalk. The lab had caught up and was leaping in front of her, still barking wildly. "Don't make me run another two blocks to your house. Your da will have your hide," she threatened.

The girl, tennis shoes flying, threw a glance over her shoulder. "Fee? That you?"

"How many FBI agents do you think we have in town? Yes, it's me," Fia answered, aloud.

Kaleigh halted on the far side of Simpson's lawn, eyeing Glen suspiciously.

"Get over here!" Fia stopped just short of the hedge, waving her hand, then shooing the dog. *Take a hike, buster, or I'll be having doggy burgers for dinner tonight,* she warned.

The lab tucked his tail between his legs and took off down the sidewalk in the direction he'd come.

Glen pulled up and walked around in a circle, trying to catch his breath.

"Did she take anything?" Fia asked him.

"No, I don't think so. I don't know, but she ran when she saw me."

"You probably just scared her. Let me handle this," she said. Then to Kaleigh, "I said, get over here." She pointed to the grass beside her.

Kaleigh squeezed between two bushes, still considering the male FBI agent warily.

"He's with me," Fia assured her.

"Something of interest to you in the post office, young lady?" Glen demanded.

"Special Agent Duncan, please," Fia said. "This is Kaleigh Kahill."

"Another relative?"

"Distant."

Glen studied the teenager. She glared back.

Please, be careful, Fia warned telepathically. "Kaleigh, do you mind telling us what you were doing in the rear of the post office? Didn't you notice the door was taped off? Surely you knew you didn't belong there."

"I didn't do anything wrong," the redhead flung back. "I was just looking around."

"Do you know something about Mr. McCathal's death?" Glen asked.

"No more than anyone else in town."

Fia brushed her hand against the girl's arm. "You didn't touch anything?"

"No. I just wanted to see if the blood was still there. Meg said her Uncle Mahon said there were gallons of blood. I said she was lying because you don't have *gallons* of blood. Everyone knows that!"

Fia glanced at Glen. He seemed to be relaxing a little. He was obviously pissed off, but she could see that he was beginning to see what this was, and that was nothing more than a nosy teenager being at the wrong place at the wrong time.

"Where's your mom and dad?" Fia asked.

"I don't know. Home, I guess."

Fia looked to Glen. "Why don't I walk her home, speak to her parents. You better get back to the sisters. Officer Hill was the only other person left in the building and those ladies are liable to tag-team him and take him down with their armored purses."

She said it with a straight face and heavily laced with sarcasm. To her surprise, Glen grinned.

She liked being surprised by humans. They didn't do it often.

"Count yourself lucky this time, Miss Kahill," he warned Kaleigh with an accusing finger. "I catch you poking around my crime scene again, I don't care who you're related to, you'll be arrested."

Kaleigh opened her mouth to respond, then, wisely, clamped it shut.

Fia grabbed the teenager and steered her to the sidewalk and toward home. "Give me a couple of minutes, Special Agent Duncan. I'm going to escort Kaleigh home and speak with her parents. You can tell Miss Ross—my Miss Ross—she's free to go. I don't have any more questions for her."

He hesitated, then lifted his hand and headed off in the opposite direction. Fia hustled Kaleigh down the street, waiting until Glen was out of earshot before she spoke.

"What do you think you're doing?" Fia demanded from between clenched teeth. "Didn't you hear me telepathically?"

The girl looked up with bright blue eyes. "No, I *didn't*," she said in the same indignant tone Fia heard from human teenagers. "I'm only ten months old, remember?"

Chapter 5

Fia halted, looking down at Kaleigh. This was always awkward—when sept members of prominence were reborn and had to repeat the first stages of their lives. Had to grow back into the men and women they had once been.

The girl thrust out one hip and planted her hand on it. "The *gift* hasn't come yet," she said, speaking as if Fia was an idiot. "I can't hear you. I can't hear any of your or anyone else's babbling."

Fia grabbed the teen's upper arm none-too-gently and started down the sidewalk again. "You shouldn't speak rudely to your elders."

"If you *recall*, I'm *your* elder."

"Well, I'm on the High Council and you're not, smart-ass."

Kaleigh pulled her arm from Fia's grip. "I don't know what the big deal is. I was just looking around. I wanted to know what happened to Bobby."

"So do the rest of us." Fia glanced at the teen. "And you don't have any idea? No visions?"

"Derek says somebody watched one too many slasher movies and went on a rampage. He's this human boy I met when I was working at the diner. He goes to my school. He's pretty cool."

"You shouldn't be talking to human boys."

"I go to school with them, how can I not talk to them?" Again, *the tone.*

For many years, teenagers were homeschooled in Clare Point, but eventually, with the arrival of the twentieth century and the state's control over education, it had been a General Council decision to allow teens to attend the public school in the neighboring town. Though tricky at times, it was a good way for the newly reborn to assimilate into human society again.

"We're supposed to try to fit in," Kaleigh observed. "Remember?"

"So you've gotten nothing on Bobby? Not even a *feeling?*" Fia asked.

Kaleigh was the sept's wisewoman. She had powerful telepathic abilities and unheralded wisdom which seemed to increase with each life cycle. Unfortunately, because she had only recently been reborn, her gifts had not yet returned. After rebirth, it took most vampires eight to ten years to become adults. It was always a vulnerable time for the sept when Kaleigh began a new life cycle, because they relied on her a great deal to guide them and keep them safe.

"Derek's really cute, too," Kaleigh went on. "He surfs. He keeps saying he's going to teach me." She shrugged. "I don't know when. He has this friend Kyle and he works at a surf shop in Rehoboth Beach. He says he can get me a good deal on a used board. He goes to my school, too. You ever surfed, Fia? Derek says if I go with him, he'll let me use his board. He's been trying all summer to get me to go with him."

Fia looked at her, perplexed. "Go where?"

Kaleigh rolled her eyes. "Not *go* somewhere. Go *with* him. You know, like go out."

"You're fourteen. How old is he?"

"Fifteen," she said, defensively.

"So how can you go on a date? Neither of you can drive."

Kaleigh rolled her eyes again and groaned. "It's not like back in the day when you were this age, Fia. We'd just go out . . . you know, hang out together."

"You mean have sex?" They reached Kaleigh's front yard and Fia lifted the latch on the gate of the white picket fence. "Because you know very well that's forbidden. Nothing has changed. You have to reach twenty-one again, and then only with a consenting sept member."

Kaleigh closed the gate behind them. "I know, I know, because I might lose control, bite somebody, drink their blood, and then he'd be one of us." She rattled off the warning she'd no doubt heard a hundred times. "But does that *really* happen?" she scoffed. "Or is that just one more story you guys tell to scare us?"

"Kaleigh, a year ago, *you* were one of us, warning teenagers of the dangers of sex with humans."

"But I don't remember that." She threw up her hands in exasperation. "All I know is what you guys tell me. Mandy says you're all lying. It's all a big conspiracy."

"What is?"

"The whole story about how we can make one of them into one of us."

"What about Victor? Shannon?"

"Maybe that's all lies, too. To keep us here. Keep us *down*." The teen dropped down on the white-washed step of her front porch. "Guys are really into us, you know. Girls from Clare Point. We have a reputation for not putting out the way human girls do, so I guess that makes us celebrities or something."

Fia glanced away. She really didn't want to get into a conversation about vampire sex with Kaleigh. Not now, not ever, if she could help it. The whole subject made her uncomfortable because she still had her own struggles with it.

But Kaleigh obviously wanted to talk and it was Fia's responsibility as a member of the community to help one of their own through this difficult time. Reluctantly, she sat down beside the teenager on the top step. She removed her sunglasses from her suit jacket pocket and slid them on. The whole thing about vampires not being able to stand the light of day was pretty much a product of Stoker's fiction, but the sun's glare did give her a headache sometimes.

"Kaleigh . . ." Fia attempted to choose her words carefully so as not to extend the conversation any longer than absolutely necessary. "No one is lying to you. Why would we? We've all been through this time and time again. We know how hard it is to be reborn and lose so many memories and abilities, and how dangerous."

"But they're so cute."

Fia looked at Kaleigh, not following.

"The human boys." The girl shrugged slender shoulders. "Different than sept boys. Cuter." She looked at Fia earnestly. "Don't *you* find human men crazy hot? Like . . . almost irresistible?"

Talk about a loaded question.

Fia clasped her hands, threading her fingers, lowering her head. Kaleigh didn't remember Ian, yet. Didn't remember the night that he and his vampire slayers murdered so many Kahills. Didn't understand that it was Fia who had brought them. Fia who had betrayed her own people by loving a human.

One of the hardest things for Fia about being a vampire was that your past never stayed in the past; it had to be retold again and again . . .

"It doesn't matter if we find them attractive, Kaleigh. It's dangerous. For us. For them. We now exist to protect humans; a great responsibility has been placed in our hands."

Kaleigh leaned back on her elbows against the step and stared up at the blue sky. "Where do you think Bobby's head is? And why take his feet?" She looked quizzically at Fia. "Derek said there was this guy in the Midwest back in the fifties who used to kill women and cut their heads off and like, put them on his bedposts and stuff. Do you think the head smelled? I mean, did he spray them with disinfectant or something?"

Fia exhaled, rising from the step, wondering what had made her think she could ever have a serious conversation with Kaleigh in the first place. The girl was like any fourteen-year-old human right now: unable to focus, with irrational priorities. "Stay away from the post office and Special Agent Duncan, and stay away from the humans. I'm warning you."

"And if I don't?"

"Take it from a person who knows from experience. If you don't, you'll be spending the next couple of centuries trying to make up for it."

That night, Fia waited, stretched out fully clothed in the motel room until one A.M. Then she slipped out of the room. As she walked down the center of the vacant street, other adult sept members joined her in her silent march. Heads bowed, they wove single file down the street, around the massive old brick church, to the cemetery behind it. Shrouded in heavy, dark shadows, the above-ground graves and mausoleums looked like stacked dominoes. All of them empty graves, dug over the centuries to facilitate the lie they all lived.

Bobby McCathal would be the first Kahill to be buried in this churchyard who would not rise from the dead on the third day following his death. It was difficult to kill a vampire, almost impossible. The only way to prevent the soul from reentering the body after a fatal injury was to separate the head from the body and destroy the flesh with fire. Some called it God's curse. Others believed it was God's last gift to his outcast children, for so long as they could retain their earthly bodies, there was still a hope of salvation of their souls.

Inside the gates of the graveyard, the group huddled together under a weeping willow tree that had been planted by Fia's grandfather, the sept leader, more than two hundred years ago. Crickets chirped. Rodents scurried in the tall grasses beyond the black iron fence. The waning half-moon hung low in the sky, casting yellow light through the trees of the wildlife preserve beyond the churchyard.

At first, everyone kept their thoughts to themselves, fingers of the moon's shadows playing over their faces. Some prayed, some held hands. Bobby's two Marys wept softly, holding hands, united tonight in their sorrow. Fia wished she had not come, but she had been compelled like all Kahills but the very youngest and oldest of the sept. One by one they joined the group until they were close to two hundred strong. Then the thoughts began to flow and Fia was caught up and swept away in the tide of their fear and sorrow.

My Bobby, my dear, sweet Bobby.

How could such a thing happen? How, I ask ye?

'Tis impossible. This is impossible, isn't it?

My dear Bobby, my dear, sweet son.

The killer couldn't have known what Bobby was.

An accident. A coincidence. So many madmen in the world today.

Couldn't know who we are. . . .

Fia felt bombarded by those around her. Men and women she had laughed with, cried with, loved, hated, for centuries. It wasn't just the words hounding her conscience, it was their emotions. Like her dad, she had never been good with her own feelings or anyone else's, but after Ian, it had become even worse. Harder. It was one of the reasons her career choice in this life cycle suited her so well. FBI agents didn't have to rely on emotions, not when they had investigative techniques, forensic science, and political pull.

How?

Why?

Who could have done this?

Have they found us?

Found us at last?

The proverbial "they". But in this case, the threat was very real. "They" were the vampire slayers. The men the sept had been hiding from on the peaceful shores of America for the last three hundred years.

What if it's worse?

Worse? What could be worse?

One of us.

Hearing the words in her head made Fia shudder. It had been a possibility she had been trying to avoid for two days. Mungo was right. To be killed by one of their own *would* be worse. But she still wasn't convinced by the evidence that this crime, however horrendous, was anything more than the killing she had seen in the alley in Lansdowne the other night. Some sick bastard.

"Please, everyone." Their chieftain, Gair, dressed in plaid shorts and a SURF THE NET T-shirt emblazoned with a surfboard, held his thick, wrinkled hands high in the air. At the age of seventy-three and nearing the end of this life cycle, Fia's grandfather resembled Spencer Tracy—not when he was young, but as he appeared in *Guess Who's Coming to Dinner* and *Inherit the Wind.* The resemblance was so uncanny that in the summer months he was something of a celebrity among the summer visitors.

Fia loved Spencer Tracy. She loved her grandfather more. In all these years, he was one of the few people who she believed had truly forgiven her for her transgression.

"Please," Gair repeated, trying to speak above the voices. "We cannot stay here long. There are still humans among us."

Human police.

Not just police. Visitors. Mary Kay's got a couple at the inn.

Not police. FBI.

That's even worse.

Fia brought him.

She shouldn't have brought him.

There was so much disorder, verbally as well as telepathically, that Fia only caught bits and pieces. She couldn't tell who was speaking or thinking what. What she did know was that her people were frightened. And angry.

"I know you have questions," their chieftain said, lowering his hands. "We all do, but for now, there aren't that many answers." He turned around to face Fia, who had been standing several rows back, trying to remain as inconspicuous as possible. "Fee, have you something to say? Something to comfort us?"

She looked down at her feet, then up again. All eyes were on her. Some supportive, but many accusing. "Um . . . as you know, the FBI has launched a full investigation into Bobby's death."

Shouldn't have 'em here. Should settle the matter ourselves. Find the feckin' bastard who did this ourselves.

She glanced in the direction of Victor Thomas, a cantankerous, grizzled old fisherman who hated Fia, but no more than he hated the rest of them. "Because Bobby worked for the federal government and the crime—"

The murder . . .

"The crime took place," Fia continued, "on federal property, we had no choice in the matter. But Bill . . . Senator Malley was looking out for us. He made sure I was called in, even though Clare Point isn't in my jurisdiction."

"What about the other agent?" a woman demanded. "The human? Why is he here?"

"A minor snag in the bureaucracy. This is his jurisdiction."

"We don't want him here."

It's not safe.

"I don't like him being here any more than you do," Fia assured the crowd. "But I promise you, I'm keeping an eye on him and he should be out of town by tomorrow, the following day at the latest."

"Still no idea who did this, Fee?"

She turned in the direction the voice had come from. "We're doing everything we can, but so far, as Gair said, we have little information."

"Tell us this." Her father stepped forward, his voice grave. "Was it a coincidence, Bobby bein' beheaded, or do we have a bigger problem?"

She knew what he was thinking without reading his thoughts. The same thing they were all thinking. Had Bobby been killed by one of the maniacs the world was so full of these days, just a sick coincidence that he was murdered in the one way that could actually kill him? Had one of their own killed him, a crime that had only been committed three times in all these centuries? Or did a human know Bobby McCathal was a vampire?

Chapter 6

Fia was in her cubicle in the bull pen in the FBI office in Philly by nine-thirty Friday morning. She would have been back earlier, but Glen had insisted on sitting down to breakfast at the motel and reviewing the case before they went their separate ways.

She had thought the meeting a waste of time. Both of them knew exactly what they had, or more importantly, didn't have. Bobby McCathal's body, released this morning, would be buried in the town's cemetery the following day without his head and feet. The body parts had not been located, and there were no leads as to where to look for them or who could have committed the crime. Fia knew that Glen knew that with every twenty-four hours that passed, it was less likely the case would be closed quickly. Often, if a suspect was not immediately apprehended, the murder would be solved not by superior detective work, as on the TV shows Sean Kahill watched, but by the perp telling someone who would tell someone else. The criminals couldn't keep their mouths shut. It was never a matter of *if* they would tell, but how long it would take. Eventually, a lead would get back to the police. Nonetheless, over hot tea and a cold bagel, Fia let Glen talk. They both took copies of the file and the photos and left Clare Point by 7:30 A.M.

Fia slipped out of her suit jacket and threw it over the back of her chair. When she sat down, the chair popped and lurched to one side, nearly throwing her to the floor. "Son of a bitch. Moron!" She got out of the chair, dragging it out of her cubicle and into the one beside her.

"What?" Her fellow agent Jeff Morone glanced up innocently from his computer monitor.

"Get out of it," she threatened.

He chuckled and rose from his seat. Charlie Alston, in the next cubicle over, laughed, but didn't dare show his face.

Fia grabbed the desk chair Jeff had been sitting in and wheeled it around the half wall to her desk, biting back the threats and curses—some literal— on the tip of her tongue. She knew the more she said, the more the agents would laugh and the more likely it would be that they'd play another practical joke on her the next time she left the office. With only four female agents on the floor, the office was like Boy Scout camp; the practical jokes and farting and burping contests never ended.

She plopped back down in her own chair and hit a series of numbers on the phone on her desk, retrieving her messages. Twenty-two calls, but nothing earth-shattering. She listened to each one, making notes, deleting, saving. She'd half hoped she would hear from Lieutenant Sutton on the Lansdowne murder; it had been on her mind on and off all week. She kept going back to the dead woman, splayed in the alley, and the oddity of the familiarity she couldn't shake, but she couldn't identify, either.

Nothing from Sutton. Two messages this morning already from her mother asking why she wouldn't be returning to Clare Point for Bobby's official funeral. Despite the truth of Bobby's death, with all the outsiders poking around, it was necessary for the sept to go through the motions of a funeral.

One disturbing call.

Fia played it back twice to be sure she had identified the caller correctly, then she spent the next two hours returning phone calls and following up on several projects she'd left on her desk. She finally called him around noon. She got his voice mail. There was no doubt in her mind it was him. She left a curt message that she would see him at ten-thirty at the designated meeting place. She spent the rest of the day cleaning off her desk, her thoughts bouncing between Bobby's missing head and Joseph's resurrection.

Fia strode into the dark, smoky bar, ignoring the gazes that followed her. The low whistles, the single bold catcall. She liked the fact that New Jersey hadn't yet banned smoking in public places. She knew it was bad for her lungs, but the haze served as a shroud, distancing the patrons from each other. From themselves. Here, in a crowded bar on a Friday night in August, Fia, like so many others, could lose her identity. Take on another.

She smelled him before she saw him and it stopped her dead. She closed her eyes for a second, breathing deeply. His scent was different from Ian's, from Arlan's, from Glen's. Somewhere mingled in the aroma of desires, hers and his, was the sharp bite of regret.

She was almost on him before he turned on the barstool. His instincts were good, though not as sharp as hers. Never would be, but still, she knew he felt her presence.

"Fia." He looked her up and down, his gaze somewhere between that of a hawk's and a vulture's. "You're looking good."

He hadn't aged a bit. He had used money and facials to his definite advantage. He was movie star good-looking; dark haired, blue eyed with a patrician nose. Nice clothes; slacks, a designer oxford and Italian loafers. He reeked of sex appeal and expensive cologne.

"Not bad yourself." She made a point of imitating his scrutiny, eating him up with her eyes.

"Still teetotaling?"

She slid onto the polished chrome bar stool beside him, giving the gawking men a glimpse of her bare inner thigh before swinging her legs around. The motion got an audible response. Humans didn't have nearly the sense of smell that vampires had, but there wasn't a man between the ages of thirteen and ninety-three that couldn't recognize the scent of a woman wearing no panties.

"Perrier with lime," she told the bartender, who stared at her breasts spilling over the lacy bodice of the black camisole she wore.

He poured the drink, still watching.

"Another." Joseph pushed his low ball glass across the bar, toward the bartender.

"Why are you here?" She stared straight ahead, purposely avoiding eye contact with him, watching the reflections of the crowd in the massive mirror over the bar. "What do you want?"

"Still the warm, fuzzy gal I knew."

"We agreed it was best if you stayed on the West Coast."

"Best for whom?"

She sipped her sparkling water, savoring the sharp, clean flavor. Though they were not touching, she could feel the warmth of his skin and when she turned to look at him, her gaze settled on the pulse of his throat. She could feel his heart beating, almost see the blood pumping through his jugular. There were other places equally efficient to harvest blood, but it was blood from the jugular that always seemed the sweetest, the most satisfying.

"You didn't answer my question," she said, looking down into her glass.

"You didn't answer mine."

"Joseph—"

She felt his hand on hers and she looked down at it on the bar. It didn't seem real, but waxlike and disembodied. Her thoughts drifted.

Why had the killer taken Bobby's feet? Was the fact that his feet were missing an indication that the beheading had been a mere coincidence? She wanted to think so. Sweet God of St. Patrick, she wanted badly to think so.

Joseph squeezed her hand and his face came into focus. He had that look of a man who knew how attractive he was. He knew how to manipulate people with his sexy good looks and charm.

It was hard to believe now that Fia had once thought herself in love with him. She had once adored everything about him; his voice, the way he moved, the way he spoke. It had not been just his face that she had thought beautiful, but also his thighs, his chest, his arms, and especially his hands. As perfect as a Da Vinci drawing. They looked like the hands of a surgeon.

"A physicians' conference or something?" Fia sipped her drink, her voice intentionally detached. As cool as the sweaty glass in her hand. "That why you're here? Thought you'd check out the old stomping grounds?"

He sipped his vodka on the rocks, his sensual lips forming around the rim of the glass. "We're opening a new office, my partner and I. Here on the East Coast, I think."

She lifted her gaze, locking with his as she pulled her hand out from under his. "Joseph, you can't do that."

"I can. I have."

"It's not safe," she insisted, pushing off the barstool. She hadn't expected this, not even after his phone call. Not now; she couldn't handle Joseph's return now.

Suddenly she was suffocating. The smoke. The scent of the humans and their pulsing blood. The reflections in the mirror over the bar had suddenly turned hazy. They were no longer human, but ghosts of her past floating by, some uncannily silent, others shrieking in her head.

"Once again," he said as he watched the ice cubes dance in the bottom of his glass. "Not safe for whom?"

Overwhelmed by the sudden emotion that welled inside her, Fia strode away. She ignored his voice calling her name. Ignored the ghosts-turned-men-and-women-again that stared. She walked out of the bar and into hot, humid night air. She had fully intended to go straight to her car, but found herself, minutes later, on another barstool. The man next to her was not nearly as good-looking as Joseph, but he wore a nice suit and he was drinking an eighteen-year-old scotch. She let him buy her a Perrier.

The darkness, the closeness of the humans, the sound of the suit's voice whirled around her, pulsing to the beat of the music blaring through the speakers cleverly hidden in the ceiling. The suit was a litigation attorney. In half an hour's time, she knew the name of several of his socialite clients, that he made in the high six figures annually, and why he and his wife had divorced. Lack of sexual adventure was, of course, a major issue with him and Penny . . . Peggy . . . Pilly.

She didn't catch his name either. Didn't want to be able to recall it in the morning.

Fia didn't know what she was going to do about Joseph. She had an appointment with her shrink next week. Dr. Kettleman would want to talk about it. They'd talk about Bobby, too. About Fia's feelings of inadequacy when she went home. About how guilty she felt about the fact that her father was still disappointed in her.

The suit continued to talk, continued to order himself drinks. He was pretty loaded. At first, he had taken her for a high-class hooker, which had amused her. She guessed they didn't see many professional women in Jersey wearing skirts as short as hers. He kept telling her how beautiful she was, how intimidating she had to be to some men. He was not, however, intimidated. Too drunk or too stupid, she guessed.

Fia sat there listening to him ramble on about his accomplishments and how he had just bought a penthouse apartment overlooking the river. It was probably Pottery Barn furnished with a small wet bar in the living room and six-hundred-count sateen sheets on the bed.

When he asked her if she'd like to come back to his place to see it, she had known she should say no. Known she had to, but he made it so easy. They could walk, he said, which immediately made her think of the dark streets, poorly lit alleyways.

And he was so stinkin' drunk. . . .

As she walked out of the bar on his arm, she considered warning him of the dangers of picking up women in bars. From a law-enforcement point of view, he was playing with fire. In his state, he could easily be robbed, worst-case scenario, murdered, not to mention the risk of blood loss. . . .

They walked past the bar where she had met Joseph earlier. She no longer sensed his presence. Angry with her for walking out on him, he had probably gone off hunting on his own. She doubted Joseph had any trouble picking up women in bars.

The suit was polite enough. He walked on the street side of the sidewalk and when they stopped to wait for a light, he moved to kiss her. He was only a little clumsy. His mouth was cool and smoky-tasting. The scotch. And when she slid her palm over his chest, beneath his suit jacket and up to the pulse on his throat, he moaned, thinking her good at foreplay, no doubt.

Her own pulse quickened and she felt the first prickling of desire.

They crossed the street.

"There a shortcut?" she whispered huskily in his ear. Once the urge began, it built quickly, urgently.

She knew she shouldn't do it. . . .

He laughed and stopped in the middle of the sidewalk to kiss her again, this time awkwardly groping her breast.

She pushed his hand away, pretending to be playful.

Walk away, the voice of reason urged. *You get caught hunting humans and you'll be sanctioned. You'll be removed from the High Council and ordered to return to Clare Point where you'll be forced to remain until your next life cycle.* But already her head was buzzing, her fingertips tingling in anticipation.

"This way," the suit said, taking her hand, leading her between a deli and a flower shop.

Halfway down the alley, deep inside the shadows of the two-story buildings, she halted. He stumbled, reached out and grabbed her around the waist, laughing. He thought it was all part of the pick-up game. She let him kiss her, let him thrust his human tongue into her mouth and then she let him caress her breast to distract him as she drew her mouth to the pulse of his neck. He must have shaved very early in the morning because he already had beard stubble.

She licked his skin, testing the waters, as it were, giving his groin a stroke for good measure. He threw his head back, exposing his neck even further, groaning with pleasure.

They were so easy when they were intoxicated. . . .

Excitement washed over Fia, an excitement akin to the moment just before orgasm when every nerve was tingling, every fiber of muscle tensed. Heat rose in her face, her nipples hardening beneath the lace of her bra.

He barely flinched when she sank her teeth into him and it was her own moan she heard in her ears.

She gripped him tightly in her arms as his body went limp and he slipped into unconsciousness. His blood was hot and thick and sweet on her tongue. Somewhere, in the depths of the honey was the taste of the scotch he had drunk. Fia had to struggle with every ounce of restraint she possessed not to take any more.

She had to stop . . . but just one more sip . . .

She groaned as she forced herself to release him and ease him to the ground, taking care she didn't leave him in a rotting pile of garbage or animal excrement. He would wake up soon, unharmed, without memory beyond a tall, attractive redhead in a short skirt, and hopefully, tomorrow he would think better of drinking too much and picking up strangers in bars.

Fia hurried off into the darkness of the alley, running for her car. Shame burned on her face and the heat mixed with the thrill of the deed until she could no longer separate one from the other.

Back at her apartment, disgusted with herself, Fia undressed in the dark and stuffed her clothes in the back of her closet. At first, she tried not to think about what she had done, but the denial never lasted long. Her face was warm and flushed with the shame of what she had done. By the time she showered, dried off, and slipped into gym shorts and an old T-shirt, serious remorse had begun to set in.

Lying in bed, surrounded by the scent of fabric softener, she stared at the ceiling fan, watching the blades spin. Her cat, Sam, a fat old Persian with thick black fur and a sagging belly, lay beside her, purring contentedly, making no judgments. Fia was able to do that all on her own.

She had been doing so well. It had been weeks since she had taken a human's blood. What was wrong with her? Why had she allowed Joseph to push her buttons that way? Why had she taken it out on the suit in the bar, an innocent bystander?

She thought about Special Agent Glen Duncan and the way he had looked at her that night when they walked back to the motel. The craving for human blood had started then. She hadn't recognized it at the time, but in hindsight, she knew it was true. It went hand in hand, sexual desire and the thirst for human blood.

Fia's cell phone, on silent mode, vibrated on the nightstand and she stared at the glaring red numerals on the digital clock beside it. It was 3:05 A.M. She rolled onto her side, her back to the phone. It was the third time Joseph had called in the last hour.

Chapter 7

Joseph called her cell phone twice more Saturday. She ignored the calls, deleting his messages without listening to them. Juvenile, perhaps, but an effective form of avoidance.

Properly contrite for what she had done to the attorney, she worked Saturday through the day, giving the taxpayers of America a good return on her salary. Work seemed more a refuge than usual. Fia found herself thankful the office was so blissfully quiet; thankful to be so engrossed in her paperwork that she didn't think about Bobby's headless body, now stored in the cooler of the only funeral home in Clare Point.

Turning off her cell phone, she stayed in Saturday night with a rented DVD and Chinese takeout. Sunday, she slept in, changed the cat's litter box, cleaned the bathroom, and took her elderly neighbor, Betty, to the grocery store.

She and Betty Gold were good companions. Betty didn't know Fia's history, Fia didn't know the German woman's, and they both seemed content to leave it at that. Neither asked questions of the other. Betty never asked Fia why she came in so late so many nights a week dressed like a high-class hooker and Fia never asked her about her glass eye or the numeral tattooed on her forearm.

Monday, Fia went through the motions at work. She followed up on cases and resisted pulling Bobby's file out of her left-hand bottom drawer to study images of his headless, footless torso. Nothing had come back yet from forensics, not that she expected any worthwhile evidence. The scene had been too clean.

That night, curled on the end of the couch, laptop balanced on her knees, she entered the tombs of FBI files and researched the decapitation of bodies. There were more recorded in the U.S. in the last twenty years than one would like to think. No mention of vampire decapitations.

She took notes on the possible psychological reasons for removing and carrying off body parts and played with the idea of giving Special Agent Duncan a call, just to let him know what she learned, which was really very little. The human psyche was complicated and became even more complicated when murder was a factor.

She thought about Glen. Wondered if he was on his laptop, sifting through the hundreds of pages of data available to agents or if he was out having a mai tai with his fiancée. It would be silly to call him at home. Inappropriate.

When the phone rang at eight she saw her parents' number on the caller ID screen and, against her better judgment, she answered. It was her mother, of course. To her recollection, her father had never called her, not since Alexander Bell's invention of the telephone.

"You're home?"

"I'm home, Ma. That's why I answered my home phone." Fia switched screens, closing the FBI file on a 1967 beheading in Louisiana—voo doo related—and opened her e-mail account.

"You missed Bobby's funeral. Your father said you wouldn't come."

"I told you Thursday before I left I couldn't come. I had cases on my desk; I worked all weekend."

"It was nice."

"Ma, how nice could it have been? You buried him without his head. His soul is burning in everlasting limbo, caught between this world and the next."

"I made soda bread to take to the wake. Tavia said it was the best I'd ever made. You didn't find out who did it yet, did you? Killed Bobby? Your da says a drug-crazed teenager; the big cities are full of them."

It was her mother's way of reminding Fia that she did not approve of her daughter living in the *big city*, even after all these years. It was Mary Kay Kahill's belief that all of her children should live within the safety of the Clare Point city limits.

Relative safety.

Fia deleted e-mails on her computer screen offering financial independence and extended erections. "We haven't found the killer yet. It's only been a week. Forensics haven't come back. How are the Marys?"

"Taking it hard, especially Mary McCathal." Her mother took a tone of arrogance. "She was always weak, Mary McCathal. Taken easily to spells."

Fia wanted to suggest to her mother that she, too, might be "taken to spells," should her husband, the father of her nine living children, be beheaded and his body burned, his soul condemned to eternal unrest, but she thought better of leading the conversation down that path. Then she'd never get off the phone with her mother. "Heard from Fin and Regan?" she asked, thinking the subject safer.

"Not since Belfast a week ago." Her mother's Irish accent was generally faint, but her pronunciation of the capital city was thick, weighted by a mixture of hatred and longing. It had been three centuries since she had seen the meadows of her birthplace.

"But you're expecting them home soon?" Fia asked. "Last time I talked to Fin, he said the investigation wouldn't take more than two to three weeks."

Her brothers were following a lead on a pedophile Scotland Yard had been unable to see convicted. It was the council's practice to fully examine a case before a name could even be brought to the Watch list. Young, adventurous, and ambitious, though with different motivations, Fin and Regan were competing to take the next opening on the council's kill team. Fia and Fin were close, had been since the beginning. It was different with Regan, the baby of the family and her father's favorite, but Fia tried to keep the peace with him, mostly for Fin's sake. The two brothers were more than brothers, they were best friends.

"They'll be home when they're home," her mother said, rather philosophically. "Regan said something about Romania."

"Anyone talk with them? From the council, I mean." Fia set her laptop aside and Sam jumped down off the back of the couch and climbed into her lap. He kneaded her inner thigh with his broad paws. "Do they know about Bobby?"

"You know I'm not privy to the council's whims." Her mother made no attempt to keep her resentment out of her voice. The seats on the council changed periodically. Upon death and rebirth of a member, he or she was replaced. Mary Kay had been replaced and though it had happened fifty years ago, her daughter being appointed had just added fuel to the flames of her indignation.

"Ma, I should go. I've still got work to do."

"You work too hard. Arlan was asking for you at the wake. You like Arlan don't you?"

"Ma."

Her mother was silent on the other end of the phone for a moment and Fia raised her guard. Her mother's psychic abilities had never been particularly strong, and they were even less effective with her daughter, but Fia could feel her probing.

"What's wrong, Fee?" her mother pressed.

"I'm just tired." With the next exhalation of breath, Fia let her guard down. "And Bobby. Ma, I know I see this kind of thing more often than most, but it still scares me. Scares me more because it's one of us."

"That's it?" She didn't sound as if she believed her. "Nothing else going on?"

And just like that, Fia raised the bars she had carefully constructed around her years ago to protect herself. "That's not enough?" Fia pushed the cat off her lap and got up from the couch. "Tell Dad I said good night. I'll call you in a couple days."

"Promise?" It was as close as her mother ever got to tenderness.

"Promise."

* * *

"You should have called me right away," Dr. Kettleman said.

Fia shrugged, shifting on the edge of the couch. "I already had the appointment. I didn't think a day or so would matter."

Kettleman didn't reply, forcing Fia to eventually look up at her across the coffee table. They were sitting in the lounge, as the psychiatrist referred to the area of her office set in an alcove away from her desk and bookshelves. It was supposed to be a place where a patient could pretend she was at home and in a comfort zone where she felt free to speak. To feel. Fia wondered if she was alone among Kettleman's patients in thinking she was far more comfortable in this lounge than in any living room her family possessed.

Dr. Kettleman waited for Fia to begin the conversation. It was an annoying but effective technique. The scent of her Chanel perfume drifted.

Fia studied the psychiatrist for a moment. She was dark-haired with a conservative shoulder-length bob and a structured gray suit. Wire-frame glasses in a world where most people wore contacts. She reminded Fia a little of Tony's psychiatrist on *The Sopranos*, enough so that she wondered if Kettleman had done it purposefully.

Fia was an HBO fan. She appreciated the stark reality, the irony, the dry humor.

"If you'd have asked me a week ago, I would have told you there wasn't a chance I would fall off the wagon," Fia heard herself say. "I've been doing so well. It's been months . . ."

"And how did it make you feel," the psychiatrist asked, watching Fia. "This *fall*."

Fia thought for a moment. The office was overly

warm and she considered removing her jacket, but the psychiatrist was also wearing a suit jacket and she didn't seem to be hot. "I felt like a failure, of course," she said. "The loser my father always knew I could be."

"Pretty harsh judgment," Kettleman observed.

Fia studied the woman's eyebrows. She had nicely shaped brows. Fia wondered if she had them waxed.

"Do you feel this was a minor setback, Fia, or are you falling back into your dependence?"

Fia thought about the tangy, sharp taste of the suit's blood, the incredible rush it had given her. She suspected his blood was as intoxicating to her as any recreational drug on the market. "I'm not going to fall back into my old habits, if that's what you're asking," she told the psychiatrist. "I've worked too hard to get where I am to take the chance of losing it all." She sat back on the caramel-colored leather couch. "This is a minor setback. Nothing more."

Dr. Kettleman was silent again. *It was the silences that could kill a woman.* Make her want to kill herself.

Suicide? Fia almost laughed aloud at the irony of it. If God had given the Kahill sept the option, wouldn't they all have killed themselves a thousand years ago? It was one of the conventions of the *mallachd* that made it so cruel. Not only was it nearly impossible for a human to end a sept member's life, but they could not end their own. On good days, Fia knew it was also a blessing from God.

"Tell me about the other night. What happened with Joseph?" Kettleman asked in her passive psychiatrist's voice.

"I told you. He called. I met him. We had a drink and I left."

"What did he want?"

Fia's gaze drifted to the wall of diplomas behind the woman's head. Undergraduate degree from Temple University. Medical degree from Johns Hopkins. The woman was no slouch.

"I don't know what he wanted," Fia said, her own reflection in the glass over one of the diplomas making her uncomfortable. She needed a haircut. Her shoulder-length auburn hair was losing that razor-cut edge she liked. "I didn't hang around long enough to ask."

"So you drove to New Jersey to meet your ex-boyfriend you haven't seen in fifteen years and you didn't stay long enough to ask why he called you?"

Fia had to admit it sounded ridiculous when put that way, but obviously she had issues, otherwise she wouldn't be paying for twice-monthly hour-long sessions with a shrink, would she?

"It was harder than I thought it would be," Fia said softly.

"What was?"

"Seeing him." Fia was surprised by the emotion that caught in her throat. She picked at the shell button of her Ralph Lauren linen suit jacket. "Hearing his voice again."

"Do you still love him?"

Fia looked up. "Of course not."

"Because . . ."

"Because . . ." She looked down at the button between her fingers. "Because we were bad together. He was . . . it wasn't a healthy relationship."

"And yet after all these years, he calls you and you still come running."

Fia frowned. "I'm not finding any of your comments today particularly helpful. You know I come here to feel better. To get you to help me figure out how to live day to day with who I am."

"How have the last six months been?" Dr. Kettleman crossed her legs. She had nice gams. "Just in general."

"Not bad. Pretty good," Fia conceded. "At least until I was sent to my hometown to investigate a murder. Until someone I knew turned up decapitated and two exes came back from the dead to haunt me. All in one week, I might add."

For the first time since Fia arrived today, Dr. Kettleman smiled. "I don't think you really need my help, Fia. You know your own weaknesses; the substance abuse, the sexual addiction. You know which relationships you have that are toxic. The past relationship with Joseph. The present relationship with your parents."

Silence stretched between them again. Dr. Kettleman waited. Fia sifted through her thoughts. Her emotions.

"For months, I've felt so in control," Fia said hesitantly. "And then I go back to Clare Point and suddenly nothing is what it was. I'm not what I thought I was."

Again, Dr. Kettleman smiled. "Life changes and we have to change with it. You have to accept that not even you, Special Agent Fia Kahill, are immune to loss, to death, to the innate need to be loved."

Fia released the button on her suit. "All my training and I have no clue where to find Bobby's killer. No thought even where to begin." She knew she was hopping around, subject to subject, but her sessions with Dr. Kettleman often went this way. It took days, sometimes weeks after an appointment for Fia to sort out everything they discussed.

"You said the FBI sent a Baltimore FBI agent in because it was their jurisdiction. You said he looked like Ian. Tell me about him. Did you like him?"

Fia frowned, at once defensive. "Did I *like* him? We weren't on a date. It was a crime scene."

"You said he reminded you of the one true love you've ever had," Kettleman said. "Did you work well together? Did you like him? That's all I wanted to know."

"We get funny about jurisdiction, the FBI. The case should have been Duncan's but Senator Malley's office made a special request that I go to Clare Point. Special Agent Duncan was pretty pissed."

"You obviously got past that," Kettleman observed. "You worked on the case together."

"I don't know if we got past it, but we did work together for a couple of days. We're waiting for forensics and the ME's report right now."

"So you liked him?" the psychiatrist pushed. "Why do you think that is? Just because he reminded you of Ian?"

Again, emotion caught in Fia's throat, threatening this time to cut off her ability to breathe. "Yes, I did like him," she murmured. "Because he reminded me of Ian, but also. . . . No." She thought back, trying hard to be objective. "He was different than Ian. Not as volatile. He has a calmer presence."

"Have you talked to him since you got back?"

Fia shook her head.

Dr. Kettleman glanced at the clock on the end table beside her. "Time's just about up, Fia. We've talked about a lot of things. Anything you think we missed that still needs addressing today?"

"Nah. We pretty much rubbed all the edges raw."

Dr. Kettleman rose to walk Fia to the door, putting a hand on her shoulder. "Just once I'd like you to give yourself a little credit. You don't need to come in here to figure out what you want to do about Joseph. You know you can't risk a relationship with him." She stopped at the paneled door. "As for Agent Duncan—maybe that's a risk you are ready to take."

Fia walked out the door feeling better. Determined to call Joseph and Glen, just not sure what order to do it in.

In the end, she didn't call either. But she did decide she needed to tackle her demons in order, or in this case, in reverse order. Fia dressed in a short black skirt, killer heels, and a confidence-boosting skin-tight red tank. She added big hoop earrings and slicked her hair back with styling gel before walking out the door.

Her intention had been to cross the river into New Jersey and look for Joseph there, but her instincts told her he was closer to home. He was out there somewhere tonight, somewhere nearby. She found herself going from bar to bar near the apartment they had once shared on the outskirts of Philly.

Of course she had his cell number. She supposed she could have called him, but this needed to be done face-to-face. And she was certain that he knew she was looking for him. He was playing games with her. Toying with her. Joseph had always been all about the hunt, even when she met him.

Tonight, each time she entered a dark, smoky bar, she got the feeling he had just been there. She could almost smell a remnant of his scent in each doorway she entered, as if he had left a trail of bread crumbs for her.

It was last call before Fia dropped down onto a barstool in a place she'd never been. No sign of Joseph, but she knew better than to think he had come and gone from her life that easily. He wanted something from her and if she didn't find him, he would find her.

The guy on the barstool beside her ordered her a gin and tonic, despite her insistence that she just wanted the tonic. He was wearing a red bandana around his head, a tight black T-shirt and jeans. His wallet was attached to his back pocket with a heavy chain. It wasn't until she was sipping the tonic she'd ordered herself that she realized she'd walked into a biker bar. She wasn't even entirely sure what street she was on. She'd become so intent on look- ing for Joseph that she'd lost track of where she was.

Wandering the streets, barhopping in Philly, pro- bably wasn't the smartest thing to do. What if some- one from the Bureau saw her?

Like any of those tight-asses frequented biker bars. . . .

"Hey, babe, you like hogs?" the guy in the red bandana asked.

She glanced at his neck. It was thick. Fleshy. He wasn't really her type. But he was hitting on her pretty hard. Pushing tonics that he apparently didn't realize were minus the gin.

Hogs? The Kahill sept kept a wildlife preserve with herds of deer. Over the centuries, they had adapted until they no longer needed human blood; animal would suffice. Blood was routinely harvested from the deer to sustain the family.

It had been a while since she'd tasted pig's blood. She wondered if the biker would taste like hog.

"You tryin' to pick me up, sugar?" Fia asked sweetly, turning her full attention to the man she knew would be her next victim.

One hour and three hundred dollars shot in an instant.

The biker led her out a back door into an alleyway that stank of sour milk and rodent droppings. She'd apparently wandered farther afield in her search for Joseph than she realized. It was a seedier part of town than she normally frequented. More dangerous.

The question was, for whom?

As Fia linked her arm through her escort's, she thought of Glen. Wondered what he was doing. She knew it was absurd, but she had the sudden urge to speak to him . . . to hear his voice.

The biker beside her made a sound deep in his throat and he clamped his hand around her arm. Lost in her thoughts, Fia responded a split second too late to the sudden danger she smelled as sharply as the gunpowder that had been in the air the night her Ian had come for the Kahills.

The biker shoved her hard against a steel Dumpster and she cried out in surprise as her head hit the metal panel and bounced. The nice bandana biker dude had suddenly turned mean.

Chapter 8

"So what do you think?" Stacy swung his hand in hers as they exited the movie theater and turned onto the sidewalk. "Daddy's offer to rent the country club is tempting. We could have so many more guests, but Jamaica was our dream." She squeezed his hand. "I don't know that we should give up our dream so Mommy can have her bridge club come to our reception."

Glen tightened his hand around Stacy's, pulling her up short to prevent her from stepping off the curb as the light changed and cars shot forward. As he waited for the crosswalk to clear, he studied the crowd around him. He'd been doing some research online about decapitations. He had assumed such a violent crime had to involve a drug-induced rage. How else could one human do such a thing to another? But he'd read the files on several cases of decapitation that had taken place in the U.S. in the last thirty to forty years and often the crime was quite methodical. Planned out with definite purposes.

Last night, Glen had considered calling Fia, just to check in. But then he thought better of it. Check in about what? They really had no information to exchange and it wasn't as if she was dying to hear from him.

He'd been thinking about Special Agent Fia Kahill all week. They hadn't exactly hit it off. Even once they got past the jurisdiction issue, she'd been so prickly with him. So damned . . . unyielding. On just about everything. And so protective of everyone in that weird little town of hers.

She was wound pretty tight. Even for an FBI agent.

The WALK sign lit up and Stacy took off, still holding Glen's hand.

"I think the cost would be the same," she chatted on. "I mean, sure, we've got the plane tickets and the hotel and all, but the whole package for the cabana wedding at that one hotel is only five hundred dollars. Can you imagine just what the catering bill would be at Daddy's country club?"

Glen flexed his fingers; Stacy was holding too tightly. Despite the hour, it was still hot out and her little fingers were sweaty. He didn't want to hold hands, but it wasn't worth getting into an argument over. Not after they'd already disagreed about where to have dinner and what movie to see.

Glen supposed he'd been feeling a little uptight himself since his trip to Clare Point. He just couldn't get the images of the beheaded postmaster out of his mind. He kept thinking that someone would not commit such a grisly crime just to get a deposit bag with less than two hundred dollars in it, which was their best motive right now. Their only motive.

He wondered if the money was just a cover. What if it was about a piece of mail? The two canvas bags of mail found in the post office, both incoming and outgoing, had been sent to D.C. and looked over before they were sent out. There was nothing out of the usual there. Of course if the killer had taken what he was looking for, there wouldn't be any evidence, would there? He and Fia had discussed that possibility, but had come to no conclusions. At this point, it was still all speculation.

"So I told Daddy, we'd go ahead and meet with the event planner at the club, just to see what he has to say. What do you think?"

Glen checked his watch. It was late. He'd met Stacy at nine-thirty for dinner because he'd wanted to put a few extra hours in on the computer before leaving work. Then she'd wanted to go to a movie. He'd just wanted to return to work, or go home, have a Diet Coke, and flip on his laptop. The movie had been painfully long; a chick-flick comedy which, in his book, was worse than anything in the un-requited-love or dying-of-cancer genres.

It was almost 2 A.M. and the streets were beginning to thin out. Last call had already come and gone at the bars.

He rubbed his eyes. He was tired. Not getting enough sleep. He shouldn't have agreed to a mid-night movie. What was he thinking? Stacy only worked part-time. She had nowhere to be tomorrow. He'd wanted to get to work early. He always liked to get into the office early when the bull pen was still quiet and he could think.

"Glen?"

He looked down, realizing that was the second time she'd spoken his name. They were standing outside her apartment building. He hadn't noticed how many blocks they had walked. "I'm sorry." He took his hand from hers and flexed his fingers. It was too hot a night to be holding hands.

"Did you hear a word I said?"

"Country club or destination wedding in Jamaica? You decide."

"Oh, baby." She lifted up on the toes of her sandals and kissed him. "You're coming up, aren't you?"

He hesitated.

"Come on, baby," she whispered in his ear. "You haven't come up in days, not since you got back."

Sometimes it was just easier to let the current sweep you along than to fight it. He let her lead him through the front doors.

"What the hell do you think you're doing?" Fia demanded, shoving the guy back. Bandana Biker Boy was heavier than she was by a good sixty pounds, but she was taller and she bet she could leg press more than he could. Surely he didn't think he could take her on? Surely he didn't think she was just some poor, unsuspecting chick in a Versace skirt?

"This how you treat a lady?" she asked him. "Back off!"

"Lady my ass," he grumbled, reaching out and grasping her neck between one plump thumb and forefinger.

She was really·going to be pissed if he broke the Czech crystal choker Fin had brought her back from Europe last year.

His fingers tightened around her throat, beginning to cut off her air passage.

Fia was definitely not in the mood for this tonight.

She drew one hand around, balling it into a fist. She struck him squarely in the temple and he stumbled back.

"Motherf—" His foul language was lost in a grunt

of pain as he lunged at her again, and she made a quick sidestep, causing him to hit the Dumpster full force.

"You offer a lady a drink,"—Fia told him, slamming him face-first against the Dumpster again as she twisted his hands behind his back—"you offer to walk her safely to her car." She raised her knee to pin him against the metal wall so she could reach into the cute little black purse she carried and pull out one of the plastic zipper ties law enforcement used as emergency handcuffs. "You *do not* lead her into a dark alley and then try to have your way with her. You understand what I'm trying to tell you here, buster?"

He made one last feeble attempt to wrestle himself free, but a well-placed cuff to his left ear calmed him down, and the stale air in the alleyway was filled with the satisfying sound of the handcuff tie tightening over his wrists.

"What the hell? You crazy, lady?"

She grabbed his arm and whipped him around, using another tie to secure him to the Dumpster as she debated what to do next with him. She obviously couldn't just let him go, but he'd gotten a pretty good look at her. She doubted he could ever identify her looking the way she did now, compared to her FBI file photo, but it would be foolish to take the chance.

She knew what she *should* do, but the idea turned her stomach a little. She just wasn't up for sport tonight any longer. And then there was the pudgy neck. The red bandana.

She leaned over him, grabbing his thin ponytail to pull his head back and expose his neck.

"Getting kinky, are we?" he said as she pressed her lips to his throat. "Why the hell didn't ya just say—"

Fia sank her teeth into his flesh and he made a little yelp of a sound as his knees buckled.

She stepped back and let him fall, his hands flying over his head, his wrists still tied to the Dumpster. She spat out the blood. Then, wiping her mouth with the back of her hand, she leaned over him and fished in the front pocket of his jeans. She made the call to 911 and then dropped the phone at his feet. He'd be the police's problem now. She knew they wouldn't arrest him, not without a witness, and him with no memory of what had transpired after he left the bar with her. But the police would at least keep him in a holding cell overnight, until he sobered up. After a night in jail, maybe he'd be a little nicer to the next chick he picked up in a bar.

As she walked down the dark alley, the sound of a police siren in the distance, she wondered what Glen Duncan was doing right now. Sleeping, if he had any sense. Dreaming, maybe.

It was funny, but she wondered what kind of dream he was having and hoped it was pleasant.

Stacy made a little mewing sound beneath Glen and he thrust into her again.

He wondered if he should give the lab a call tomorrow. Even if they couldn't put a rush on the few samples of blood, fiber, and soil he sent them, he could at least check to be sure the whole envelope hadn't been set aside because someone else had called about a more pressing case.

"Baby," Stacy whimpered, holding him tightly around the neck.

He picked up the pace.

But what if Fia already called the lab? You made too many calls, pissed them off, and you ended up getting your results back the end of next week instead of the end of this.

Maybe he should call her.

"Oh, baby, baby . . ."

Wouldn't be any harm in that, would there? Just a quick call to touch base? Let her know what he'd found interesting on past decapitations. Make sure she'd gotten the fax concerning the mail from the post office that had been examined and sent.

"Now . . . now!" Stacy squealed.

Glen lowered his head, balancing his weight on his hands and feet. She would complain if he didn't. She said he was too big, too heavy. Of course she didn't like to be on top, which had been his suggestion as a compromise.

He drove hard into her and released, more out of habit than urgent need. As he lowered his head to kiss her cheek, Stacy tapped his shoulder.

"Get up, you're all sweaty."

He rolled off her, onto his back and the clean sheets and she bounced up, pushing down her cotton nightie. "You want to take a shower before you go?"

In the bathroom, he heard her turn on the water. She always showered after they made love. She liked to be clean, she told him.

He lifted his head, settling it on a white lace pillowcase, and wondered if Special Agent Fia Kahill jumped out of bed after orgasm and washed the smell of her lover off her skin.

He somehow doubted it.

* * *

Fia was surprised that Dr. Caldwell got his autopsy report to her so quickly. It was properly filled out, sent by e-mail to be followed by hard copy. For a fifteen-hundred-year-old country doc, he was still pretty sharp.

The report provided the victim's name and other typical government information, then a description of the state the body was found in. She skimmed all that quickly, moving to the line where a medical examiner must give his or her best guess as to the cause of death.

There had been no wounds on Bobby's torso, but Fia and Glen had guessed there must have been blunt trauma to the head. With all the blood spray, he had probably been hit with something hard; baseball bats and two-by-fours were both popular with rural murderers. Fia didn't know exactly how an ME figured out how a person died in cases like this . . . when the head was gone, but last week Dr. Caldwell had seemed confident he could figure it out. It had to do with when the heart stopped pumping, where the blood pooled, and in what manner. She guessed he might even be a little better at blood analysis than most MEs.

The Cause of Death box simply stated *Sanguination (Acute blood loss due to the severing of the jugular.)*

She was so surprised that she read it twice. Bobby had died of blood loss from the actual decapitation?

She reached for the little notebook on her desk that she had used at the scene last week, flipped through several pages and punched numbers into her desk phone. She worked her way through an automated answering system.

"Special Agent Duncan," he said on the other end of the line.

It took Fia a second to regroup. His voice had caught her off guard. Even though she had been the one to call him, she hadn't expected him to sound so much like Ian. Even more so on the phone than he did in person.

"Agent Duncan . . ." Feeling foolish, she started again. "Glen, it's Fia. Fia Kahill." That sounded silly, too. How many Fias could he have known?

"Hey," he said, seeming glad to hear her voice. "I was just going to call you."

"Yeah? What's going on?" She was surprised by how relaxed he sounded. There seemed to be none of the tension she had felt back in Clare Point. Maybe he'd finally just accepted the fact that they would be handling the case together. Or maybe it was her. Maybe she was more relaxed with a couple of beltways between them. No fear of losing control, having wild abandoned sex with him, and drinking so much of his blood that she turned him into a vampire. Not with all the rush-hour traffic and those beltways to traverse.

"No, you go ahead," he said. "You called me."

"You get the ME's report? It was just e-mailed. You should have gotten a copy," she said, glancing at her computer screen.

"Hang on. I haven't checked my e-mail this morning yet. I hate e-mail."

"I love e-mail," she said, hearing the tap of his keyboard.

"Nothing but a long list of stuff I have to do."

"I love long lists of stuff to do," she came back. Their conversation almost sounded like banter.

He was in a good mood. She wondered if maybe he had gotten laid last night. That always put her in a good mood. Since she started seeing Dr. Kettleman, her good-mood mornings weren't nearly as frequent. She was still having a little trouble with the taking of humans' blood, but she'd cut way down on the sex with strangers. She liked to think it was progress.

"Here we go," Glen said in her ear. He was quiet for a second and Fia considered saying something. Anything, just to keep up the tenor of the conversation, but she knew that would be hard to do, considering why she'd called in the first place. She let him read the autopsy report in peace.

"You have got to be shitting me," he said. "Sorry," he added quickly.

"You're right. I've never heard that phrase before," she quipped. Then she moved on. "Can you believe it?"

"Am I reading what I think I'm reading? Did the postman die from having his head cut off?"

"That's how it appears," she said, the weight of what had happened settling on her shoulders again.

He was quiet for a minute and she got the feeling that even though he didn't understand the full impact of what had happened to Bobby, he still felt empathy for the man he had never known. For his family. Maybe even for Fia.

"Still nothing from the lab," he said after a moment. "I thought I'd give them a call, maybe a little nudge, but I wanted to check with you, be sure you hadn't already done it."

"No. Go ahead." She rocked back in her office chair, staring at Bobby's autopsy report on her computer screen. "But I have to confess, I'm not too hopeful. Blood that was Bobby's, stray fibers, dirt that he probably tracked in. I don't think progress in the case is going to come out of that pittance of evidence we collected."

"Yeah," he agreed. "I see Dr. Caldwell noted that the only thing he could tell about the decapitation was that it was done with a sharp instrument. I've been reading up on decapitations—"

"Me, too," she interrupted. "Great bedtime reading."

He chuckled grimly. "After what I've read, after going over the photos and interviews again, I can't help thinking our next lead is going to come directly out of Clare Point."

Chapter 9

Fia knew the call was from Clare Point before she answered it. There was a sudden buzzing in her ears and a feeling of lightheadedness as she lifted the handset.

Something was wrong. No one ever dared called her at the office, not even her mother.

"Special Agent Kahill," she said because it was how she always answered the phone. "Ma? Are the boys all right?" she whispered.

When she had talked to her mother two nights ago, she had learned Fin and Regan had still not returned from their fact-finding trip. What if something had happened to them? Vampires were at far greater risk in Europe than in the U.S. Americans were too modern, too *technologically advanced* to believe in the supernatural, but the Old World knew the Kahills and a few other families from different parts of the world were still out there. There still remained small pockets of human slayers which stayed well-concealed and unknown to the contemporary world.

"Ma?" Fia repeated, glancing around her cubicle to be sure no one was passing by.

"Nay. Fee, it's not your ma. It's yer Uncle Sean, it is."

"Uncle Sean?" She leaned over her desk, keeping her voice low. From this distance, it was impossible for her to read his thoughts. All she was getting was a low hum of jumbled words and emotions, but there was no mistaking the fear in his voice. The terror.

"Fee, Fee, ye have to come quick," he said, his accent thick. He sounded near to tears.

"Uncle Sean, what's happened?" *Not Fin,* she thought. *Anyone but Fin.*

"It's happened again," he blubbered. His next words were unintelligible, just a jumble of pitiful sounds.

"Uncle Sean," she interrupted. "Uncle Sean, listen to me. You have to calm down. I can't understand what you're saying." Her heart raced, but she was already thinking more clearly. It wasn't Fin. Fin was safe. She would know if he was dead. She'd know because a part of her soul would be gone. "*What* happened again?"

The moment she repeated his words, she knew what he meant.

No. It was impossible. Bobby's death was the single, solitary act of a strung-out junkie looking for cash. A second beheading would establish a pattern. It would indicate that the random, unprovoked murder of Bobby McCathal, member of the Kahill Sept, had not been random.

"Uncle Sean, take a deep breath and tell me what's going on or put someone on the phone who can."

She heard him take a deep, strangled breath. "He was found less than half an hour ago on the game preserve. Head and hands gone. Jesus and Mary and Holy St. Joseph, Fee, it's a bloody mess."

"I'm coming, Uncle Sean. Give me three hours. I'll call you as soon as I reach town."

It wasn't until Fia hung up that she realized she hadn't asked who had been murdered.

"I disagree with you, sir," Fia said calmly. "It doesn't make sense to split up the investigation this way, especially now, with a second murder." She gestured. "Some info being sent to Baltimore, some here. Copies all over the place."

"I don't give a fat rat's ass what you think, Kahill." Jarrel stuffed a forkful of spinach from a Styrofoam take-out box into his mouth. He was reading e-mail as he ate. Thousand Island dressing.

Fia despised Thousand Island dressing.

"Call Agent Duncan. If his office wants to hand the case over to us, fine, that's up to them. But Senator Malley's office green-flagged this bipartisan team, and I'm not screwing with it." There was a spot of pink dressing on the corner of his mouth.

Fia wondered what he would do if she leaned over his desk and licked off the fleck of dressing. She could bite his carotid artery and he'd be dead in less than three minutes.

She touched the corner of her mouth, wondering what the hell was wrong with her. She was usually in control of her thoughts. She rarely allowed them to stray so far.

"Why are you still standing there, Kahill? You need me to make the phone call for you?"

"No, sir." She turned to go. "I'll call to touch base before you leave the office today."

"You do that." He munched a mouthful of salad. "And Kahill . . ."

"Sir?"

"Don't screw this up. Don't let this petty territorial shit get in the way of your investigation. We can't afford it, not with a U.S. senator's office involved."

"I won't, sir." She looked back at him over her shoulder as if she was with him on the whole Bureau politics thing, but in her mind she was already forty-five miles south, trekking through the forest, looking for a head.

"Those your hiking clothes?" Fia glanced back at Glen, who was struggling to match her pace. The dirt road was no more than a three-foot-wide deer path, cut through the forest.

The woods were thick and heavy with undergrowth and the oppressive September heat. The trees, mostly hardwood—ash, birch, poplar, and elm—hung in a canopy over their heads, blocking direct sunlight. The humid air was heady with the rich, damp scent of leafy vegetation, thick moss, and rotting humus.

"You didn't tell me we were hiking anywhere." He swatted at a mosquito.

"I told you the body was on the Clare Point Wildlife Preserve, a mile off the main road."

"You didn't say *road* as in the *only* road." He blocked a branch she released just before it snapped back and caught him in the groin. "I assumed there would be a dirt road, a pickup truck, some way to get back here."

"I told you, my uncle's arranging for ATVs. It's a federal preserve; deer, fox, raccoons, they don't need paved roads." She ducked under a tree limb that had grown out over the path and shifted the pack she carried on her back. Inside was her camera, a notebook, plastic bags, and other items they would need to collect evidence. She had her cell phone with her, too, although it would do her little good. There were no towers nearby, so poor or no reception.

"And you're sure we're going the right way? Your uncle said there were almost four hundred acres of woods, here."

"I'm going the right way."

Fia could have followed this trail in the dark or with her eyes closed. She'd run it many times in the night, over the years. Deer had been running it for the last three hundred years and at least as many before the Kahills' arrival. An old Lenape Indian village was said to have once sat on the crest of a small hill to the northeast. As a teenager, she and others combed the forest floor for stone artifacts like axes, spear points and arrowheads. Many had been found in the first one hundred years they had lived here, and were now displayed in the town's museum.

"You want to go back?" she asked, pushing on, refusing to slow down to allow for his polished loafers and creased pinstripe pants. At least he'd had the sense to leave his suit jacket in his car. At her apartment, after throwing a bag together, she had dressed in a pair of khakis, an FBI polo, and sneakers. She was hot in the pants, but they protected her legs from the greenbriers and mosquitoes. "You could wait for the ATVs. Uncle Sean said his cousin Malachy had at least two we could borrow."

"It's been almost four hours. We need to process

the scene and get the body out of there." He wiped the sweat on his forehead with the back of his hand, but kept moving.

"You a city boy, Glen?" she asked, trying not to think about the body ahead on the path. They were almost there. No more than fifty yards from the hangman's tree, Uncle Sean had told her. He'd left Petey Hill to guard the body.

"Suburbs of Baltimore."

"Ah, the American dream. White picket fence. Dog in the backyard."

"Hey," he grumbled, double slapping mosquitoes. "I saw plenty of white picket fences back in your hometown. You didn't have such a bad life yourself."

"My father is an alcoholic." It came out of her mouth before she had time to take it back. She didn't normally *share* with coworkers.

"Mine, too. Was. He was killed on the job."

She glanced over her shoulder at him, holding back a sycamore branch. *On the job* echoed in her head. In an instant, she had a connection with Glen's father, a man she had never known. They were all connected . . . law enforcement agents of every kind, all over the world. A silent brotherhood. Sisterhood. Whatever. "A cop? You're kidding."

"Bureau. Firearms deal gone bad. Seventies. I was in middle school. A long time ago."

Fia nodded. She probably should have said something like how sorry she was, or how much respect she had for agents who had given their lives for their country, but the words seemed unnecessary. Part of the connection they all shared.

She slowed her pace, not sure if it was because she felt bad for giving Glen a hard time about keeping up or because she knew the body wasn't far.

She caught a glimpse of pale blue on the green canvas of the forest. A uniform. "Officer Hill?" she called out. "Petey? It's Fia Kahill. I've got Special Agent Duncan with me."

"Ah, Jezus," he swore, approaching them. "About time someone got here. I been alone with him for an hour." *I was scared here alone, Fee, and I'm man enough to admit it,* he telepathed. *What in Sweet Jezus Christ's name is goin' on here?*

Not here, Petey. Not now. Not with the human present.

She consciously blocked out his thoughts, trying to concentrate on the crime scene. On her job.

She heard the flies before she saw the body. They were already beginning to lay their eggs. If the body wasn't refrigerated within the next few hours, the white eggs would begin to appear around the edges of any open wounds or bruises. Within a week, maggots would begin to hatch. As she walked closer, the stench of burnt human flesh, with underlying hints of the first putrid stages of decomposition, grew stronger in her nostrils.

Sometimes enhanced senses weren't all they were cracked up to be.

Petey met them on the path. He was a nice guy. Late thirties. Married to her Aunt Ruthie. He had a teenage daughter, Katy, who she heard through the grapevine was giving him a run for his money. Drinking. Violating curfew. The usual teenage bad behavior.

"It's this way."

"Pete," she said softly. "You don't have to show me—" Because I can smell him, she was going to say, but as he drew back the branches to reveal the headless, handless body, sour bile rose in her throat.

"Ah, hell," Glen muttered, turning his head away to catch his breath.

This close, even a human could smell it.

"Is that—"

"It must be eighty-five out here. Ninety-five percent humidity. Decomposition starts immediately." She tried to breathe through her mouth as she took a step back. The body lay in a small clearing, just off the path. When Pete let go of the hawthorn branch, her view of the body was blocked again.

She looked to her uncle's officer. "Officer Hill, how about if you take a few steps back, give Special Agent Duncan and me some room?"

"You want me to cut back some of those thorny branches?" Pete needed no further invitation to move out of the direct vicinity of the body. "Chief said to leave 'em be. Possible evidence, but—"

"No. You did the right thing."

In another two hours the sun would be setting. They'd have to move fast to process the scene or be forced to haul in generators for light. Two old ATVs wouldn't be near enough then and she didn't want to have to call the office for additional backup and equipment. She didn't want anyone else from the Bureau here.

She swung her backpack off her shoulder and felt for the digital camera in the front zipper pocket. "Officer, why don't you begin a perimeter check, make a circle around the body, then a bigger circle and so forth. You see anything that could be evidence—blood, a footprint, a piece of fiber, even a broken branch—you holler. I want it photographed and marked clearly."

"Weirdest thing. No blood outside the clearing."

"Look anyway."

"Will do, Fee."

Petey walked away and she looked to Glen, standing beside her. "You want to take the photos?" She raised her camera.

Generally, when two agents worked together and one took photos, it was the other agent who truly observed the crime scene. As odd as it sounded, the photographer could distance himself or herself from a grisly setting, concentrating on recording it. Without a camera in one's hand, without the lens to soften the edges, a body in this state could be overwhelming.

"I'm no good at high-tech crap. It will take me an hour to upload them onto my laptop. You get the pictures." He reached around her, brushing her arm with his fingertips as he pulled back the prickly branches of the hawthorn.

Fia stepped through the natural wall into the small clearing. The leaves and dry pine needles, now singed, were tamped down. It was most likely a place deer bedded at night, or in the heat of the day. Perhaps even gave birth.

Twenty-three-year-old Mahon Kahill was lying in the very center of the clearing, his torso on its side, his legs bent, poised as if still running, even in death. His head was gone. Both arms severed at the wrists, his hands nowhere in sight. His flesh was blackened, but not to the degree Bobby's had been. It was likely little or no accelerant had been used, just dead leaves and whatever the killer could find nearby.

What was distinctly different between this scene and the one at the post office was that good-looking, affable Mahon, who liked NASCAR and wet corn bread, had some sort of wooden rod protruding from his chest. He had been pinned to the ground, probably while still alive. It made the decapitation go easier.

Fia tried not to let the screams of the horses, the men that night, pierce her brain. Her brother Gill had been pinned to the ground by a broadsword and decapitated. She remembered the green wool of his cloak, still on his shoulders, bloody, fluttering on the morning breeze.

She heard Glen, just behind her, take a deep breath as he saw what she saw and it snapped her back to the present century. She could have sworn he said "Fuck me," under his breath and it almost made her smile. *Almost.*

"Saved the best detail for last, did you?"

She hadn't told him everything Uncle Sean had told her, but she hadn't left the impaling out on purpose. Their conversation had simply been very short when she called him from her car to tell him to meet her in Clare Point.

"Look like maybe a bit of a struggle to you?" She glanced around. Some of the leaves and pine needles on the forest floor appeared to be disturbed. A few branches were bent. A couple broken. The disturbances in the ground cover could have come from the assailant scooping up leaves to burn the body, but that wasn't the impression she got. Standing here, she could almost smell Mahon's terror in his last breath. She could *feel* him fighting for his life.

"Came in through there." Glen pointed to the northwest. "Not a lot of spatter for the quantity of blood here."

"Soaked into the ground, maybe." She crouched at Mahon's shoulder and took a close-up of his neck, the ligaments, muscles, and his trachea easily identifiable. Like Bobby's, the wound was relatively clean. He had been beheaded with something sharp. But, while Bobby had been beheaded face down, Mahon had seen what was coming.

She took a series of photos, taking care not to disturb the body, although the whole time she was doing it, she wanted to touch Mahon. To somehow console him.

It would be his family that would need comforting.

They worked for close to an hour without really talking and Fia found that Glen was easier to be around than maybe she had given him credit for the first time around. He was respectful of the body, conscientious of his work, and thorough. He carefully collected samples of leaves, blood, even snapped twigs from the immediate area, bagging them and logging where it was all found.

At the rumbling sound of approaching ATVs, both Fia and Glen took a moment to walk outside the immediate circle surrounding the crime scene. They were both bathed in sweat, their clothes damp and stuck to their skin. The mosquitoes were still buzzing in their ears but as the late afternoon lengthened into early evening, a slight breeze began to rustle the leaves of the trees. When Fia turned her head, she could faintly smell the salt of the bay more than a mile away, but the scent that was strongest in her nostrils, even stronger than the smell of Mahon's blood and his burnt flesh, was the smell of Glen's skin. His damp hair.

He smelled good and it was annoyingly distracting.

"Excellent. Two more men to help us move the body," Glen remarked.

She passed him a water bottle from her backpack. "Three."

He looked over at her, questioningly, as he twisted the cap.

"Three ATVs," she observed, watching in the direction they would appear as she gulped her water. "One's got serious transmission trouble. I hope it's not the one pulling the trailer." She screwed the cap on the water bottle, glancing away, realizing that the four-wheel-drive-all-terrain vehicles were still a good quarter of a mile away, and to the human ear probably just sounded like a bunch of noise.

She could tell Glen was wondering how she knew how many were coming. Back in the parking lot at the entrance to the preserve, Uncle Sean had specifically said Malachy had two ATVs. He'd apparently scared up a third somewhere.

"Find anything, Pete?" Fia called, not giving Glen a chance to say anything about the approaching vehicles. She'd have to be more careful. He was more observant than she'd first given him credit for, as well.

"Nothing of the head or hands. Nothing out of place except that path beat through the pines over there. I'm no expert, but it looks to me like someone was following someone else. You think you can take some of those fancy footprint molds like on TV?"

"Possibly."

The engines of the ATVs grew so loud that they drowned out Pete's voice. Fia looked up to see one come through the trees, then a second, then a third.

"Good hearing," Glen remarked, meeting her gaze.

She held it for a second, then looked away. As

her uncle and the two other officers cut the engines, she could hear the flies buzzing over Mahon's
body again. The minute she had moved away, they
had moved back in again. "Let's finish up and get
Mahon out of here."

Chapter 10

It was dark by the time Fia and Glen walked out of the woods, hot, tired, sweaty, eaten up by the mosquitoes. The parking lot was as busy as the Dairy Queen on a Saturday night in June, but the townsfolk had the good sense to keep their distance. They stood huddled in groups in the darkness, whispering, watching.

Fia and Glen waited in the gravel parking lot under the circle of light from a security lamp mounted on an electric pole as Mahon's body was transferred from the wagon pulled behind Malachy's SUV to an ambulance. He'd be transported to Dr. Caldwell's morgue.

Uncle Sean approached, hiking up his uniform pants; he appeared to have lost weight in the weeks since Fia had seen him. "I got one officer willin' to stand watch over the scene overnight, Fee, but I'm worried about him bein' in there alone, I am, *considering the circumstances.*"

As he spoke to her and Glen aloud, the police chief tried to communicate telepathically to Fia.

She blocked his thoughts. *Not now, Uncle Sean. Not here.*

"But a couple of boys from the volunteer fire company are willin' to stand shifts with him," he went on. "What do ye think?"

She rubbed her eyes. With the coming of dusk, the no-see-ums, tiny black gnats, had appeared and were more annoying than the dive-bombing mosquitoes. "Just make the rules clear. They're there to protect the scene until Special Agent Duncan and I can get back at daybreak. I don't want them touching anything. I don't even want them taking a leak within a hundred yards of that spot. And I don't want anyone else there, except those you've assigned to the watch."

"Ye got it, gal." He hitched up his pants and hurried toward his car where several of his officers waited.

The volunteer EMTs closed the doors on the ambulance.

Fia turned to Glen. "We'll get some sleep at the motel, come back in the morning." As she spoke, out of the corner of her eye, she spotted a figure standing near her car. She walked toward him. "Meet you there, Glen?"

"Fee," her father called out of the darkness. His cigarette glowed. "Your mother says you should come stay with us. Bed and breakfast is practically empty." He didn't look at Glen still standing under the street lamp. "Room for you both."

"That's okay, Dad. We've got reservations at the Lighthouse."

"She won't charge you for the rooms. Just what meals you eat. She says she can bill 'em or put it on a MasterCard or something."

"Tell her thanks, Dad. It's nice of her to offer, but—"

She felt Glen's fingertips brush her shoulder blade. "It wouldn't be such a bad idea," he said quietly, coming up behind her.

"Excuse me a minute," she told her father, walking away from the car. Glen followed.

"We should stay at the motel, out of the fray," she said. "Her kitchen is like Grand Central. Everyone in the town stopping by for coffee. Talking, conjecturing."

"Could be a good thing."

She could hardly see his face in the dark, but she knew he was watching her. She glanced away. Her father's cigarette grew brighter then dimmer as he puffed.

"People coming and going," he continued. "We might overhear something pertinent to the case. Let's face it, two beheadings in a town this small, Fia. *Someone* has got to know *something*."

"My mother's nosy. She likes to get into my business."

"So keep your briefcase and your overnight case shut." There was a hint of amusement in his tired voice.

He was probably right. At the motel, they were isolated. No one there but a couple of tourists and old Mrs. Cahall who owned the place. With word of Mahon's murder hours old, the bed and breakfast would be as packed as the pub tonight. Busier tomorrow morning, as the first coffee pot percolated.

Of course, staying at the B and B would mean taking more chances with Glen. Her parents were pretty good around humans; they'd had a lot of years of tourist trade to practice. But with the end of the season in sight, and with what was happening in the town, Fia wasn't sure how well they were keeping their guards up.

As she stood with her hand on her hip, vacillating, the decision came sauntering their way, hips swaying, cherry-cheesecake lip-gloss mouth pursed.

"Special Agent Duncan," Shannon cooed. She was wearing a tight pink T-shirt and denim shorts that appeared to be without an inseam. Her pale, untanned butt cheeks glowed in the dark. "I was hoping you'd be back in town. Not that I would wish such a thing on anyone, God forbid." She giggled. "But you know what I mean."

Glen barely glanced at Shannon, but there was no way a human male couldn't notice her. Be attracted to her. It was chemically impossible, and Shannon, of all people, knew that.

"Okay, we'll have it your way," Fia said to Glen, walking back toward the car. "Shannon. Go back to work."

"It's my night off," the blonde called after her.

"We'll follow you into town, Dad," Fia told the glowing cigarette. "Special Agent Duncan, you coming?"

"Right behind you."

As Fia guessed, the kitchen of her mother's place, the Sea Horse Bed and Breakfast, was packed. The good citizens of Clare Point mulled around, helping themselves to coffee and iced tea and her mother's famous pecan sticky buns. They spilled out of the kitchen and dining room onto the wide veranda that circled the rambling Victorian home Fia had grown up in. Twice.

It would have looked like a party except that there were few smiles. Even less laughter.

"Special Agent Duncan, I'm so glad you could join us." Mary Kay Kahill, who was actually Mary K., to keep her straight with the other Marys in town, met them on the veranda's wide front steps.

"It's nice to meet you, ma'am." Glen passed his small duffel bag from his right hand to his left so he could shake her hand.

"Mom." Fia passed her on the steps.

"Fee."

"Which rooms?"

"The Starfish and the Blue Gill. There's only two other rooms occupied so you both get your own bathroom."

Fia had always thought the Blue Gill was a silly name for one of the rooms; after all, bluegills were not saltwater fish. Her mother insisted it didn't matter; most tourists didn't know it and didn't care. Mary Kay, forever the pragmatist, said it beat calling the room the Oyster Cracker Room. Looked a darned sight better on her Internet site and on the hand-painted nameplate on the door.

"Lot of people here, Fee," her mother called after her. *A lot of people wanting to know what you're going to do about this.*

Fia tried to ignore the hint of accusation in her mother's voice. After all, she hadn't actually spoken the words out loud.

"You got something quick to eat, Ma? Special Agent Duncan and I need to get some sleep. We want to be back on the preserve by dawn. We get any rain and evidence out there will be washed away."

"No rain in the forecast. I've got a fresh chicken

salad I can put in a wrap or I can make up a nice plate with some fruit."

"Either would be fine, Mrs. Kahill." Glen followed her up the steps.

"No big-city formalities, here," Fia's mother said, cutting her eyes in her daughter's direction. "My guests just call me Mary Kay. Would you like me to set you a place at the dining room table, Special Agent Duncan?"

"It's Glen. The dining room would be—"

"Just have one of the boys send it up, Ma," Fia interrupted. "*Glen* probably wants to grab a shower. It's been a long day." In the front hall, she dropped her car keys in the basket on the marble-topped table, an old habit, and made a beeline for the grand staircase that wound its way to the third floor.

"Thank you, Mary Kay," Glen said, taking his cue to follow Fia up the stairs.

"Be sure to come down for a nightcap, Glen," Mary Kay called.

Fia made the first turn on the staircase. The thoughts of the sept members in the rooms below echoed louder between her ears than their voices. Everyone was scared. Angry. *Why were they angry with her?* "Early start in the morning, Ma."

On the third floor, Fia pointed to the door marked THE BLUE GILL ROOM. "Key's in the door," she told Glen. "Mom will send one of my little brothers up with a tray. Stay clear of the iced tea unless you want to be awake for the next three days. She brews it strong."

He rested his hand on the doorknob to his room. "You going down tonight?"

She looked up as she pushed open her door. "You?"

"Nah, I'm beat. I think I need to clear my head

before I start interviewing again. You've got some odd characters in this town, Fia."

"This town?" Somehow she managed a chuckle. "What about this house?"

"Night."

She waited until he entered his room and closed the door, then slipped into the room heavily decorated in a seahorse motif and made a beeline for the shower.

It was after midnight and even though Fia hadn't partaken of her mother's killer iced tea, she couldn't sleep. She lay in the dark, in the queen-sized bed, surrounded by ruffles and pillows with sea urchins embroidered on them, thinking of all the times she and Mahon had had a good laugh over a pint at the Hill. In Ireland. In the days before the *mallachd*.

Mahon had been special to her. He had known Ian, maybe even called him his friend. It was Mahon who had locked her in the root cellar that horrific night. Saved her life for certain because Fia knew with all her heart that she would have faced Ian, had she been able to get to him.

Sometimes, just before she fell asleep, or in that moment before she became fully awake, she liked to think that Ian would have set her free that night if he had come upon her. Or she would have faced him, accused him, but her love for him would have kept her from killing him. But she knew the truth, just as Mahon had known the truth the night he had forced her through the hole in the ground and closed the hatch over her head. Either she or Ian would have died that night. Possibly both.

As she thought of Mahon and her last conversation with him only ten days ago, images of Joseph's face began to appear superimposed over his. The two men had been nothing alike, and yet she thought they would have liked each other, had they met.

The idea was absurd, of course. She didn't even know what made her think of it.

She wondered where Joseph was now. Why he hadn't returned her calls. Had he thought better of his decision to return to the Philadelphia area?

She doubted it. It wasn't like him to give in so easily.

Fia rolled onto her side, pushing her fist into her pillow, making a dent for her cheek.

It had been after eleven before the downstairs had cleared and people had said their good nights. Her mother had only locked the front door half an hour ago, but she knew she and Fia's father were already sound asleep, lying stiff and still beside each other in the double-sized bed. The two could barely stand the sight of each other after fifteen hundred years. Fia didn't know why they didn't at least get a king-sized bed.

An unidentifiable sound in the hall caught Fia's attention and she rolled onto her back, gazing at her door. She listened. The house was quiet. No footsteps. No creaking floorboards.

Had she imagined the sound?

She thought about Bobby and Mahon. No matter how she tried to convince herself otherwise, she knew two beheadings weren't a coincidence. They were not random acts. Someone had known what both men had been, known how to kill them.

She wondered if Bobby or Mahon had heard their attacker approach. Had they known what was coming? Mahon must have. There had been obvious signs of struggle, and then there was the four-foot stake driven through his torso to pin him to the ground.

She heard a sound outside her door again and in a single fluid motion, she rolled onto her side, grabbed her firearm from the bedside table and rolled onto her back to face the intruder. As she rolled, the doorknob turned and two men burst through the doorway.

Blood pounding in her ears, she sprang up, raising her pistol, flipping the safety.

The two figures hurled themselves toward her, landing in her bed.

"Jesus, Mary, and Joseph!"

Chapter 11

"**I** could have blown your heads off, you feckin' assholes." Fia flipped the safety on the pistol, her heart pounding in her ears. Thank God her vision was good, even in the dark, or she might have seriously injured one of them. Kahills couldn't die, but they still bled, got infections, suffered like humans.

"You're getting slow in your old age," Fin teased, straddling her at her hips and pinning her on her back, arms to her sides.

"I told him you'd shoot him. I told him it was a bad idea." Regan dropped beside them, his head on her pillow.

"I should have shot you." She struggled against Fin's hold, managing to set her firearm on the table again. "Get off me!" She slapped at him. "When did you guys get back? Mom—"

Distracted by her brothers and the hum of the window air conditioner, Fia didn't hear the bedroom doorknob turn. She didn't realize someone was there until the three of them were staring into the barrel of a Glock pistol at the end of the footboard.

Fia shoved Fin off her and sat up. "Glen—"

"Fia, are you—" Glen lowered the drawn pistol, obviously not understanding exactly what was going on, but realizing he'd mistaken the situation. "I heard you . . . the door . . . the male voices."

Boxer briefs. Nice. She would have pegged him for a baggy boxer man. "My brothers, Fin and Regan." She introduced them awkwardly. She knew it had to look bad; her in her bra and panties, two young men in her bed, one on top of her.

Glen took a step back. "Okay, so I feel like an idiot."

She scrambled off the bed, grabbing a T-shirt off the chair and dropping it over her head as she walked toward him. In the dark, he had probably barely seen her in her state of undress.

No, she could tell by the look on his face. He *definitely* caught a good look.

"I . . . they're asses." She gestured lamely toward the identical twins in her bed. Twenty-eight in this life cycle and dangerously good-looking, Fin and Regan seemed to be closer to eighteen or nineteen years old and used it to their advantage when they traveled for the sept. While they appeared to humans to be harmless college students, they actually hunted the world's rapists, murderers, and child molesters.

"Who the hell is this? Jezuz, Fee." Regan snapped on the bedside lamp. "He looks just like—"

"This is Special Agent Glen Duncan," Fia cut in. "My . . . my partner on the case."

She wished Regan hadn't turned on the lamp. In the light, she and Glen both looked even more ridiculous, her in her old Temple T-shirt that didn't come close to covering her red lace panties, and him in his tight boxer briefs that left nothing to *her* imagination either.

Heat prickled the back of her neck. Glen worked out. He wasn't so muscle-strapped as to look like a gym monkey, but he had excellent definition: shoulders, biceps, pecs, abs. She suspected he was far stronger and more agile than he appeared in his gray pinstripe suits.

Fia's gaze drifted from his flat abdominals to the dark line of hair that led from his belly button south.

Glen backed up, his face flushed. "I really am sorry."

She followed him into the hall, arms crossed over her breasts, making an effort not to look at him. She felt vulnerable, the two of them standing awkwardly in their underwear in her mother's hall, and it left her off-balance and unsure of herself. Not a state she found herself in too often.

"No, it's okay. I'm the one who should be apologizing." Unable to suppress a chuckle of nervous laughter, she covered her mouth with her hand. "College kids," she explained. "They have no idea of the hours the rest of us keep."

Glen stepped into his room. "Five-thirty?"

"Five-thirty in the dining room," she agreed. "Good night."

She waited until the paneled door closed and then, groaning, strolled back into her room. "Thanks a lot, guys."

The door behind her swung shut and the lock clicked. Both Fin and Regan had strong telekinetic powers, among other gifts. It used to gall her that some sept members could walk through walls, move an apple across the table without touching it, shapeshift or make objects burst into flames while she could do none of those things. But Gair had once told her she had the gift of humanity and that was what made her special to the sept and vital to their survival. Days like today, she wondered if he had just said it to make her feel better. . . .

"What did we do?" Fin asked innocently.

Her brothers lay on their backs in her bed, arms tucked comfortably under their heads.

"You have to be careful around him," Fia warned, a full step past annoyed.

Regan frowned.

"No, I'm serious." She kept her voice down. "He's pretty perceptive for a human. And whether I like it or not, he and I are working together until we solve this case."

"I can't believe Mahon and Bobby are both dead." Fin sat up, running his fingers through his dark, short hair. "You think slayers have found us again?"

"There's no evidence to suggest it." She perched on the edge of the bed. "With Bobby, I was hoping the beheading was just a sick coincidence, some strung-out doper, but now . . ."

"You think he has something to do with it?" Regan nodded in the direction of the wall.

Regan never made any bones about who he liked and who he disliked and she could tell he disliked Glen Duncan for no reason other than the fact that he resembled and carried the same surname as Ian had. "He was called in *after* Bobby was murdered."

"I don't care. The resemblance is just too weird."

"Jesuz, it's not that great a resemblance." Fin got out of the bed. "All the Scots look alike, you know that. Inbreeding. Come on." He waved to Regan. "Fee needs to get some sleep."

She followed them to the door that unlocked and opened without anyone touching it. She placed her hand on Fin's shoulder as he followed Regan out the door. No words passed between them verbally or telepathically, but his smile told her she had his support. Hers told him how much she appreciated it.

Fia sat on the front step of her parents' house and checked her voice messages at the office. She and Glen had had soup and sandwiches at six-thirty in the dining room and then he'd excused himself to make phone calls. They had decided to head over to the pub to have a pint and he'd offered to meet her there, but Fia was waiting for him. The less time he spent alone with the Kahills, the safer she thought he'd be. They'd all be.

That especially held true now that Regan was back in town. Although he'd been behaving himself for years . . . decades, he had a reputation for exploiting humans. It was Regan who had turned both Victor and Shannon into vampires. He'd found Shannon in an eighteenth-century tavern; she'd been a serving wench who had chosen the wrong traveler to share a roll in the hay. Victor had been a nineteenth-century ship's captain who had befriended Regan, given him safe passage from Europe when Regan had been on the run. Regan had rewarded Victor's friendship by holding him captive, and on a blood binge, taken the man's life, replacing it with everlasting damnation.

Shannon had accepted her lot in life, and held no ill will against Regan or any of the other Kahills, but Victor resented Regan's intervention. Despised him for it. Hated them all. At least twice a winter,

Victor got drunk and walked up and down the darkened streets of Clare Point, threatening to *"Murder ever damned last one of 'em, while they slept in their beds."*

Because Regan had slipped not once, but twice in recent years, there were many in the sept who didn't believe he was ready to participate in the committee that exterminated the men and women they hunted. Regan was trying hard to win the town over, saying all the right things, demonstrating the right actions, but Fia wasn't falling for it. She didn't believe he could be trusted and she believed in the age-old adage that a leopard did not change his spots.

Then she wondered, was she being hypocritical? Perhaps. But her circumstances were far different than Regan's.

Fia skipped through several messages on voice mail; all matters she could see to when she got back to the office.

She and Glen had spent half the day in the woods, then returned to town for interviews. They'd combed the wildlife preserve for any possible evidence and taken additional photographs. As with Bobby, they had been unable to locate the head and extremities. The few footprints Petey had discovered the day before were of such poor quality that Glen had been unable to take a cast. It appeared that some common gasoline *had* been used as the accelerant again, though they would have to wait on the lab test results for confirmation.

The only concrete evidence they had in the case, so far, besides Mahon's body, was what appeared to be a rake handle, the rake portion broken off, which was used to impale him, and a small cardboard box found in the woods. The empty box had contained generic, lawn-sized garbage bags. No other trash was found within half a mile of the crime scene, which made them both suspect that the box was connected to the murder. Had the killer placed Mahon's head and hands inside garbage bags? It would account for the lack of a blood trail.

Both the rake handle and the box had been bagged as evidence and sent by courier to the lab in Baltimore. They had a few more people to interview in the morning, but Fia didn't expect any surprises. Mahon had left his house on Tuesday morning, his day off after working Labor Day weekend, to go bird-watching on the game preserve. Everyone in the town knew Mahon was an avid bird-watcher. Year round, he could be found once or twice a week on his days off, walking the paths of the Clare Point preserve, or one of the other parks in the state, such as Bombay Hook.

Nothing had been different about Tuesday morning except that Mahon had not come back in time to make his ten-thirty dental appointment and when his wife had been unable to get him on his cell, a neighbor had offered to look for him.

As Fia listened to her office messages, she methodically saved and deleted. There was a call from Lieutenant Sutton in Lansdowne; she didn't say what she wanted, only that it was in reference to the Casey Mulvine case. *Casey Mulvine.* Fia now had a name to go with the image of the dead girl in the alley.

Joseph had also called, cheerfully asking her to give him a ring when she got a chance. He spoke as if nothing had happened in the bar. As if he didn't know that she'd been looking for him for the last two weeks.

Finishing her messages, Fia set her cell on the step beside her, drawing her knees up into her arms. She honestly didn't know which call disturbed her more, the one from Joseph or Lieutenant Sutton. Joseph for obvious reasons, but what was it about the girl's case that had gotten under her skin?

She pressed her thumb and forefinger to her temples, fighting a flutter of panic in her chest. She felt as if her life was crumbling around her. A short month ago, she'd been happy, confident in her job. With help from Dr. Kettleman, she felt as if her personal life was in check . . . or at least getting there. And now—

The front door opened and closed and Fia heard Glen approach behind her. "Hey," she called lightly. "You ready to go?"

"How do you do that?"

Still seated on the step because she was drop-dead tired, she glanced over her shoulder. "Do what?'

"Know who's behind you. Any one of half a dozen people could have just walked out that door, yet you knew it was me."

She shrugged. "Aren't cops supposed to be observant?"

"Yeah, but you're creepy observant, Fee."

It was the first time he had ever called her that. She knew he'd heard others call her by the nickname, but from him it seemed more . . . personal. "So I've got good hearing." She stood.

"So I've noticed."

She looked back at him and started down the sidewalk. "You talk to Stacy? You were gone awhile." She had no idea why she'd asked, why she even cared, but she suspected that was why he had excused himself. So that he could talk with his lover in private. She wondered if they had phone sex.

"Yeah, the conversation got pretty intense. Eggshell or white linen."

"Pardon?"

He walked beside her. The sun was beginning to set and the air had cooled off a little. The neighbors had cut their grass and the sweet scent filled Fia's nostrils, mingling with the aroma of steaks cooked on the grill somewhere on the same block. She relaxed a little. It felt good to be in the open air, away from the stench of Mahon's blood and burnt flesh that she had still been able to smell in the woods today.

They crossed the street, stepping back onto the sidewalk. The quaint streetlamps were beginning to come on, but not in unison, so as they walked, sometimes his face was illuminated, other times it was in shadow.

"My fiancée," Glen explained. "She's trying to decide what color tablecloths to rent from the linen service for our wedding reception."

Fia glanced at him, unable to suppress her disdain. "And you care?"

"Not a damned bit."

He grinned and she found herself smiling. "So when's the big day?"

"April tenth."

She wanted to comment that he didn't seem all that excited, but she held her tongue. Fia was finding that, while she resisted, while she tried to remain professional and removed, she was liking Glen more than she wanted to. She appreciated him for his similarities to Ian, but she also appreciated his dissimilarities. Glen was a little more easygoing. He took himself less seriously. He smiled more.

They walked the next block in comfortable silence.

"You know, you didn't say anything about last night," she said. "My brothers."

"I thought I'd already embarrassed myself enough."

"Why should you be embarrassed?" She stopped at the end of the sidewalk and waited for a car to crawl by. Uncle John waved from the open window of his pickup. "I thought you looked pretty fine wearing nothing but your underwear and a Glock, Special Agent Duncan."

"You have a pretty fine ass yourself, Special Agent Kahill."

Fia was searching for a snappy response when she spotted a couple of teenagers standing in a huddle outside the Quick-Zip Market. Columns of cigarette smoke snaked over their heads. It was Kaleigh, Petey's daughter Katy, one of the Cahall girls, and three human teenagers. At once, Fia raised her guard.

There were anxious whispers and one of the boys flicked a cigarette butt onto the sidewalk, grinding it out with his flip-flop. Another butt landed in front of the soda machine.

"Kaleigh." Fia walked up to the group; Glen hung back a few steps.

"Fia," Kaleigh's shoulders were stiff, her tone resentful. "Agent Duncan." She acknowledged him with a lift of her chin.

Fia looked to the teenaged boy who stood closest to Kaleigh. Had to be the one she had mentioned. The surfer. "Special Agent Kahill, FBI, and you?" She offered her hand.

The dark, shaggy-haired teen had a surprisingly firm grip. "Derek Neuman, ma'am."

"My partner, Special Agent Duncan."

The teen reached around one of the girls to shake Glen's hand. "Sir."

The boy seemed polite enough, better mannered than most teens, but that didn't change the fact that he was a human.

"So what are you up to?" Fia asked, addressing Kaleigh but meaning the whole group.

Kaleigh shrugged. "Going to get an ice-cream cone, I guess."

"You being careful?" Fia glanced at the others, now including them in the conversation. "Even if you don't read the papers or watch the news, I know you're aware of the recent homicides."

Derek looked from Fia to Kaleigh and back at Fia again. "We figured we were safe." He hooked his thumbs in the pockets of his cargo shorts and slumped. "You know, as long as we were hanging out together. Safety in numbers and all that sh—" He started to say *shit*, but finished with a mangled version of *stuff*.

Glen appeared amused. Fia wasn't. Hadn't she and Kaleigh just recently discussed the dangers of human boys? And Derek Neuman certainly looked older than fifteen to Fia.

You know this is dangerous, Kaleigh. Didn't we talk about this? Fia telepathed. *Someone's going to get hurt.*

Fia could have sworn Kaleigh flinched, but if she understood Fia's thoughts, she gave no indication.

It's okay, Fee. Katy's thoughts were clear and strong. *It's just ice cream. We won't let anything happen to her.*

"Isn't it a school night?" Fia looked back to Kaleigh. "Don't you have to be home?"

"It's not even nine yet," Kaleigh groaned. Then, to her friends, "Come on, if we're going."

Fia watched the group of teens move down the sidewalk, more as a single entity than individuals. "I can't believe their parents are letting them wander the streets."

"Come on, they're teenagers and invincible. I know I certainly thought I was at that age. And they're right. They probably are pretty safe. Both of our victims were alone."

They halted at the door to the Hill and Fia watched the teens as they appeared to get smaller and smaller. They were not headed uptown in the direction of the ice-cream shop or any market that might sell ice cream. They walked toward the bay and the docks. Fia sensed trouble in the air but couldn't get a take on what was going on in the little group. The teen girls' thoughts were too muddled, too unfocused to read, as was often the case at their age.

Glen opened the pub door and music and voices tumbled into the semidarkness of the street. "Come on, stop worrying," he urged. "Let me buy you a pint."

Fia drank her single pint, and again Glen had three. But this time, unlike that first night after Bobby's death, when they walked home, Glen seemed completely in control of his faculties and kept well away from her. They briefly discussed the case and the decision that they would return to their respective offices tomorrow. Both were frustrated by the lack of evidence, but were hoping that once Mahon's autopsy report and the lab reports from the evidence were back, they'd have some direction to go. There had to be some similarity between Bobby and Mahon's deaths, beyond the obvious.

As they walked up the sidewalk of the B and B, Fia spotted a form that suddenly morphed into the silhouette of a man. It . . . he stood on the front porch, watching. Waiting.

Glen spotted him a second later. "I think I'll head upstairs," he said, mounting the steps. "See you in the morning."

Fia waited until Glen closed the door behind him before she turned to the dark figure. "What do you think you're doing?"

He glanced at the door Glen had just walked through, taking his time before he spoke. "I was wondering the same about you."

Chapter 12

Fia walked up onto the porch. "You can't do that around him."

"Do what?"

"You know very well *what*." She slugged him in the arm.

Arlan laughed and draped his arm casually around her shoulder. "I was messin' with you. He didn't see me. He didn't see anything. Humans never do. I don't know why you waste your time with them."

She moved toward the railing, but not entirely out of his reach.

"He was assigned to the case. I didn't have any choice in the matter."

"I'm not talking about the case and you know it, Fee. I saw you at the Hill. You're involved."

"I'm not *involved*. He's my partner. *On this case*," she clarified. "There's just no way around the jurisdiction issue, not with another body. Not now."

He was quiet for a moment. "I haven't really gotten time to talk to you. To tell you how sorry I am about Mahon." He paused. "I . . . I know you were friends."

Lovers. He knew they had been lovers once, too. But that had been a long time ago.

Fia was surprised by the tears that stung the backs of her eyelids. "Thanks. He was good to me after . . ." She let her sentence trail into silence.

Arlan's fingers found the nape of her neck and teased a sensitive spot.

"What do you think's happening? Slayers, or worse?"

The weight of his arm on her shoulder was comforting, but a part of her wanted to shrug him off. Maybe she didn't want to be comforted. Maybe she didn't deserve it. Her family needed her and she wasn't coming through for them. "Worse? There's worse?"

"What if it's one of us?"

"Arlan, that's a horrible thing to say."

"You were in the pub. You heard them. Everyone is thinking it, even if they're not coming out and saying it."

"I don't listen in on people's thoughts, *uninvited*," she said, chastising. They were both quiet for a minute. "Besides, it wouldn't be possible. How could someone keep something like that to themselves? We'd know. One of us would know."

"I'm just saying, whoever did this knew what they were doing. The first time, coincidence, maybe, but now with Mahon—"

"I can see what's happening," she cut in. "Don't tell me how to do my job, Arlan."

They watched a bat flutter past the porch. The streetlamp was attracting insects and the bats came to feed on them.

"I wasn't telling you how to do your job," he said.

"I was just thinking out loud. This makes two of us. We haven't lost two so close together in a very long time."

Fia had been thinking the same thing tonight as she watched family members move around her in the pub. It was a strange relationship she had with the Kahills. She despised the sept for what they were, for what they had made her with their warring, and yet she loved them fiercely. Like it or not, she was one of them. Would be, perhaps, for all of eternity and she had no doubt in her mind she was willing to give her life for any one of them, even Victor, even Shannon . . . even her brother, Regan.

"I'm going to figure this out, Arlan." She watched as a second bat was drawn toward the swarm of flying insects around the lamp pole. "I'm going to find out who did this to Bobby and Mahon."

"I know you are." He drew his finger along the ridge of her collar bone. "So, you want to come back to my place?" He leaned forward and brushed his lips against her neck. "Just for a taste. . . ."

She felt a shiver of pleasure, but she resisted it. With vampires, sex always involved bloodletting, but it didn't *have* to be that way. Did it? "I can't." She looked back at him, studying his gaze. "I need to keep my eyes on my partner. Shannon was circling him again tonight. I don't put it past her to climb through his third-story window to get to him."

Arlan sighed and moved back. Not away, just back a few inches so that while their clothing still touched, skin did not. "He's not Ian, Fee. He just looks like him. Distant relative or something, maybe, but it's not him. Ian was mortal and is long in his grave."

"I know that." She prodded him with her finger. "What makes you say that? What makes you think I think it's him?"

He looked down at her, his gaze unwavering. "Because I know you." He sighed. "Look, good or bad, it's not him and that human can't alter the past. You can't change it. Nothing will bring Ian back and nothing will change what happened that night in that village."

His words brought an ache to her chest and a lump to her throat. She wished that she could love Arlan. Wished that she could let him be to her what he wanted to be. He was such a good man. He would be good for her.

But she wouldn't be good for him because she would never love him the way he deserved to be loved.

"Come home with me," he urged her.

She rested the flat of her hand on his chest. "Not tonight, Arlan."

"You sure? Just a little release?" He lifted her hand to his mouth. "I'm not asking for anything more."

"Good night, Arlan and thanks." She stepped toward the door.

"Change your mind, stop by."

She chuckled as she watched him morph into a sleek gray cat and slink down the porch steps. "Good night, Arlan."

Upstairs, on the third floor, Fia lay down but she didn't sleep. She listened to the rumble of Glen's voice for a long time as he talked on the phone. She didn't hear him speak Stacy's name, but she knew he was talking to his fiancée. Eventually he hung up.

She imagined him on the other side of the wall,

stretching out on the bed, reading for a while. And after he shut out the light, she imagined him lying in the bed with the blue ruffles, nude. She imagined herself lying beside him. She remembered Ian and the taste of his skin, the feel of his body against hers. She wondered if Glen would feel different.

Okay, so obviously she was attracted to him. There was no sense denying it any longer.

Fia thought about what Arlan said. Obviously the initial attraction, subconscious or otherwise, had to be about Ian, but was this just about her past lover? Did she just want to have sex with Glen, to taste his blood, so that she could feel her Ian inside her again? So that she could pretend for a short time that the only man she had ever loved had not betrayed her, causing her to betray her family? Or was there something else going on here?

Fia didn't care what Dr. Kettleman said, anonymous sex was beginning to seem appealing. . . .

They had agreed to meet at 2 A.M. Fia had wanted to wait until three, but Little Johnny, Fia's seventy-seven-year-old great-uncle, had insisted that *some people* were too old to be staying up half the night. *Some people* needed their sleep.

Walking to the museum, she took shortcuts through yards and back alleys. It was still hot during the day, but nights were beginning to cool and there was the faintest hint of the coming fall in the air. A tiny sliver of a moon cast dim, white light. As Fia made her way across town, dogs and cats that prowled the neatly cut backyards ignored her. At this time of night, only humans would have disturbed them; they were used to sept members moving after midnight, especially in the summer when they were forced to be more careful. Everyone kept supplies of blood in their freezers, but occasionally even the most disciplined felt the need to hunt.

As she walked alone in the dark, she wondered if she should be afraid. What if someone was hunting *them*? Could she be a target? Were they all?

At the museum's rear door, Fia punched a series of numbers into the security keypad and let herself into the rear hallway. As a teenager she had dreamed of being one of the honored eleven members of the high council, which also made her a member of the larger, general council which was meeting tonight. The high council's sole responsibility was to make decisions concerning the humans they watched, hunted, and sometimes executed. The general council was responsible for the more mundane, but no less important, day-to-day running of the town and governing the sept.

Fia entered the main room of the museum. The room-darkening shades had been drawn, unlike the last time she had been here for high council, when ceremony had to be adhered to, and tonight the room was blazing with fluorescent light. Someone had made coffee. There were donuts and other snacks set out on a tray and instead of sept members being dressed in hooded robes, they sported shorts, T-shirts and flip-flops. The chieftain wore plaid pajama bottoms and a Captain Morgan Rum T-shirt with a bikini-clad girl and a pirate on it.

"Gair." Fia acknowledged her grandfather as the sept's leader as she entered the room, as was proper.

He nodded, shuffling toward the snack table. "There's banana-nut bread. You should try it."

In a rare impulse of affection, she kissed his weathered cheek.

"Been a hard day," he acknowledged, piling slices of sweet bread on a napkin.

She could tell he was pleased by the kiss, even if he didn't say so.

"You see cream for the coffee? I hope the hell it's decaf or I never will get any sleep tonight."

Fia gazed around the room. Council members were filing in, breaking into groups, chatting quietly. "Doc coming tonight?" she asked, her glaze flicking from one face to the next. The people in the room were nervous, scared. It didn't take ESP to figure that one out. She could see it in the tight lines around their mouths, hear it in the laughter that wasn't quite genuine.

Gair shook his head, carrying his coffee and napkin of sweets to one of the folding chairs set in a circle. "No, but he says he'll have the autopsy report by morning for you, all official, *i*'s dotted. *t*'s crossed. Toxicology reports and such will take longer."

She sat down beside him, taking a deep breath. "I'm not expecting any surprises."

Gair blew on his coffee. Slurped it. "Me either."

She sat back in her chair and gazed around the room. The museum had been built in the late sixties to encourage the town's burgeoning tourist trade. Portraying Clare Point as a pirate's den in early colonial days, the museum mixed fact with fiction, displaying many objects that had actually been on the ship the sept had traveled aboard from Ireland. When the vessel had wrecked on a reef in a storm and they were all washed ashore, they had collected these objects as well as the scrap wood from the splintered hull. They had built their first homes with those warped planks; portholes had become windows and the simple white bone china now displayed had been used on dining tables.

There had been a small colony of wreckers living in lean-tos on the beach when the Kahills washed a-shore, but once Gair declared that they had reached their final destination, the Kahill women had bared their fangs, the men had raised their swords, and the pirates who made a living luring ships onto the rocks had moved south to Virginia, to safer ground.

The glass cases in the rinky-dink museum, identified by printed signs, sometimes with humorous sketches, were filled with pieces of china, brass candlesticks, and other assorted junk, mostly brought from the ship, although some of it was bounty the wreckers had left behind in their eagerness to escape a colony of vampires. There was also a small exhibit of arrowheads and spear points from the area's earlier history, when Native Americans had hunted and fished the area. Some items were displayed on the round table that had come from the ship's captain's cabin; the same table that was used when high council took an *aonta*.

During the museum's operating hours, a five-minute movie was shown in one corner of the room and there was a small gift shop off the hall, near the bathrooms. There, plastic swords, eye patches, fake coins, tomahawks, and other assorted souvenirs were sold. On rainy days, in the summer months, the museum made a surprisingly tidy profit.

"Fee . . ."

She felt a small hand on her shoulder and she turned to see a tall, slender, redhead with a short, spiky, hip haircut and heavy black eyeliner. She had to consciously block her thoughts and stifle a groan. "Eva."

The woman, in her late twenties, kept her hand on Fia, giving her a little massage. "It's good to see you," she purred. "I got word of what was going on when I was in Istanbul. I came straight back. I can't imagine how hard this must be for you."

Fia leaned forward, trying to escape Eva's grip. The woman, a professed lesbian, had had the hots for Fia for at least a hundred years, maybe longer. It wasn't that she had anything against lesbians. She even felt sorry for Eva, she being one of only two in the Kahill sept, but it just wasn't Fia's thing and Eva wasn't taking no for an answer.

"It's been hard for all of us." She started to turn back to her grandfather, but Eva slipped into the chair beside her.

"But especially for you," she emphasized. "You know, I've always admired you, Fia. You've always been one of the strong women."

Fia groaned inwardly, glancing at her grandfather, hoping he might bail her out, but he was ignoring them, intent on his banana bread and coffee. She turned back to Eva. "So . . . you were in Istanbul. How was your trip?"

"It was fine. But I missed home, you know, especially after I heard." She scooted up on the chair until her knee was touching Fia's. "You know, I was thinking, with Mahon . . . gone . . . there'll be an opening on the police force. I was considering applying. What do you think? Do you think I'd make a good cop? I mean . . . I know I could never be as good as you, but—"

"I think we're starting," Fia said with relief as

Peigi Ross tapped the side of her chair with a Bic pen to get everyone's attention. Gair was the chieftain and would be the leader of the high council until the end of time, or a time at which God forgave the Kahills and called them home. Whichever came first. In the meantime, sept members took turns serving as the governor of the general council. Peigi had held that position for the last fifteen years or so.

"I know we all want to get home so the sooner we get started, the sooner we can get out of here," Peigi called to the last stragglers, still loading up at the refreshment table.

"Sorry," Fia said under her breath.

"Maybe we can talk later." Eva reluctantly swung her legs around in the chair to face the center of the circle. "Maybe I could buy you a pint at the Hill tomorrow night."

Fia gave a quick smile and turned her attention to Peigi. Peigi wore her gray hair short and cut close to her head. In baggy stretch shorts and a flowered top, she looked like any fifty-something, lumpy, bumpy human female. Running into her in the grocery store, or on the Rehoboth Beach boardwalk, no one would have guessed she had the ability to set a box of cereal or a moving car on fire, or that she made the best chicken enchiladas Fia had ever eaten in all her lifetimes.

"I know we had several issues on the agenda for tonight, but in light of Mahon's death, I think we can table most of that stuff for two weeks. Soon as Dr. Caldwell releases the body, we'll know when the wake is, but I talked to Sarah tonight and she thinks it'll be Saturday night, her place. Everyone's welcome, of course."

"And that's it?" Mary Hall rose from her folding

chair, her eyes red and puffy. "We just bury 'm like we buried poor Bobby?"

"What about Victor?" Rob Hall asked her. "Not a month ago, he got rip roarin' pissed and threatened to take my head off with an axe. You know, that old one he uses to chop wood at his place."

There were murmurs of agreement.

"What about Victor?" a voice echoed.

"He's not one of us. We all know that," Rob went on. "Maybe we need to look in that direction."

"Look in the direction of that little tart is what I say," Rob's mother put in. "That Shannon. I don't care what anyone says, I don't trust her. She's not one of us, either."

"Now, now, let's not get ahead of ourselves." Peigi balanced a clipboard on her knees and raised both hands. "Victor and Shannon may not have been one of us once upon a time, but they are now and it's unfair to accuse them like this, not without any evidence."

"But there is no evidence. At least that's what we're being told," someone called out.

"Nuthin' we can do," someone else murmured.

"Sure there is. We can stop it from happening again," Mary Hall argued. Her gaze honed in on Fia. "So how are we going to do that, *Special Agent Kahill?* That's what I want to know. How are we going to protect our loved ones?"

All of a sudden more than twenty pairs of eyes were staring at Fia. Thoughts bounced all over the room. Harsh, accusing, angry. They hit her so hard that they could have been fists.

Gair slurped his coffee beside her as if the recipe for the banana bread he was making short work of was being discussed.

It's okay, baby, Eva telepathed. *I'm here for you.*

Fia didn't know which was worse, being attacked by the council or comforted by Eva.

Fia stood, though why, she wasn't sure. Easier to defend herself maybe, if the blows became physical? She looked to Peigi for permission to speak, as was proper protocol, although everyone seemed to be ignoring it tonight.

Peigi nodded, sitting back in her chair, pulling her clipboard to her sagging breasts.

Fia cleared her throat. "I know everyone is upset—"

There was mumbling. Some spoke aloud, others didn't, but no one made any bones about the fact that they were not pleased with her investigation.

"But I want you to know," Fia went on, "that the FBI . . . *I'm* doing everything possible to find out who did this, and quickly."

"So you admit it. You don't know anything?" Mary Hall demanded.

"We found some evidence this week that could be very helpful," Fia said to Mary. "It's being sent off to a crime lab." As she spoke, she tried to direct her answers to each and every person on the council, meeting their gazes. But with each passing second, she felt less capable. "In the meantime, there are things all of you can do. I need you to go over in your minds the contact you had with Bobby and Mahon in the days before they died—"

Were murdered, you mean to say, someone telepathed.

"Go back weeks, months if you have to," Fia continued, trying to block everyone's thoughts. "Was there anything out of the ordinary you heard or saw? Something Bobby or Mahon said. Something an outsider might have said or done. And you need to call me. I'll leave cards for everyone. Don't hesitate to contact me. No matter how insignificant it might be."

"And that's it?" Tavia asked. "That's all we can do?"

Doesn't seem like much to me.

Seems like nothing.

Seems like no one's doing anything.

"What about putting a group together like we used to in the old days?" Tavia suggested. "To hunt the slayers."

"Don't know why we need the FBI at all," someone else said. "That's not how we used to do things."

"No, it's not." Fia turned to her great-uncle, who had spoken. "It's not the way we used to do things. But the way we *used* to do things didn't work either, did it? Vigilantism is how we ended up in a sinking ship in the Atlantic Ocean, fleeing for our lives. That's how we ended up here."

"And following this country's justice system has worked," said a deep-timbered voice from beyond the circle. "It's worked for three hundred years."

Everyone on the council, including Fia, turned toward the hallway. It was Fin. Fin to the rescue.

You're a little late, Fia threw in his direction.

But not too late. Fin grinned as he entered the circle and stopped in front of an empty chair. He had a way about him that she had always admired. He was dressed casually in jeans and a black T-shirt with a bad-boy five o'clock shadow on his chin. But the facial hair only seemed to make him more attractive. Fin had that charismatic presence that could be felt but not explained. When Fin Kahill spoke, people listened. People, humans and sept members, believed.

"Fia's right. We need to let the authorities deal with this, at least for now. We need to stay calm and not panic."

"Easy for you to say, young man," Mary Hall snapped. "It's not your lover rotting in a grave without his head!"

"I'm sorry, Mary." Fin turned to her, meeting the older woman's gaze. "I can't imagine how you feel except to compare it to the loss of my Lizzy and my sweet Fiona."

His voice was so gentle, so compassionate that everyone in the room seemed to relax a little. Fia took a deep breath. She wasn't going to be lynched. At least not tonight.

"So what do we do?" Tavia asked.

"Yes, what should we do, Fin?" another questioned.

"We should do what Fia asks. We stick together and don't make unwarranted accusations, and we should keep an eye on each other."

People nodded. A few made sounds of agreement. A hush was settling over the circle of men and women in the room. A calmness.

"Thank you, Fin," Peigi said, smiling at him.

Fin smiled back, taking the empty chair.

Peigi checked her clipboard. "The only other subject we really need to discuss is the increasing complaints about the teenagers on the streets at night. I understand a dinghy was stolen the other night and it was found filled with shaving cream. And there's the trees at city hall getting TPd again."

Someone chuckled.

"It's becoming a serious problem," Rob argued defensively.

"Kids roaming the streets, kickin' over garbage

cans, horsin' around, trampling flower beds," Little Jimmy injected. "I for one think it's time we did something about it. I been sayin' for years, we need a curfew for these kids."

"Jimmy, you've been complaining about the teenagers for at least five hundred years," Mary Hall moaned. "Which is interesting, because I recall a certain person raising hell in his day."

Everyone began to talk at once, all having a story about a teenager they knew or a prank they had pulled when they were teens. Thankful the attention had shifted to another subject, Fia slipped into her chair. Peigi let the conversations go on for two or three minutes and then began to strike her pen on the side of her chair, getting everyone's attention again. "If you have something to say, give me a nod, raise your hand, I'll call on you."

"Exactly what is the complaint?" Tavia asked. "Vandalism?"

"Here and there, some graffiti on the boathouses, a few stolen crab pots," Peigi responded.

"Human shenanigans," Rob scoffed.

Several more comments were thrown into the ring.

"Yes, Mungo," Peigi said, recognizing the portly man in the madras plaid shorts.

The voices died down.

"I for one, in light of what's been going on around here, am concerned for the safety of these kids, not our damned dinghies. They're at a vulnerable age. The boys are mostly out chasin' deer, stealin' rowboats, harmless stuff, but the girls are who we ought to be worried about. There's a group of them spending an awful lot of time with human boys."

"You know what they're doing don't you?" Eva spoke up, amusement in her voice. "Same thing we were all trying to do at their age."

"It's forbidden," Mary Hall said flatly. "Sex is strictly forbidden before the age of twenty-one and certainly with humans."

"I'm not saying it's right." Eva shifted her long legs. "I'm just saying we all know that's what it's about."

"It's mostly flirtation," Rob threw in. "Harmless teenage stuff. We all did it. Those girls aren't having sex with those boys. They know better."

"Right. Just like you weren't jumping that cute little blonde back when we were in high school?" Rob's brother Joe teased. "What was her name? Samantha W—"

"I think we're getting off the subject here," Rob interrupted, his face reddening. "I don't know that we need to set a curfew, but it wouldn't hurt to talk to the teenagers, would it?"

"Maybe talk to Kaleigh?" Mary Hall crossed her arms over her chest and sat back in her folding chair. "She's the one I see out at all hours of the night. Flirting with those human boys who work at the diner and the ice-cream shop. She ought to know better!"

Fia glanced across the circle at her brother. Though Fin wasn't smiling, she could tell by the twinkle in his eyes that he was amused.

"I have a suggestion," he said.

At once, everyone quieted.

"Why don't we all make a point this week to talk to our teens, those of us who have them in our homes or in our families? I don't mind talking to my little brothers. Rob, you wouldn't mind talking to your niece, would you? And Mary, you've always had a way with our teens. You'd be surprised, but I bet Kaleigh might listen to you better than her own parents right now. She's always admired you."

Mary Hall sat up straighter in her chair. "She has?"

The meeting only ran another ten minutes and when it was over, Fia was quick to grab her chair, add it to the stack against the wall, and make a bee-line for the door. As she slipped down the hall, she looked back, thinking that if she could catch Fin's attention, she'd tell him she'd wait for him outside. But when she saw him surrounded by several women, all vying for his attention, she knew he might be another hour.

Just as she was about to turn away, he saw her and held up his hand, telling her to wait.

She didn't really want to. She wanted to go back to the B and B and get some sleep. She just wanted to put the council meeting and the whole day behind her. But she couldn't say no to Fin. Never could.

He was out in record time and breezed past her on the sidewalk. "You coming? We're late."

"Late for what?" she asked suspiciously.

"You know." He turned to face her and in the dim yellow moonlight she saw him arch his dark eyebrows comically.

"Oh, no, Fin." She hurried after him. "Absolutely not." She glanced behind her to see who was coming out the door. It was hard-of-hearing Little Jimmy, talking loudly to one of the Marys. Fia hurried to catch up to her brother. "We can't. You can't," she whispered under her breath. "Fin, that's been outlawed for two hundred years."

Chapter 13

"Fin, this is a bad idea. Fin!"

He veered off the street, cutting through an alley.

"Come on." She practically begged him. "Let's go home. Please? It's late. You don't need any blood tonight."

"What I *need* tonight . . . what you *need*," he shot over his shoulder, "is a little fun."

"Fin!" Fia sprinted to catch up. Once her brother made up his mind, she knew she had two choices. She could go back to the B and B and let him find his own way out of the mess he'd get himself into, or she could go with him and attempt to keep him out of trouble.

Only four blocks from their parents', on a street that overlooked the bay, they entered a dilapidated house through the back door. Though it was close to 3 A.M., the elderly Mrs. Hill, Eva's mother, Petey's aunt, was seated at her kitchen table. Dressed in a flowered, cotton nightgown, she was eating chocolate-chip cookies and drinking blood from a cut-crystal claret glass while she read a tabloid newspaper that sported the headline "Hollywood Werewolf Party Crashed by Rappers."

"Good evening, Mrs. Hill," Fin said with his usual charm.

"Evening, Fin." Mrs. Hill looked up over the rims of her pink rhinestone-studded reading glasses, her cheeks coloring.

"Good evening, Mrs. Hill." Fia followed Fin through the kitchen.

The old woman returned her gaze to the paper.

Fin opened the creaky white paneled door that led into the basement of the turn-of-the-century house. Heavy metal music wafted up the staircase. Judas Priest.

Fia darted down. Sweet Mary, Mother of Christ, she hadn't heard Judas Priest in twenty years.

Fin followed, pulling the door shut behind him, enveloping them in darkness. The walls pulsed with the heavy, pounding music and lights flashed below, reflecting rhythmically off the mason jars that lined the shelves on both sides of the stairwell. Mrs. Hill had canned peaches, green beans, beets, and what appeared to be pickles. The canning jars had to have been there for at least forty years.

"Since when did you start hanging out with Eva?" Fia whispered, glancing over her shoulder at him as she tried to make it down the steps without breaking her neck. "And Mrs. Hill? She's *ar mire.*"

Fin shrugged. "Not any crazier than the rest of them. And she's nice to me."

"Everyone's nice to you," Fia grumbled.

"She makes me cookies."

Fia stepped out of the stairwell into the room and was instantly transported through time, back to the eighties and her teenage years. The old brick basement looked just as it had the year Eva's parents remodeled it in the late seventies: cheap paneling, a clumsy, stained-pine bar built against one wall, plaid Berber carpet under her feet. There was gray pleather modular seating along one wall, a pool table on the other.

The room was smoky and smelled of mildew, beer, cigarettes, and vampires on the prowl. "Who are all these people?" Fia marveled, repelled and yet fascinated at the same time.

The basement room was wall-to-wall with men and women dressed in black leather, chains, tight T-shirts, fishnet stockings, and bustiers. Their inky dyed hair was sleeked back in bizarre styles and many of them, their faces painted white, wore black lipstick and heavy eyeliner.

"You know, brother dear, these aren't real vampires," Fia whispered loudly in Fin's ear. "What are they doing here?"

He flashed a mischievous grin. "What do you think?"

She gave him a none-too-gentle shove. "Fin, you can't do that. It's not allowed."

He shrugged. "Gray area. They're here of their own free will. They say they're vampires. They want us to drink their blood." He pointed to her as he passed her. "You want a beer, sugar britches?" he asked with a sweet southern accent. Fin had a way with languages and accents; he could imitate anyone on earth from a southern belle to an eighty-year-old Mongolian yak herder.

She shook her head furiously. "No, what I want is for you to—" Her voice was lost in a sudden rise in the volume of the music as the lead vocalist worked himself into a frenzy.

"You came. Oh, God, I can't believe you came!"

Fia felt a hand on her shoulder and spun around.

Eva threw herself into Fia's arms and smacked a wet one on her lips. It was all Fia could do to not wipe her mouth with the back of her hand as she stumbled back. "Eva."

"I'm so glad you came." Dressed similarly to the vampire impersonators, Eva clasped Fia's hand. She was wearing black lace fingerless gloves.

Fia pressed her lips together, tasting the waxy black lipstick that had smeared off Eva's lips onto her own.

"I wanted to invite you myself, tonight, at the council meeting. I really did," Eva gushed. "But I didn't want to put you in a bad position, you know, you being on the high council and all, but I told Fin you were invited. I told him I *really* wanted you to come."

She sounded high. On what, Fia was unsure; drugs, alcohol . . . maybe just human blood. In small amounts, it caused euphoria. Too much, and a Kahill became downright intoxicated. Fia eyed Eva. She must have performed quite the vanishing act to have gotten here and dressed so quickly. She couldn't have been more than ten minutes ahead of Fia and Fin. But Eva had the rare gift of being able to teleport small objects as well as herself. A regular *Samantha Stevens* among them.

"I . . . I just stopped by for a minute." Fia attempted to extricate herself from Eva's grip. "I really shouldn't be here. The council . . ." *Not to mention the Bureau.* It wasn't specifically mentioned in the agent guidelines, but she was pretty certain rounding up humans en masse and drinking their blood was a no-no.

"Just stay a minute," Eva begged, taking Fia's hand again.

Fia tried not to stare at Eva's getup but it was hard not to.

The redhead sported fishnet stockings and a black knit dress that appeared to have been spray-painted on. She was wearing no bra or panties and four-inch stilettos. Her hair had been gelled and sculpted into a point on the top of her head and white plastic skulls dangled from her earlobes. She finished off the Halloween-costume-gone-bad with thick black eyeliner and the apparently requisite black lipstick.

Fia was so stunned by Eva's getup, by the room of "guests," that she didn't know what to say. She hadn't realized anyone had this kind of party in Clare Point anymore. Sure, once in a while she caught wind of a *feasta oíche* somewhere in Europe, but she hadn't thought anyone dared hold them at home anymore. Leave it to Fin and Eva.

In the 1920s, at the height of prohibition, the general council had banned all *feasta oíche,* or feast night, celebrations after a party had gotten out of hand and humans had died. Fortunately, no one was turned into a vampire. But the bodies had to be disposed of and the sept had been in an uproar for weeks afterward, as local law officials searched for the fourteen family members that had all vanished from a silver-anniversary party. Their bodies were never found and the mystery was never solved. The cases remained unsolved to this day.

"Let me get you a drink." Eve grabbed Fia's hand,

squeezed it and let go, darting into the crowd. "Be right—"

"No, E—" It was a waste of breath. Eva was gone and the music was so loud she couldn't have heard Fia anyway.

"Good evening," a man in his late twenties greeted Fia in a poor Eastern European accent as he approached her. He bared his canine teeth, which had apparently been chiseled to points.

Fia had to draw her lips tightly to keep from laughing aloud. "Hi."

He circled her, flapping a black and red satin cape behind him.

She covered her mouth with her hand. Where did Eva find these people?

"I like your outfit," he told her. "Very . . . *subtle.*"

She looked down. Black sweatpants and a man's black Calvin Klein T-shirt. Flip-flops.

"Where did you—" She couldn't help herself. "How did you . . . get invited here?"

He pulled his black lips back to bare the cosmetically altered teeth again.

And to think, Fia had had her canines *filed down* at the age of sixteen when they became more pronounced than was acceptable among humans, even in their retracted state.

"First time at one of these parties?" He moved closer, drawing his cape around her.

"Actually . . ." Fia found herself at a loss as to what to say. She couldn't fathom what bad movie or what character he was imitating. He was just so ridiculous looking. As he circled her, she continued to turn so that she could face him.

He reached out to rest his hand on the wall,

trapping her with his cloak. A flash of strobe light crossed his face and she saw that he was wearing black contacts. He looked silly, but he smelled . . . *inviting*.

She glanced around the room and spotted Regan on one end of the modular couch, a human woman dressed in black on each arm. He flashed a smile; not warm like Fin's. Cold. Arrogant. Challenging.

"Hey, Fee, I didn't expect to find you here." Arlan wove around two human females who were doing some sort of striptease dance to Iron Maiden. "Drink?"

She took the bottle of pale ale he offered and tipped it. She knew it was a mistake the minute she tasted the yeasty, mild brew. There were reasons why she didn't drink.

"Who's your friend?" Arlan cocked his head at the ridiculous looking guy in the cape standing beside her.

"Jeremy." The cape offered his hand.

"Get lost, buster." Arlan drew back his lips and long saber teeth appeared. He snarled like a lion.

The guy in the cloak flinched. Blinked. Ducked off.

"That wasn't very nice." Fia took a drink from the bottle.

"He'll never remember a thing in the morning." Arlan's teeth morphed back to normal as he snatched the beer from her.

She watched the way his mouth fit around the brown glass.

"Pretty naughty of you to be here, Special Agent Kahill. Especially with your boyfriend back at the house."

"He isn't my—"

"Hey, Fee, it's okay," he whispered, moving closer so that she could hear him over the pulsating music. "I get it. It happens to all of us once in a while, and him looking like Ian . . ." Arlan shrugged. "Just my bad luck."

"Arlan—"

"Shhh. I'm talking." He pressed his finger to her lips. "So you listen." He drew back his hand. "See, I been thinking. And I've decided I'm not going to ask you to my place anymore. I'm cutting you off."

"You're what?" She tipped the beer back. It tasted entirely too good.

"I'm cutting you off. Cold turkey. No more hot stud vampire for you, Missy."

She laughed, but she knew he was being serious. At least half serious. "Arlan—"

"No, no, hear me out. I've decided I can wait until you're ready. Until you come to me." Holding the beer bottle with one hand, with the other he traced her pale flesh above the collar of her T-shirt.

Fia's heart rate soared.

"I'm going to give you some time. Some space. Let you come to your senses."

She had to smile. He was such a damned good guy.

"And you will, Fee. Because you always do." He lowered his hand, looking into her eyes. "You'll realize it can never work with a human, just the way I've realized it. And you'll know." Another shrug of his broad shoulders.

"I'll know?"

Again, he leaned close, still holding her gaze with his big brown eyes. "That I'm the only man for you." He brushed his lips against hers . . . the sweetest kiss.

Then he was gone. A bobbing head in a sea of bodies twisting on the dance floor.

Fia finished the beer and made her way to the bar, hands in the air over her head, trying to squeeze through. There were so many people, bodies pushing, brushing, gyrating. The music throbbed in her head. The strobe lights in the corner of the room flashed. Someone had already taken human blood . . . she could smell it in the room. Was it Regan? Eva? Both of them?

She set the empty bottle on the bar.

The young woman behind the bar looked up. She wore a tight black T-shirt with a graphic of red lips on it. "Fia!" She laughed. "I have to say, you're one of the last people I would have guessed I would see here tonight."

Fia plopped down on a barstool. "Are you talking or serving?"

Sorcha grinned and reached for a bottle of ale in a bucket of ice. "Serving." She popped open the top with a bottle opener and passed it to Fia. "So how have you been?" She leaned over, elbows on the bar. "Well, not so great lately, I guess, with what's going on here, but you know—how's life in the big city?"

Fia felt totally out of her element; the music, the wild atmosphere, the beer, someone asking her to talk about herself. She didn't know what to say.

"I miss you, you know."

Fia leaned over to hear her better. "Miss me?"

Sorcha was Fia's age and pretty with pale red-blond hair, blue eyes, and killer cheekbones. Her lover and soon-to-be husband had been killed in Ian's raid, so she'd never had the opportunity to be married, or give birth, either.

"I miss talking to you, seeing you," Sorcha said. "You used to call me . . . or least return my calls."

"I'm sorry." Fia looked down at the dark bottle in her hands. "I've been busy. You know, long hours at work."

"I know. But not any busier than the rest of us." Sorcha grabbed a beer for herself and leaned on the bar again. "I just figured you had your life in Philadelphia. Your FBI career." Her voice sounded wistful. Hurt. "We were good friends, Fia. For a long time. What happened? What did I do wrong?"

Fia made herself look at Sorcha. "You didn't do anything," she said softly. "It's me." She was quiet for a minute, thinking. She *had* shut Sorcha out. And Eva. And Alana. They had all been such great friends for a long time. Hundreds of years. And then, Fia had gotten caught up in her life with Joseph, then the FBI . . . her human life . . . and . . .

She wasn't sure what had happened. Why. She had just pulled back from Clare Point and everyone here, including her friends.

Sorcha waited, sipping her beer.

"I don't know what to say." Fia grimaced and looked up. "I'm sorry?"

Sorcha grinned, sliding her bottle across the bar to clink against Fia's bottle. "To old friends."

"Old friends," Fia agreed.

As the two talked, the party around them gained momentum. Maybe it was just the beer and lack of sleep, but as the hours passed, the music seemed to Fia to get louder, the movement of the bodies around her more frantic.

By her fourth beer, Fia was beginning to think it was time she made her exit. Sorcha had wandered off with Eva to dance with a human couple sporting plastic, glow-in-the-dark fangs and Fia was left alone on the bar stool to finish the last of her beer and find enough energy to walk out.

She was watching a woman dance . . . actually, watching the woman's Gucci shoes—they were really cute—when her buddy from earlier in the evening swooped in, satin cape flapping.

"A dance, *madam?*"

She was going to say no. She had no intentions whatsoever of dancing with him. How *did* one slow dance to Def Leppard, anyway? But then he drew his hand down his throat, catching Fia's attention, and she slid off the stool, mesmerized by the steady pulse in his throat.

"Billy's Got a Gun" throbbed in her head as Jeremy wrapped his arms and his cloak around her. It was just so easy . . . easier even than with the men she picked up in bars. This guy *asked* her if she'd like to taste his blood.

Everything, everyone, was spinning around Fia. She brushed her lips against Jeremy's throat and he moaned. She bit gently, testing the waters. He groaned.

She'd only intended to take a tiny sip. No sex of course, and just a taste. But he *wanted* it. Wanted her. It was what all the humans in the room wanted.

Jeremy's blood warm and sweet and tangy on her tongue, she caught him in her arms as he passed out. Realizing what she had done, she glanced around, afraid someone had seen her. But there were other young sept members on the dance floor supporting their unconscious partners.

There were humans lying on the couches, on the floor. Sorcha was kissing a good-looking human wearing a costume straight out of the movie *Bram Stoker's Dracula*, including the spectacles and top hat.

Fia eased Jeremy's six-foot frame onto the carpet. As Arlan said, he'd remember nothing in the morning. If this party was like the ones in the old days, while still unconscious, the humans would be transported back to where they had come from and in the morning they would be weak, hung over. They would remember nothing of where they had been or what they had done. At the very most, they would all talk about the weird dreams they had had.

A human, lying half under an end table, caught Fia's hair and twisted it around his fingers. She crawled toward him. He lifted his chin, groping her breasts and offered his neck, already dotted with punctures. She only took a couple of sips. She didn't know how much of his blood had already been drained. Then Eva, stretched out on the end of couch, beckoned her.

Fia half crawled, half dragged herself to the couch, where a human male lay passed out in Eva's lap. Eva smiled, her mouth red with the man's blood.

Fia lowered her head and drank greedily.

Fia didn't know how long she was on the floor or how many humans she sampled or how many vampires she shared her own blood with. It had been a very long time since she had overindulged this way and after a while all the faces faded. She saw nothing but blood. Smelled nothing but blood. Tasted nothing but sweet, forbidden, human blood.

It was almost dawn when she stumbled up the cellar steps, missing one flip-flop. She left the other under Mrs. Hill's kitchen table. In the gray dawn, Fia cut across yards and slunk into her mother's house. She thought she would do better just to shower, get dressed, and get on with her day, but by the time she let herself into the Seahorse bedroom, she was so tired that she decided to lie down. Just for five minutes. Then she would have to get up. She was meeting Glen for breakfast. She had work to do. A life to return to. A *real* life.

Fia must have dozed off. She missed breakfast, grabbed a shower. A glance at her neck in the mirror while dressing made her realize that the tank top she had intended to wear under her suit jacket was definitely not going to do today. She stole one of her little brothers' turtlenecks out of the laundry room. Maroon. She hated maroon. She found Glen on the front porch in an antique glider. She dropped down beside him. "Mornin'."

He glanced at her. Then a double take. "You okay?"

Sounded like genuine concern.

She lowered her sunglasses from her damp hair and sipped from the white mug in her hand. Mornings like this, she wished she drank coffee. She could have used the extra kick of caffeine. "Fine."

"You don't look fine. You look . . . hungover. I thought you said you didn't drink."

She would have smiled had her head not felt as if someone were driving nails into it with a pneumatic gun. What she had told him was that she didn't drink *alcohol*, at least nothing beyond a good Hill stout. She'd never said anything about overindulging in blood.

"I don't. Just a bad night." She tugged on the too-tight collar of the ridiculous-looking turtleneck and leaned her head back on the swing. "Old haunts, shall we say?"

He studied her for a moment and then gazed out over the well-manicured green lawn. The fishpond in the side yard gurgled. Midmorning traffic crawled by. No one in Clare Point was ever in a hurry. It wasn't as if they were going to grow old and die before they completed their task. They had all the time in the world . . . and maybe then some.

"You went out last night," he said quietly.

She opened her eyes, cut them in his direction. Pain knifed through her head.

"I couldn't sleep either. I heard you go out. One forty-five. Pretty late for a small town like this."

Not knowing what to say, Fia said nothing. She sipped her tea, making a mental note to be more careful about slipping out at night while in his vicinity. Of course it probably wouldn't matter after today. He was returning to Baltimore, she to Philadelphia. Cases would get solved. Lives that had intersected would never cross again. It was the nature of an FBI agent's job. Life.

Glen was quiet beside her and she watched him through the dark lenses of her Maui Jims. "Guess these walls are thinner than we realized." She hesitated. The bites on her neck burned and she tugged at the turtleneck again, wondering if they really hurt or if it was just guilt that stung this morning. She should never have gone to the party last night with Fin. She was a member of the high council, for sweet Joseph's sake. She should have shut the party down.

"I heard you talking to your fiancée," she said, trying to keep her tone light. "Table-linen matter still not settled?"

He watched a nuthatch teeter on the edge of a stone birdbath in a flower bed. "Old haunts?"

"What's that?" she asked. Her mind was working sluggishly this morning.

"You said *old haunts* kept you awake. You mean an old boyfriend?"

She crossed her ankles and watched the nuthatch. "Something like that."

"The guy waiting for you on the porch last night?"

"Yeah," she heard herself say. Then, before she could catch herself. "No . . . not really. It's . . . complicated, Glen."

"You're telling me."

Again, silence.

"Did you love him?"

"Who, Arlan? No. It was his friend. His best friend." Fia didn't know why she was saying these things, but it was as if once she started talking, she couldn't stop herself. "They were practically brothers growing up." She lifted the mug to her lips. "I loved Ian. Arlan loved me. Ian . . . mostly he just loved himself."

Emotion thickened her voice. It was the first time she'd ever admitted that fact. To herself. To anyone. Sweet Mary, Mother and Joseph, what had she drunk last night? Some sort of bizarre truth serum?

"Where's Ian now?"

"Gone."

She said it with such a finality that he didn't ask where. She didn't think he realized she meant dead. She knew he didn't realize she meant dead hundreds of years ago.

Hundreds of years? Had it been that long? Why then, did it still hurt so much?

"And Arlan's still coming around?"

"Yeah." She gave a little laugh, but there was no humor in it. It made her sad. Sometimes angry, but this morning . . . just sad.

"And you and he . . ." Glen left the sentence for her to finish.

"Arlan and I . . ." Fia searched for the right words. "I . . . I love him for what he's been to me, for how he's been there, but—"

"You're not in love with him?"

Fia lifted damp lashes to watch the birdbath again. The nuthatch was gone, but two female cardinals had come in its place. She couldn't believe she was having this conversation with Glen on her mother's front porch in broad, blinding daylight. Wasn't this the kind of talk people who were practically strangers, like themselves, had late at night in bars, half lit? Wasn't the anonymity what made them talk outside their usual boundaries of comfort? Fia couldn't count the number of times men had confessed to her they didn't love their wives or they hated their daddies or they were wearing pink silk panties under their gray Armani suit.

"No, it's not settled," Glen said.

She shifted her gaze from the birdbath to the good-looking man beside her. Again, the sluggish brain. "I'm sorry?"

"The linens. Stacy and I. We didn't agree on the

table linens. Hell, I don't even know if we agreed what country we're getting married in." He looked away from her, squeezing his temples with his thumb and forefinger.

She couldn't see his eyes because he was wearing sunglasses, too, but she sensed unrest. Unhappiness. "Trouble in paradise?"

He chuckled. "Something like that."

"So you fought over white versus ivory napkins. So what? Weddings are stressful, or so everyone tells me. You'll work it—"

"It's not the damned napkins, Fia."

His forceful tone startled her. Then she realized that he didn't want her to placate or reassure. He just wanted her to listen. She drew her knees closer to his, angling her shoulders so that she was looking directly at him.

"I don't know . . . I'm not sure . . ." He stopped and started again. "It's not as if I ever really made any decision. You know what I mean? It just all fell into place. We started dating. Sleeping together. I liked her fine."

But there was no passion between them. She could hear it in his voice. Smell it on his breath. And her heart gave a trip.

For what earthly reason, she had no idea.

"You don't love her but you're going to marry her?" she asked softly.

The conversation was so surreal. This was not the kind of exchange she was used to. In fact, she wasn't used to exchanges at all, really, at least not of the personal sort. In bars, she listened to men's confessions because they always wanted to come clean before they asked her back to their place. She had no real girlfriends, not in the outside world, at least. And here in Clare Point . . . well, everyone already knew all her deep, dark secrets.

"I don't know." He lifted his hand and let it fall. "I don't know if I love her. I don't know if I want to marry her. I don't know if I'm getting cold feet because every forty-two-year-old man who's never been married does get scared at some point, or . . ."

Fia wanted to reach out to him. She wanted to rest her hand on his knee. On his arm. She wanted to draw him to her breast, smooth his hair, and whisper to him that it would be all right. That he would figure it all out.

She stayed on her side of the porch swing. He stayed on his, but there was a sudden crackle of energy in the air. A sexual tension that hadn't been there before. He *wanted* her to touch him . . .

"Glen—"

"Hey, I'm sorry. I didn't mean to get emo on you, here." He got up awkwardly. "I was waiting around thinking we should talk before we go back, but we're good, right? Waiting on the autopsy, the tox reports, lab results, etcetera."

"Right. Yeah. Sure." She got to her feet, pushing the swing back as she rose. It drifted forward. She felt like a complete idiot. A dweeb, her teenage brother would have called her.

"So I guess I'll be on my way." He hooked his thumb in the direction of his car, parked on the street. "We'll talk next week, right?"

She followed him to the steps, resting her hand on a white porch column. "Sure. Talk to you next week."

On the sidewalk, he raised his hand in a half-wave.

Fia couldn't decide if she wanted to run and tackle him and kiss him, or bite him. Either would have worked.

Chapter 14

"I appreciate you taking the time to meet with me, Special Agent Kahill. I know this isn't the way we usually do business." Lieutenant Sutton glanced up at the guy in the paper hat behind the deli counter. "Smoked turkey on whole wheat, sprouts and mayo, please. But this is the kind of thing I feel weird talking about over the phone, if you know what I mean," the policewoman continued, looking to Fia.

"Roast beef on rye with brown mustard. No, not that piece. The rare stuff." Fia pointed at the slab of meat in the glass deli case.

She had been surprised when Lieutenant Sutton had called Monday morning and asked her out to lunch to talk about the case. It really *wasn't* done often, dialogue between FBI and local cops, but Fia's curiosity was piqued.

Even though Jarrell had passed the task of researching similar past crimes for the Lansdowne police on to Morone weeks ago, Fia hadn't been able to set the woman's death aside the way she usually could. It was a technique cops learned early, had to, to stay sane, and it worked most of the time. But not always. Once in a while there was a case, a victim, or maybe a surviving family member who stuck with you long after the case had been solved or officially left open.

"It's not a problem, Lieutenant. A woman's got to eat." Fia watched the deli guy slice her roast beef with an electric slicer. Rivulets of bloody juice ran over the sides of the blade. "I needed to get out of the office for a few minutes anyway."

"Tough case?" Sutton accepted her paper plate from gloved hands.

"The beheadings in Delaware."

A woman in brown BCBG pumps in line behind them cut her eyes at Fia.

So beheadings weren't polite deli-line conversation. Why was the chick eavesdropping, anyway?

Sutton spotted Brown Pump Chick and moved up to the cash register without saying anything more. She waited for Fia at a table in the front, next to the window. The deli was a dump, but the roast beef was always excellent and it was only a couple of blocks from the Bureau's office on Arch.

"You were saying you were on the beheading cases."

"Know anything about what happened?" Fia opened the cap on her bottle of iced tea.

"Mostly what I read in the paper."

"First a postmaster. Then a police officer."

"Jesus." Sutton bit off a corner of her sandwich.

"Thing is . . ." Fia looked down at her sandwich wrapped in waxed paper. "I'm *from* Clare Point."

"And they put you on the case?"

"Long story involving federal bureaucracy at its finest." Fia dropped a napkin into her lap and reached for her sandwich, realizing she was famished. "So what's going on with the Mulvine case?"

"Nothing, and that's what's irking me." Sutton nibbled at the crust of her bread. "Nothing came back on the forensics. I did dig up this file." She pulled a manila envelope out of her leather bag and slid it across the table. She wrinkled her nose and reached for her sandwich again. "You probably want to wait until you get back to the office to have a look."

Fia stared at the envelope, getting that weird feeling again. She looked up at Sutton. "Don't take this the wrong way, but—" She stopped and then started again, thinking that no matter how she phrased it, it was going to come out rude. "I'm not sure I know how I can help you."

"I know. Not your case. Not your jurisdiction." Sutton held out one hand, sandwich in the other. "The other agent who contacted me was not very helpful."

Fia frowned. "Really? He find anything of use?"

Sutton looked up, chuckling. "Not a thing. Not even sure he looked, but that's neither here nor there." She looked down at the envelope, then back at Fia. "Truthfully, I don't know why I called you." She groaned. "This sounds stupid, but I'm at such a loss with this case, it's so disturbing and . . . I felt as if you and I made some kind of connection that night at the scene." She grabbed her napkin, lowering her voice. "And no, I'm not coming on to you, Special Agent Kahill. I'm strictly heterosexual, although I don't get the chance to demonstrate it nearly as often as I'd like."

It was Fia's turn to laugh. In another life, if she

had another life, she might like to have been friends with this woman. "I didn't think you were. And it's Fia."

"Ann," she said. "Look, Fia, I called because I'm at that point in the case where it's time to box up the evidence and stick it on a shelf and I don't want to do that. I was hoping you could look at this other case"—she tapped the manila envelope—"and tell me if you think this is the same guy."

Again, Fia eyed the envelope. She remembered feeling that night as if she had seen the girl . . . the alley . . . *something* before. "How old is it?"

"Fifteen years in October. Crime scene was only two blocks from where Casey Mulvine was found. I'd like you to look at these photos. It didn't occur to me at the time, but if you compare them to the Mulvine crime scene photos, I think maybe these girls were posed. She hesitated. "By the same killer."

"Serial killer who hasn't struck in fifteen years?" Fia tried not to sound too much like the arrogant, doubting FBI agent she could sometimes be when dealing with local police.

The lieutenant shrugged. "Told you, I'm grasping at straws. But I can't get anyone in my office to bear with me long enough to consider the possibility and you . . . you were there. You got the vibes."

Fia wanted to crack a joke about the "vibes," but she didn't. Sutton's observation was too accurate. Accurate enough to make Fia uncomfortable.

"Serial killer," Fia mused aloud.

"Look . . . I know you don't know me," Sutton said, "but my instincts are good and I'm telling you, this is the same man. I don't know if he's killed others in the area and we just haven't put it together, or if he's been out of town or in jail, or happily married until his wife dumped him last month, but he's done it before." She paused. "And I'm afraid he's going to do it again."

"I'll have a look," Fia agreed, reaching for the envelope. As her fingertips touched it, she felt that same eerie tingling she'd gotten the night she entered the alleyway to meet with Sutton.

So, was it the crime or was it the cop?

It's the mature thing to do, Fia told herself as she cruised the block for a parking spot. *It's the only way to settle things between us. For good. The only way to put this relationship behind so I can move forward.*

She hadn't really come up with the mantras on her own. All she was doing was repeating the things Kettleman had said in their session yesterday.

Fia rounded the block again and braked behind a UPS truck double-parked. She glanced at the manila envelope on the seat beside her. She didn't have to slide the faded photos out to see them. They were burned into her mind, the brand still sizzling at the edge of her tender flesh.

Maria Pulchecko, age twenty-one. Blond, like Casey Mulvine. About the same height and weight. She was found in the alley behind what had been the Clover, a pseudo-Irish pub, in the eighties. The place had since been sucked into the city's creeping blocks of renovations, old brick buildings that had been divided into one bedroom and studio apartments.

A nursing student, Maria Pulchecko had also been raped and strangled, but with her bra, not bare hands. A slightly different MO than Mulvine's killer. But what was giving off the creepy vibes was that she was found lying in the alleyway in a position almost identical to Casey's. And, as Sutton had observed, she didn't appear posed . . . not until you compared the two women. Then, they eerily appeared to be the same woman . . . the same crime scene.

A copycat killer? Possibly. Who? A cop, an emergency technician, a neighbor who had seen Maria Pulchecko sprawled in the alley fifteen years ago and had been dying to mimic the crime?

Fia laid on her horn. What was the UPS guy still doing out at eight o'clock at night? She craned her neck, trying to figure out if she could squeeze by him, but there wasn't a chance. A massive SUV prevented that escape maneuver.

More horns began to sound behind her and she glanced up in the rearview mirror. Being an agent, seeing dead women in alleys and men without their heads made her suspicious. Any one of the drivers behind her could be ready to blow a gasket, could pull a gun from his or her glove compartment and start taking potshots.

A young Asian woman in a brown uniform jogged across the street, waved to Fia, and jumped into the UPS panel truck.

Five minutes later, Fia had parked her car and was walking into the bistro where she had told Joseph she would meet him. It had to be somewhere public, she had insisted. And not a bar. He had a table for them in the back. She slipped into her chair, glancing at the candle flickering on the table between them and the single red rose in a bud vase beside the chrome salt and pepper shakers.

"Could you have found a better-lit table?" she asked, tossing her bag on the chair beside her. Joseph had always been a romancer. And he'd been good at it. And he'd known it.

"Hey, you picked the restaurant," Joseph replied smoothly.

She looked to the waiter. "A tonic water, please." She glanced at Joseph. He'd shaved before he'd come and still smelled of expensive shaving cream. He'd always had a problem with a five o'clock shadow but he'd only ever shaved in the evening for big dates. "He'll have another of whatever it is he's drinking."

Fia waited for the waiter to walk away before she leaned back in her chair, crossing her arms over her chest. "Okay, enough of this. I want to know why you're here and when you're going."

"Why I'm here?" He opened his arms innocently. He was wearing a designer linen shirt that was impeccably smooth, not a wrinkle to be seen. No tie. Entirely too much charm. "I told you why I'm here. Scouting out a new place for my partner and me to set up business. Elective plastic surgery has become a gold mine."

"So what was wrong with your business in California? Surely not everyone in Southern California has gotten a boob job yet."

"Fee, you're such a cynic. So distrustful. Nothing was wrong. Everything was great. So great that we want to expand to the East Coast."

She didn't like it when he called her Fee. That name was personal. Private. He no longer had a right to it. Hadn't in a very long time.

The waiter brought the drinks, but walked away without offering a menu.

"I already ordered the foie gras and feta filo sachets." He sat back, resting his ankle on his knee.

"I told the waiter we would see how things went before ordering the entrées."

"I don't think I'll be staying long enough for an entrée." Fia leaned forward. "Tell me what's going on and don't lie. You're not a good liar."

He smiled. "Actually I am, Fee."

Actually, he was, but she wasn't going to admit it. "You can't be here. Not in this city. You agreed with me. We *agreed*, Joseph."

"We agreed, we agreed." He reached for his fresh drink. "Years ago, Fee. We were kids." He sipped from the glass. Something clear on the rocks. "Can't we let bygones be bygones? Kiss and make up?"

"There will be no kissing. No making up, Joseph." She studied his face for a moment. He was very good at blocking his thoughts. It was as if she were standing in front of a brick wall when she tried to read his mind. Mentally, she stabbed at him. It was definitely a wall, but one with the tiniest chink in it . . .

"What did you do, Joseph?" she hissed.

He blinked. "Do?"

"In LA? Why did you have to leave?"

For the first time since he'd reappeared in her life, she saw a flash of uncertainty on his face. Self-doubt. Maybe even self-loathing.

"Joseph?"

"It was nothing. A misunderstanding," he said quickly.

"But a big enough one that you had to move across the country?"

"My partner and I really had been discussing opening another office." He was practically whining when he said it.

"So you're admitting it. You did do something you shouldn't have done."

He met her gaze. "Haven't we all, Fee?"

It was a direct accusation.

"Oh, come on." He slid forward, trying to take her hand, resting on the table. "I had a little problem with addiction. But I'm fine now. I'm great. And I'm ready to make a fresh start."

She pulled away.

"We're adults. Surely we could live in the same *city*."

"We *couldn't*," she insisted.

He caught her hand and she didn't pull away, not because she wanted him to touch her, but because she didn't want to cause a scene. Not here, not this close to her office. Not so public. This wasn't like in a bar where smoke and alcohol made people forget who and what they saw.

"I need you, Fee," Joseph whispered, holding her hand tightly in his. "I really need you. I'm still in love with you. I swear I am."

"Do you need help, Joseph? With this addiction? Because I know someone who's really helped me. She's an excellent psychiatrist that specializes in this sort of thing."

"You, a shrink?"

Spotting the waiter approaching with two plates, she slipped her hand out of his and slid back a little in her chair. Joseph served both of them small portions of the foie gras and toasted bread rounds.

"I'm serious," she said. "I think you should see Dr. Kettleman. I think she could help you. Help you see that the two of us together isn't going to work."

"You mean like the two of us go together? Like couples counseling?" He licked his fingers. "The foie gras is excellent, isn't it?"

Couples counseling was not what she had in mind.

What she had in mind was for Joseph to pack up and leave town. Tonight. "I guess that's a possibility," she heard herself say. "Do you want me to call Dr. Kettleman? Make the appointment?"

"How about if I think about it?" He winked and then pushed her plate toward her. "You've got to try the foie gras, Fee. It's absolutely lovely."

Fia didn't stay in the bistro long enough to order an entrée. She went back to her apartment intending to clean the litter box, change into a pair of boxers, and watch an old movie on TV. But at her apartment, she found herself restless. And before she really had time to think it through, she was getting out of her car in Lansdowne, just blocks from where Casey Mulvine had been murdered.

Dressed in her favorite leather miniskirt and boots because the weather had turned cool, she hit two pubs, then wandered into a little pool hall that was blaring punk music. She took a seat at the bar between a guy with pink hair and another shaved bald. Mentally, she flipped a coin. Pink Hair was the lucky winner . . . maybe loser. Just depended on how you looked at it.

He said his name was Drummer, which more than likely had something to do with the fact that he pounded the bar top, his leg, her leg, with his fingers. It was nonstop and got pretty irritating by her second tonic. But by then her other candidate, the bald guy, had moved on.

Drummer was drinking shots of vodka. By the time she watched him down his fourth, she knew all about his band, his mother charging him rent to live in his own house, and his cat that had run away last night and he still hadn't found him. She didn't feel bad for him, but she did for the cat. Hoped it hadn't been hit by a car or gotten into a fight with a dog.

Fia didn't have to suggest they go to his apartment in the basement of his mother's row house, he invited her. Conveniently, it was in the direction of her parked car.

There was a shortcut to his place. There always was. When she stopped him in the alley, grabbed the lapel of his leather coat, and pulled him against her, he swayed drunkenly.

"Want me, don't you babe?" he muttered, slobbering on her cheek as he tried to find her mouth.

She wasn't in the mood for small talk tonight. She grabbed him from behind by a hank of his pink hair, tilted his head back, and before he could say "mommy," she sank her canines into his throat. As he fainted in her arms, she lapped up the oozing blood.

Fia expected that hot rush of excitement, the trembling in her knees, the ripples of pleasure. She got none of it. It was if she were drinking lukewarm bathwater. Annoyed, she let him slip unceremoniously to the ground. Stepping over him, she wiped her mouth with the back of her hand. She thought it was the first time she'd ever *not* enjoyed human blood.

Maybe it was the bad aftertaste of the cheap vodka he drank. Or guilt. She didn't know which one tasted worse.

Chapter 15

All week, Fia's finger itched to punch Glen's phone number into her cell. But she couldn't come up with a good reason to call him, no matter how much negotiating she did with herself. Nothing had come back on the crime-scene evidence, and there were no unusual findings in the *wet* autopsy report. The impalement hadn't killed him, but mostly because he was then beheaded.

Fia did e-mail Glen to let him know he should have received a copy of the report as well, but he hadn't responded. She'd kind of hoped he'd write back, but when he didn't, she couldn't decide why. She knew it wasn't her imagination; they'd definitely made a connection last week. But he was engaged. Maybe he wasn't interested in connections. Or maybe she was reading entirely too much into his lack of response. He *had*, after all, warned her that he wasn't good at e-mail.

Thursday evening, Fia was surprised to hear from Sorcha. She called to invite Fia for a "girls' night" Saturday at her place. She also made mention of a matter they needed to discuss, but wouldn't give any details, promising she would explain when Fia arrived.

Fia surprised herself by agreeing to go. Maybe she was intrigued by the matter Sorcha referred to. Maybe she just wanted to get out of Philly and away from Joseph. Or maybe she was beginning to realize how homesick she was. Clare Point wasn't all bad; the people weren't all that bad. And Sorcha was right; they had been good friends. Fia thought maybe she missed her more than she realized.

Fia showed up at Sorcha's little duplex house on the beach Saturday night, just as the sun was setting, with a bottle of vodka and a tray of good sushi she'd picked up at a gourmet deli near her apartment.

"You came!" Sorcha met Fia on the front porch with a big hug. "Come on in. We're making martinis, then I thought we'd sit out here. The weather's so divine." She grinned, seeming tickled with herself as well as with Fia.

Fia caught a snippet of Sorcha's thoughts. Something about Fia having the guts to come. Fia wondered what she meant, but didn't want to know the answer badly enough to ask.

"Last renters for the season left this morning," Sorcha bubbled, waving Fia inside. "I've got the place all to myself until April!"

Fia followed Sorcha into the large eat-in kitchen that had recently been remodeled. "This is great," she said, feeling a little awkward. She didn't socialize much in Philadelphia beyond bar stools and grocery shopping with Betty, who was too hard of hearing to expect much in the way of conversation.

"I'll be damned." Eva, who was standing at the granite counter pouring liquor into a martini shaker, pointed to Sorcha. "I owe you five bucks." She looked to Fia. "I bet Sorcha you wouldn't come."

"I said I was coming," Fia protested, laughing as she set down her hostess gifts.

"I still bet you weren't coming." Eva picked up the bottle of vodka Fia had brought. "But Belvedere? Glad you did."

"Hey, there." Shannon came out of the powder room. "I thought that was your voice I heard." She surprised Fia by throwing her arms around her and giving her a big hug. "Glad you could come."

"You are?"

Shannon made a face as she slid onto one of the stools on the far side of the breakfast bar. "You bet. I'm going into the woods tonight after midnight, believe me, holy Saint Mary, I want an FBI agent with me."

"We're going into the woods?"

"I didn't tell her." Sorcha pretended to whisper a secret to the other two women.

"You didn't tell her?" Eva put the lid on the antique glass-and-chrome martini shaker and began to shake it.

"Didn't tell me what?"

Shannon peeled back the plastic wrap on the tray of sushi and chose a piece of tuna and seaweed. "You gotta tell her."

"And I'm going to." Sorcha carried four martini glasses to the counter.

"I think maybe I'll pass on the martinis." Fia raised her hand to stop Eva from pouring her one. After her behavior at the party last weekend, Fia was thinking that "no alcohol beyond Tavia's ale" was a good rule of thumb.

"Come on, you have to have a martini," Sorcha protested. "How can you come to girls' martini night and not have a martini?"

"You're going to want a drink before you hear this one." Eva elbowed Fia. "Shannon thinks that Kaleigh and some of the other girls are practicing some kind of witchcraft on the game preserve."

Fia reached for a glass. "Maybe just a small one."

"So do you really think there's such a thing as witches?" Shannon whispered in the dark, only a stride behind Fia.

The four women had retired to Sorcha's front porch with their martini shaker and talked until after midnight. Fia had managed to say no after one green-apple martini and one wedding-cake martini, so her head was clear as they entered the game preserve. Her weapon, strapped into the leather holster she wore over her black Nike T-shirt, was loaded. For what, she didn't know, but ever since they left the parking lot, taking the same deer trail into the woods that she and Glen had followed a little more than a week ago, she'd had a bad feeling.

"Witches? I don't know," Fia said softly.

They didn't need a flashlight. All four women saw almost as well in the dark as they did in the daylight. A perk of being one of the living dead.

"Yeah, sounds a little out-there, doesn't it?" Shannon ducked under a poplar branch that hung over the path.

"I guess. But maybe not any farther out-there than vampires." Fia glanced over her shoulder to be sure that Sorcha and Eva were keeping up. "Who knows? Maybe there is such a thing as witches and they don't believe in us, either."

Shannon giggled. She was tipsy. They all were, except for Fia. And considering the fact that no one had pushed her on rounds three through five of the martini menu, Fia suspected the women had planned it that way. She sensed she made them feel safe. With her in the dark woods with them, none of them seemed to be afraid they might come upon Bobby and Mahon's killer. Or if they did, they had confidence that their own homegrown law-enforcement agent would protect them.

"Come on, you two. Keep up," Fia called over her shoulder. They were more than half a mile into the woods now, and approaching the place where Mahon's body had been found.

Eva giggled. "Gotta pee. Hang on, Fee. Sorcha and I need a potty stop."

"I told you to go before you came, kids," Shannon sang as the two women stepped off the path to relieve themselves.

"How about you?" Fia asked Shannon.

The blonde grinned. "Went before I left, but thanks for asking, Mommy."

Fia could have taken Shannon's comment as an insult; on Fia's age, her bossiness, any number of things. But she knew Shannon meant nothing by it and she found herself able to let it slide. She'd never particularly liked Shannon, but she was discovering that if she could just get past the big-boobed blond cocktail-waitress image, the young woman was actually kind of nice. Not at all the ditz she appeared to be at the Hill.

"So, how's that hot FBI agent? *Special Agent Glen*

Duncan," Shannon said as if announcing his name on TV.

"Fine. I guess." Fia was so surprised by Shannon's sudden change of topic that it took her a second to regroup. "I don't know. I haven't talked to him since we left here last Friday."

"Haven't talked to him?" Shannon walked to Fia, looking up at her. "Are you nuts, girlfriend? He's mad for you."

Fia frowned.

"Oh, please. I know." Shannon raised her palm. "He's a human. Humans are dangerous. We're dangerous to humans," she chanted. "Well, I say it's all a bunch of bull."

"You do?" Fia asked. Then realizing that the way she said it made it sound like she *was* interested in Glen, she pulled back a branch and called softly into the woods. "What's taking you two so long? Come on." She looked back down at Shannon.

"Sometimes you just have to take chances, Fia. Maybe sometimes with humans. Sometimes with yourself."

"He's engaged," Fia said.

"So what?" Shannon shrugged. "You like him. I think you should go for it. The way I saw him looking at you the other night in the pub, I don't think that's as big a problem as you might think. And as far as him looking like . . . you know, so what? Who cares? That was hundreds of years ago. People in this town have too much to say about too many things. You have a right to a little happiness. Same as anyone else in Clare Point."

Fia crossed her arms over her chest. She'd been warm, hiking through the woods, but now that she was standing still, the slight breeze cooled her.

She could hear Sorcha and Eva crashing through the brush toward them, giggling.

Fia looked down at Shannon, meeting her gaze. She had light brown eyes. Almost golden. She really was pretty when she wasn't all tarted up. And smarter, maybe even more intuitive, than Fia had given her credit for in the past.

"You know, I was just goofing around with him in the pub," Shannon said. "It's just what I do. I would never go after a guy I thought you cared about. One any one of you girls cared about."

Eva and Sorcha pushed through a holly bush, squealing as the branches prickled them.

"Ouch," Eva yelped. "Glad I didn't pull my panties down there."

Sorcha grabbed her arm, and linked it through hers. "Press on, *leerless feeder*," she called to Fia. "Mission accomplished!"

"I'm beginning to think we should have left them on the porch with their martinis," Fia muttered to Shannon as she started down the path again.

There was more giggling and a few stumbles, but Eva, Sorcha, and Shannon all stayed together and kept up with Fia. They passed only a few feet from the place where Mahon had been found dead and everyone grew silent. The sad heaviness in the air seemed to sober the women, literally. Even after a week's time and a full day of rainfall the day before, they could smell the blood and scent of their friend's burnt flesh.

Fia shivered, wishing she'd brought her hoodie from the front seat of her car. "Now which way was this thing you think you saw, Shannon?" Fia didn't question why Shannon had been on the game preserve alone in the middle of the night. Everyone in town hunted the deer, drank their blood, but it was something they rarely spoke of.

"I don't *think* I saw anything. I'm telling you, it was some kind of witches' altar," Shannon insisted. "Turn north up here at the fork in the path. Northeast."

"You shouldn't be out here alone, Shannon."

"You like hunting with a buddy system?" Shannon asked.

Fia didn't answer.

"Besides, it was last week, before Mahon was killed."

"Hey, you smell something?" Sorcha asked. "Like . . . something burning?"

"Could have been from back there," Fia said carefully. She knew Sorcha knew, they *all* knew, what she meant.

"No, not *that* smell. This is different." Sorcha stopped on the path. They all stopped. "You smell that? Something burning, like wood . . . and something sweet."

Fia did smell it now. But the source was downwind of them. The scent was very faint. Too faint for anyone with normal senses to smell. "How much farther to the altar?" she asked Shannon, beginning to get that uneasy feeling again that she'd first experienced when they entered the woods.

It was as if . . . as if someone was out there. Someone watching them.

"I don't know. Right around here, somewhere. I think we're close." Shannon didn't sound quite as confident as she had earlier, when she had insisted she could find the place again. "It wasn't very big. Just some grass trampled down and a tree stump where there was black candle wax and some rabbit fur and blood."

"Rabbit sacrifices? Poor bunnies," Eva said.

Fia halted, holding her hand up to tell the other women to be silent. Everyone froze.

The smell of burning wood mixed with that sweet smell was getting stronger. And Fia thought she might have heard voices. They were far away. At least half a mile. Just a faint murmur. "Do you hear that?" she whispered.

Eva turned slowly in a circle where she stood. "Yeah," she whispered. "Sounds as if it's coming from east of here. Toward the beach."

Without discussion, the three women followed Fia off the deer path. As they headed east through the darkness, dodging branches and circumnavigating monstrous trees, the smell grew stronger and the hum of the voices became clearer.

The women walked a quarter of a mile, maybe a little farther, before Sorcha, taking up the rear, halted. "Shit," she groaned, dropping her hand to her hip. "It's Kaleigh and Katy and . . . Marie, I think."

"How do you know?"

Sorcha frowned. "I just caught a pretty interesting train of teenaged horn-ball thought. They're not alone, ladies."

"Human boys?" Fia whispered.

As they spoke, all the women raised mental walls to block their thoughts so that the teenagers would be less likely to suspect their presence. Although Kaleigh's telepathy had not returned yet, the other two girls had at least some ability to communicate without words.

"You want me to . . . you know." Eva blinked dramatically.

"How many martinis did you drink?" Fia whispered.

"I don't know. Four . . . maybe six."

"No," Fia said. "You are not going to attempt to teleport yourself. You'll end up in the center of their bonfire. You remember the time you tried that in Rome after we'd drunk all those bottles of wine?"

"No," Eva said defensively.

Shannon giggled. "I remember it. She tried to pop back to the house where we were staying and ended up in the Vatican."

Sorcha chuckled.

"It's okay, Eva. Don't feel bad. You know me. I can't teleport a leaf stone sober." Fia squeezed the woman's shoulder.

"Oh, baby, can you do that again, big, brave FBI agent?" Eva joked, rubbing up against Fia. "Only a little lower and to the left, next time."

Fia ignored Eva's flirtation. "What do you think? Split up and surround them, or just holler and make them scatter?"

"If we sneak up on them, we might catch them sacrificing bunnies," Sorcha teased, obviously still not sure she believed there was any witch altar in the woods.

"I didn't say it was Kaleigh who made the altar," Shannon said. "I just said the kid was acting weird."

"Yes, you did."

"No, I said I *wondered* if it was them."

"Okay, so maybe we should check into what they're doing?" Fia cut in, breaking up the little tiff. She still felt uncomfortable, but she didn't get the sense that any of them were in danger. Not the women. Not the girls. But something wasn't right. "Everyone okay with splitting up? Everyone sober enough?"

"Pul-lease," Sorcha moaned, walking off into the woods. "Five martinis is nothing to a Kahill. I'll come around from the north. You guys come from the other directions. Meet you at the bunny roast."

Chapter 16

Kaleigh was so busy swapping spit with the human that she never heard the women until Fia walked up behind her and tugged off the hood of her sweat-shirt. Derek leaped to his feet.

"What do you think you're doing out here in the middle of the night?" Fia demanded.

Kaleigh jumped up from the log and whipped around. "What am I doing? What are you doing? You're following me, now?"

The other two girls, who had also been making cozy with human boys, were on their feet as Eva, Shannon, and Sorcha surrounded them. Fia could hear Shannon giving them a piece of her mind. The teens had all been sitting around a campfire, roasting marshmallows, of all things. And making out, of course.

"I wasn't *following* you." Fia lowered her voice so that the humans couldn't hear her. "We were out taking a walk"—she indicated the other three women—"and we smelled the campfire." Not exactly a lie. "We were concerned." Complete truth. "Do you have any idea how dangerous it could be for you girls to be out here in the middle of the night?"

"Mahon was alone in broad daylight." Kaleigh glanced sulkily over her shoulder. The boys were quickly gathering their belongings: sweatshirts, a football, a bag of marshmallows. Shannon was still giving them all hell, pointing a finger now at one of the boys. "And you guys are out here. You don't seem to be afraid of any vampire slayers," Kaleigh said.

Fia rested her hand on her sidearm secured in its shoulder holster. "I'm carrying a G22 loaded with a 165-grain Gold Dot. Are you?" She looked away and then back at Kaleigh. She didn't know how to make the girl understand how selfish her behavior was. How important she was to the sept, and how much they would rely on her once she reached adulthood again. "No one said Mahon and Bobby were killed by slayers," Kaleigh responded.

"No one saying it doesn't mean it isn't so."

Kaleigh's gaze bore into Fia. "Who else would know how to kill us?"

"I don't know," Fia said.

"You don't know," Kaleigh whispered. "None of us do. At least we agree on that. But I'm not going to live afraid. I'm not going to give up my life, my friends, Derek, just because someone might come out of the dark and chop my head off."

"No one's asking you to give up your life," Fia countered. "We're just asking you not to be stupid."

"You're not in charge of me. No one is." Kaleigh crossed her arms over her small breasts. "You have no right to sneak up on us like this. We weren't doing anything wrong. We were just sitting here, talking."

"You could set the whole forest on fire with that

thing." Fia nodded in the direction of the campfire which had died down to a smolder.

"Could not. We dug down to the dirt. Made that log ring to contain it. Derek used to be a Boy Scout." She said the last sentence proudly.

Fia glanced in the direction of the tallest of the boys, who was cramming an old blanket into his backpack. "That a beer can I see next to your foot, Mr. Neuman?"

The boy leaned over, snatched up the can and stuffed it into his backpack.

"Anything else you have in that pack illegal?" Fia asked. "I probably don't have to remind you that these girls, that all of you, are underage, *Mr. Neuman.*"

"Fee," Kaleigh warned under her breath. "Don't you dare."

The other two boys were already slipping into the woods, but to Fia's surprise, Derek walked toward her.

"I didn't mean to get Kaleigh in any trouble, ma'am."

Fia hated it when young men ma'ammed her. Her first impulse was to walk Mr. Neuman and his pimply-faced buddies out of the woods and have one of the Clare Point patrol cars pick them up and deliver them to their parents. But she knew that wasn't realistic. It was never a good idea to stir up trouble in the surrounding human communities, if it could be helped. This was already a dangerous time for the sept; she didn't need to make it worse.

"How old did you say you were, again?" Fia scrutinized the young man more closely.

"Fifteen. Well, now he's sixteen. He just had his birthday," Kaleigh said, jumping in.

Fia narrowed her gaze further. "You don't look sixteen, Mr. Neuman. You look older. Almost old enough to be an adult, influencing minors," she intoned.

The human stared at his big feet.

Fia let the silence grow uncomfortable before she spoke again. "Didn't I just remind you kids the other night that we have a killer in the area who has yet to be apprehended?"

"We stayed together," he said, glancing up. Sounded like a big, dumb, human kid. "And we were going to walk the girls back to town. I swear it."

"Derek, I'm really sorry." Kaleigh ran her hand up and down his arm. "We didn't tell anyone, I swear we didn't."

"Um . . . is it okay if I go?" Derek asked Fia. "I'm not sure the guys know how to get out of here."

Fia hesitated, then raised her hand, pointing northwest. "Sure. Go ahead. But don't let me catch you out here in the middle of the night with these girls again, or I will call the cops."

"Yes, ma'am." Derek leaped over one of the logs they had been sitting on and took off into the woods.

"And I better not find any beer cans littering this federal wildlife preserve, Mr. Neuman," she called after him.

Fia heard a muffled *"Yes, ma'am"* as Derek disappeared into the darkness. The women were talking quietly to the other girls.

"Didn't tell anyone what?" Fia asked Kaleigh as soon as the boys were out of earshot.

"Didn't tell anyone"—Kaleigh shifted her weight from one sneaker to the other—"about us coming out here."

Fia really wished she could read the teen's thoughts right now but there was nothing there but a tangle of emotions and random words, none of which made any coherent sense. "So exactly what *were* you really doing out here?"

"I don't know. Hanging out."

"And . . ."

"What, you mean were we having sex?" The teen crossed her arms defensively again. "No, we weren't having sex. We were cooking marshmallows and . . . and so maybe we were kissing a little."

"You weren't practicing witchcraft?"

Kaleigh looked at Fia as if she was crazy. "What are you talking about? Is that what you think happened to Mahon? Witches got him?"

"So you don't know anything about an altar? Sacrificing rabbits?"

Kaleigh wrinkled her freckled nose. "Ewww. Gross." She took a step back. "You were out here looking for people sacrificing animals?" She gave another laugh. "Lot of people out here tonight, you know. I saw Uncle Arlan a little while ago. He was like a saber-toothed tiger or something stupid like that. All creeping through the bushes spying on us, too."

A smile threatened to tug at the corners of Fia's mouth but she resisted. She could just imagine Arlan slinking around the teenagers' campfire cloaked as some prehistoric cat. Maybe he was who she needed to scare a little sense into those boys. If a four-hundred-pound saber-toothed tiger walked into their quaint little camp site, they might think twice before they entered the wildlife preserve after dark again.

"I can't believe you were so rude to Derek." Kaleigh began to kick dirt over the glowing embers of the campfire. "He's going to be so pissed at me."

"I can't imagine a fifteen"—Fia cleared her throat—"*sixteen* year old could be angry that an adult suggested you all didn't belong out in the woods in the middle of the night. And if he is, you don't need a guy like that."

"What do you know about Derek?" Kaleigh kicked the dirt. "You don't know anything about him."

"What I know is that he's human."

"I'm not going to stop seeing him." Kaleigh rubbed under her eyes with the back of her wrist. "I'm not," she repeated childishly. "Derek needs me."

"He *needs* you?" Fia groaned. "Kaleigh, that's got to be the oldest guy trick in the book. It's just something men say to get what they want out of women."

"He *does* need me. He doesn't have anyone. You have no idea what kind of life he's had." She sniffed. "His mother committed suicide when he was six. In the bathtub in their house. Can you believe that? And Derek was the one who found her in a tub of blood."

"That's very sad," Fia agreed. "But how about a father?" She didn't want to sound heartless. She did feel sorry for the kid, for any kid who had gone through something like that. But a tragic childhood didn't mean the boy wasn't trying to get in Kaleigh's jeans. "Surely he has a father."

"Sort of. If you could call him that. He works like eighty hours a week. He never went to Derek's soccer games or anything. He pretends like Derek doesn't exist, except when he wants to yell at him." The teen perched her hand on her slender, jutted hip. "It's like he thinks it's Derek's fault his mom committed suicide." She lifted her hand and let it fall. "Like that makes any sense. A six-year-old kid."

Fia hesitated for a moment. Her intention really wasn't to anger Kaleigh or to hurt her. She wasn't so naïve as to not understand that these feelings Kaleigh had for this human, no matter how misguided or doomed they were, were real. All she wanted was to keep Kaleigh, to keep everyone in the sept safe.

In the end, Fia decided that she'd probably chastised Kaleigh enough for one night; from what she had heard, the other women had done the same with Katy and Maria. She let the subject drop. "Let's take care of the fire and then we'll take you girls back to town," Fia said, scuffing dirt toward the center of the campfire.

"Sure," Kaleigh responded sarcastically. "Whatever you say, Agent Kahill."

Tuesday evening, Fia was back on Dr. Kettleman's leather couch. They'd bumped her sessions back up to once a week, "just until some of the stress was alleviated."

"So would you say it was a good weekend?"

Fia thought for a moment and caught herself smiling, remembering sitting on Sorcha's front porch in the old, battered, Adirondack chairs, listening to the crash of the incoming tide and toasting to each other with apple martinis. "Yeah," she said, nodding. "It was."

"Old friendships renewed? Fences mended?"

Fia shifted her gaze to Dr. Kettleman's. "Something like that."

"Did it feel good to be home as a member of the community rather than as a law-enforcement agent?"

"I think so," Fia said slowly. "Sunday I went to Mass and then had breakfast with my mom. It wasn't even that painful."

"And your father?"

"He never misses Mass." Looking down, Fia fiddled with her signet ring. "But then he had his coffee with the newspaper on the front porch. I didn't really see him after that."

"You can't change how he feels, Fia, you know that," Dr. Kettleman offered, following one of her long moments of silence. "Only how you react to his behavior. How you feel about it."

Fia dropped her hands to her lap. "I know."

The psychiatrist shifted in her chair. "So while we're on the subject of your men, what's happening on the Joseph front?"

"Not sure."

Dr. Kettleman waited.

Fia allowed her gaze to drift to the diplomas on the wall behind Kettleman's desk, then back. "I met him last week. He admitted he'd gotten in to a "little problem" in California and that's why he's decided to relocate. At least part of the reason."

"And how do you feel about that?"

"How do I feel? It pisses me off. We had an agreement. And . . . it scares me a little."

"Because you still have feelings for him?" Kettleman prodded.

Fia took her time before answering. There was no sense shelling out big bucks each week if she wasn't going to at least attempt to do more than go through the motions. "No. I'm not in love with him anymore, if that's what you mean. But do I feel guilty? Sure. Do I not want him around to make me feel guilty? Of course." *That's only human,* she thought, ironically. Hesitated. "The thing is, Dr. Kettleman, with our history, Joseph's and mine, we wouldn't be good for each other. Maybe we'd even be dangerous."

The psychiatrist let the word hang in the air for a moment. "And Joseph disagrees?"

"I don't know what he thinks." She groaned. "He's hard to read. A real player. Then he's got this little problem. Addiction, of course. I actually suggested he should come talk to you. Maybe you could help."

"Maybe the two of you might benefit from a joint session."

Fia scowled. "That's what he said."

Yet again, the shrink silence. The clock on the end table beside the couch ticked.

"I'll consider it," Fia finally conceded.

"I think that's wise, because what we've hit on today, yet again, is your guilt for what happened between you and Joseph. I don't think you realized until he came back just how heavy that guilt weighs on you still, after all this time." Silence. "You know, eventually you're going to have to figure out a way to forgive yourself," Dr. Kettleman said gently.

Fia looked down at her signet ring and spun it. Guilt, was it? Well, she certainly had plenty of that. Guilt over Ian. Over Joseph. The chains were pretty heavy around her neck . . .

Fia glanced at the clock. "Guess our time is up."

Dr. Kettleman didn't look at the clock, but continued to watch Fia. "It is. So you'll think about bringing Joseph in with you?"

Fia rose, smoothing the wrinkles of her suit jacket. "I'll think about it."

* * *

Fia knew when she left Kettleman's office that she was going out tonight. Not to look for Joseph. Not even to stalk. She just didn't want to go home. Not by herself, with all the thoughts and emotions bouncing around inside her. Tonight, she needed the comfort, the anonymity, of a loud, crowded bar.

But instead of going home to change first as she usually did, she walked a couple of blocks and entered an upscale pub. It was only eight-thirty, early by bar standards, but the place was crowded with suits. Suits and sling-back heels. Lawyers, CPAs, corporate executives.

Fia strode along the bar, taking the only empty seat on the far end.

"Help you?" a waiter in a wool cap asked.

"Probably not," Fia quipped. "But how about a tonic and lime?"

"Stout's good here," said the guy in the dark suit on the barstool next to her.

Fia felt the hair rise on the back of her neck.

"But the best stout I've had was in a little dive in Delaware. Place called the Hill. You know it?"

Fia spun on the bar stool. "Glen?"

He grinned and raised his glass in toast.

Chapter 17

One glimpse of her smile and all the drama Glen had suffered through in the last week was worth it. Stacy's runny nose, her sobbing tears. Her begging him to reconsider. The frantic calls from her mother, her sister, her aunt, even the stern *calling out* from her father on the steps of his apartment building. All worth it, just to be here at this moment, on this bar stool, sitting beside the tall, sexy, smolderingly sensitive Fia Kahill.

Glen had never done anything this impulsive in his life. Hell, he never did anything impulsively. A lesson learned from dear old Dad. It was his father's impulsiveness that had gotten him killed, from what Glen had been able to glean from the account of the incident, read years after the fact. It was a personality trait he had chosen a long time ago not to inherit. Over the years, the decision had served him well. Until Fia Kahill had come along.

"What are you doing here?"

Fia was so surprised to see him that for once, her response was utterly spontaneous. There was nothing planned about the lilt in her voice, her smile, or the dimples he hadn't realized were there. And he liked her this way. Slightly ruffled. Suit wrinkled. Her hair not quite so smooth and perfect.

"I'm having a beer." Glen demonstrated by taking a drink. "What are you doing?" He looked at the glass the bartender slid across the bar toward her. "Tonic and lime hardly seems worth the effort."

She was still smiling, and the memory of the red-faced, snotty-nosed Stacy was receding from his mind. The guilt was fading faster.

At this point Glen didn't care that he'd made no arrangements to sublet his apartment. Or that he didn't have a place in Philadelphia yet and was staying with his elderly great-aunt Emma. Glen didn't believe in fate or predestination or any of that happy horseshit, but the job opening in the Philadelphia Field Office where Fia worked had come up so suddenly, so unexpectedly, that it was eerie.

Another agent in the Baltimore Field Office had wanted to keep his family in Baltimore so that his special-needs child could remain in the school she was attending. Everyone in the office had thought Glen was being some kind of magnanimous, stand-up guy for volunteering for the position expected to be filled immediately. None of them had suspected his motives had been purely selfish. That they'd been all about a redhead with blue eyes and a killer attitude.

It was crazy. Glen knew it was crazy. He knew he didn't have a chance in hell with Fia. Women like her didn't go for guys like him. But he had to try. As much as it went against his nature, just once in his life he had to take a risk. He just hoped he wouldn't end up like his father, splattered all over the sidewalk.

"I'm serious." Fia turned on her bar stool until

her knees brushed against his. "You have business in the office here?"

He sipped his beer. "Transferred, effective immediately. I'll continue working the Clare Point cases with you, but I'm supposed to be a part of some new antiterrorist task force." He rolled his eyes. "How many does that make for this administration?"

"At least nine hundred and eleven," she quipped. "But this is a *new* new antiterrorist task force, right?"

He raised his beer glass. "Don't get me started. Not tonight."

They were both quiet for a minute, sipping their drinks. But she was still watching him.

"So . . . what's Stacy have to say about your transfer?" Fia asked after a moment. "She ready for cheesesteaks and the Liberty Bell?"

"Stacy's not coming." He sort of said it into his beer glass.

"Not coming? As in not coming now, or never coming as in no "until death do us part" not coming?"

"Both, I guess. Neither."

"You guess?" Fia pulled back a little, slipping the paper cocktail napkin around her damp glass. "Not that it's my business or anything, but this is a case where guessing isn't really a good idea. In this particular instance, you should *know* what's going on. Are you marrying her or aren't you?"

"I'm not." He took a chance—the second in a week—and met her gaze over the rim of his glass. She was interested. *Definitely.*

"Why not?"

She said it so softly that he wasn't absolutely sure that was what he had heard.

He took a deep breath and exhaled. This had been the hardest part with Stacy. The telling her why. Every time he tried to explain himself, she'd started apologizing for everything she'd ever done wrong or perceived she'd done wrong, from choosing the wrong color napkins for their wedding reception to drinking the last cup of coffee in the morning when she slept over. She hadn't wanted to listen to him. Hadn't wanted to know the truth, really.

"Because it wasn't right," Glen heard himself say to Fia. It was weird, but it suddenly seemed more important to him that Fia understand than Stacy.

What was it about this woman that drew him to her? That made him go against everything he knew, everything that was easy and comfortable?

"It was too easy," he said slowly, thinking his way through the words, trying hard not to get dragged down by the emotion that accompanied them. "Too comfortable. Too . . . boring, I suppose. I loved her, but I didn't *love* her. Not deeply. Not madly, insanely, like I couldn't get enough of her." He paused. "It sounds . . . sappy. But you know what I mean?"

The corner of Fia's sensual mouth turned up. "I know what you mean."

"Do you?"

She looked down, then back up at him. The ice clinked in her glass. "I do."

"That experience talking?"

"Let's just say I've been in both seats, yours and hers."

She spoke slowly, her voice husky. He sensed this wasn't easy for her, talking about personal things. But the fact that she was willing to share that tiny bit of private information only strengthened his conviction. He'd done the right thing leaving Baltimore and Stacy. Coming here. Even if things didn't work out between him and Fia.

"So . . ." she said.

"So . . ."

She made him smile. Made him think. Made him feel. And that was why he'd come to Philly, really. That was it in a nutshell. She made him step outside his carefully constructed box.

"Hey," he said on impulse. *What was that old saying, in for a penny, in for a pound?* "You want to have dinner?" He motioned over his shoulder to the tables behind them.

She looked in the direction of the restaurant area beyond the bar and back at him. "Dinner?"

It almost seemed as if it were a foreign idea to her.

"Yeah. You know. Sit down. Have something to eat. Converse."

She hesitated, but it was a good hesitation. As if she was surprised he would ask her. Again, the genuine smile. "Dinner would be good."

Fia stayed at the pub with Glen far longer than she'd intended. They had dinner. Dessert. He had another beer. They'd lingered long after he'd taken the bill out from under her hand and paid for it. They talked about Stacy. About his new job and the government's war against terrorism. About the office and the guys he'd be working with. They talked a little about the cases in Clare Point.

Before Fia realized it, it was after eleven and the

restaurant was closing. Their waiter offered to find
them a seat at the bar. Fia thought that if she'd
agreed, Glen would have gone along with it.

He was *definitely* interested in her. And it wasn't
a post-breakup interest. In fact, although he didn't
come out and say so, she got the distinct impression that she had something to do with the breakup.
Or at least his realization that he didn't want to
marry Stacy.

But afraid that too much of a good thing might
somehow curse their relationship before it ever really
got started, Fia said good night at the table. Glen
walked her back to her car and she said good night
again. No good-night kiss, but there was definite
curbside chemistry going on.

All the way home Fia thought about Glen, about
how nice it had been to just sit and talk, have dinner, laugh. Not just meaningless chat on a bar stool.
Meaningless sex afterward. Or worse, meaningless
bloodletting in a seedy alley. It had been a real date.
That was what it had been.

And it wasn't until Fia was greeting her purring
cat that she realized this was the first night in a
very long time that she had not gone out stalking,
or at least *wanted* to. Tonight she'd come home
without taking human blood, but instead of being
filled with the longing emptiness she often returned
with, she found herself content.

Later in the week, humming to herself, Fia stood
in line at the Starbucks a block from the office.
She and Glen had agreed to meet this morning in
the conference room on her floor, just to touch

base on the Clare Point cases. There was nothing new in either case and both knew it. It was just an excuse to see each other and the idea that he thought he needed an excuse to see her made her foolishly happy.

She was picking up coffee and tea for them. She knew what kind of coffee Glen liked because the morning after dinner together, his first day at the office, he'd brought her tea from Starbucks and had been drinking black coffee with caramel syrup in it. She'd played it cool yesterday, fighting the urge to bring him a coffee, but this was it, this was the morning.

The line crawled as men and women in suits ordered drinks Fia couldn't even identify. She glanced at her wristwatch. The coffee was a good idea. Being late to meet Glen wouldn't be.

"Ah, I'll have a double latte with a shot of hemoglobin."

Joseph's voice in her ear startled her, and she jerked around to see him standing behind her. "What are you doing here?"

"Same as you." He nodded toward the counter. "Waiting in line." He frowned. "Since when did you start drinking coffee?"

"Since when did you start frequenting the Arch Street Starbucks? What do you want?"

"Line's moving." He pointed at the space ahead of her.

She walked forward. "I'm serious. What are you doing here? You can't be here," she said under her breath.

"What? I can't be at Starbucks now? You're the gatekeeper of the city *and* Starbucks?" He chuckled. "I'm just getting coffee, Fee. Quit being so suspicious. I'm meeting a realtor a block from here in fifteen minutes. Checking out some office space."

Fia groaned, seriously considering just walking out of the shop. There were still at least six people ahead of her in line.

"So, how's business?" he asked congenially.

He was dressed in a sharp navy blue suit and brown wing tips. Only Joseph could get away with brown wing tips.

"Mafia, terrorists, bank robbers, and pedophiles keeping you busy?" he asked.

"Please lower your voice."

The scowl that followed somehow made him even better looking. "No one's listening to us. Everyone's too wrapped up in their own lives, their own mochaccinos, to care what we're saying."

The line inched forward a centimeter and Fia wished she was anywhere on the planet but here. And the day had started out so nicely. Warm sun on a cool September morning. A pleasant shower filled with fantasies involving a particular human in the shower with her. An easy, traffic-jam-free drive to work. A great parking space. And now here was Joseph, raining on her parade.

"Hey. You see that article in the paper about that girl who was murdered in Lansdowne? Same street where we used to go to that little bar all the time. The one with the purple bar stools and the weird chrome sinks in the bathrooms. Remember it?"

Something in Joseph's tone made her turn to look at him. The hairs on the nape of her neck bristled and her couple hundred years of experience with bad guys set off the synapses in her brain.

He was talking about the Casey Mulvine case.

But how? Why? He couldn't possibly know Fia had been at the crime scene. Her mind raced. She knew she hadn't mentioned the case to him when she'd seen him at the bar or at the restaurant. She certainly hadn't brought up the subject during their brief phone conversations. She hadn't said anything to anyone about Casey Mulvine outside the office. Had she been thinking about Casey Mulvine one of the nights she had seen him? She was usually so careful around Joseph, always putting up a barrier to prevent him from reading her thoughts. Had she slipped up?

"I was supposed to look at some office space in Lansdowne, too, but that makes you think twice doesn't it?" he went on. "Crimes like that, you used to only hear about in big cities, but now"—he glanced up at the menu hanging on the wall behind the counter—"Any leads on that case?"

"How would I know? FBI doesn't generally cover homicides in alleyways behind bars."

"Ah-ha, so you do know what case I'm talking about." He pointed at her.

He was relaxed. Perfectly at ease. Nothing suspicious whatsoever about his behavior. He was just making conversation. So why was she suspicious of him?

Because she knew Joseph. Because she knew what a mean, conniving bastard he could be.

"What do you know about that case?" She took a step closer to him, lowering her voice. "How did you know a woman was killed and left in an alley in Lansdowne?"

"Whoa. Easy there, Miss Special Agent for the FBI." He put up both his hands as if surrendering to her.

She looked around to be sure no one was watching them. There had to be other agents in the shop.

"I told you," Joseph explained. "I saw it in the paper. It caught my eye because I knew the street. It was one of our old haunts. Good memories, right?"

"Ma'am? Ma'am, may I help you?"

Fia whipped around to face the guy with the shaggy Beatles haircut in the Starbucks apron. She ordered Glen's coffee, her chai tea, waited for them, then walked around the side to add sugar to her cup. Joseph followed a minute later with a tall something.

She dropped the plastic stirrer on the counter as he pushed up beside her.

"You sure are jumpy, Fee," he said quietly.

He was up to something. She just knew. Felt it. Tasted it.

"Do I really make you so nervous?"

"Joseph, I swear by all that's holy," she threatened under her breath. She'd had just about enough of his crap and she was beginning to think it was time to move past asking him nicely to get out of town.

"Easy, girl—"

"Don't you *easy* me."

He took a plastic stirrer from a bin and slowly began to stir his coffee. "You know, I've been thinking about what you said. About possibly relocating somewhere other than Philadelphia."

This was so like him, to taunt her, to force her to draw back, then to offer a tempting morsel to reel her back in again. She waited.

"And I've been thinking about what you said about seeing your shrink. It's not a bad idea."

"You want to see her?"

"Am I dying to see a freak shrink? No." He licked the coffee stirrer. "Do I want to keep my problem from getting out of hand again? Yes."

She ignored the freak comment, not sure if it was aimed at Dr. Kettleman or her patients. "I'll get you the number; make an appointment for you, if you want." She hated to sound so overly eager, but she really wanted Joseph out of her life. Especially now when Glen seemed to be coming into it.

"I definitely think I'd like to see her." He tossed the stirrer into the trash receptacle in the hole in the counter. "But I'll only go if you go. You know. Like couples counseling." He smiled and sipped his four-dollar coffee.

So there it was. Another one of Joseph's traps. "I don't think so."

"Come on. You said you'd consider it when you brought it up. It was practically your idea."

"It wasn't my idea." She popped the lids onto the two cups and reached for a cardboard carrier.

"But you said—"

"I don't care what I said." She abruptly stepped toward him and he jerked back. "I'm not going for *couples* counseling with you, Joseph. Now if you'll excuse me"—she stepped out of his "space"—"I have to get to work."

He didn't follow her, but in her head he stayed with her the rest of the day.

Saturday, Fia decided against going to the office as she usually did on weekends. She took Betty to the grocery store, ran all her errands in the neighborhood, cleaned her bathroom, cut her cat's back claws and in a moment of utterly positive thinking, called Sorcha, Shannon, and Eva to say hi. Just to try to continue the reconnection she'd made with them the other night.

Fia and Eva chatted for five minutes and although the conversation seemed to go well, Fia wound up having to reiterate that she wasn't interested in dating Eva. Shannon was out, so she left a message on her machine. When she talked to Sorcha, it seemed like old times. They chatted for forty-five minutes and by the time Fia got off the phone, it was already getting dark. She was just taking a low-cal frozen dinner out of the microwave when her doorbell rang.

Her doorbell never rang. Betty always called. Never came by.

Fia knew who it was before she looked through the peephole. . . .

She glanced down at her ratty sweatpants and T-shirt. Her hair was pulled back in a stubby pony-tail with pieces hanging down. No makeup. Not even lip gloss.

The doorbell rang again.

"Fee? It's Glen." He lifted up a brown paper bag. "I come bearing Chinese. Food, not men," he clarified.

She smelled shrimp chow mein through the door and it had a far more appealing aroma than her low-cal dinner of Sonoma chicken.

She opened the door. "How'd you know where I lived?"

"Saw it in your personnel file." Shy grin. Way too appealing.

"You're not allowed to look at my personnel file."

He pushed past her, through the doorway. "No, I'm not. Bet you'll look at mine as soon as it's transferred, though. Kitchen this way?"

She followed him through the living room. At least the place was picked up. No bras and panties drying on the kitchen-cabinet handles. Blood, bagged in the freezer, was concealed in an empty ice-cream container.

"Glen . . ." She hesitated. She didn't want to be presumptuous, suggest something was going on that wasn't, but wasn't it obvious something was going on between them? "I don't know if this is such a good idea."

"Dinner? Dinner's always a good idea."

"You know what I'm talking about. You being here."

"It's just dinner," he protested.

Sam leaped from the countertop to the refrigerator to study the stranger, as unused to visitors as Fia was.

"I took a chance you'd be home. I'm staying with my great-aunt, my father's mother's sister, over in Chestnut Hill. Lights out is pretty early around there. She eats dinner at four-thirty." He pulled white boxes from the brown paper bag.

"You came all the way here to get Chinese?" Chestnut Hill was on the northwest side of Philadelphia; whereas the trendy neighborhood where Fia lived in Olde Kensington was on the southeast side. "They don't have Chinese in Chestnut Hill?"

"I came here to have Chinese with you. Plates?"

She opened a cupboard and pulled out two of the total of four white dinner plates she owned. "And what if I hadn't been home?"

"Guess I would have eaten Chinese in my car. Spoon? Something to get this out with?" He turned to her, folding up the stained bag. "If you want to know the truth, I was going to call. Ask you if you wanted to go out, meet me or something. But I chickened out."

She smiled, somehow flattered. "You chickened out?"

"Well, you can be pretty intimidating." He took the soup spoon she'd retrieved from the drawer out of her hand. "It takes a man a little time to work his way up from blond dental hygienists with rich daddies to six-foot-tall redheads packing heat."

She grabbed two forks out of the drawer. "You should have called. I'd have said yes. And then I could have taken a shower, gotten dressed, maybe."

He handed her a plate, looking her up and down. "But then I wouldn't have gotten to see you braless again." He walked out of the kitchen carrying his plate. "You have anything to drink? I forgot to get something to drink," he said from the living room. "I thought about wine, but I didn't want you to accuse me of coming here with the intention of getting you liquored up and into bed."

Chapter 18

Turned out he wasn't being presumptuous and he didn't need the wine. He probably could have had his way with her without the charm or the chow mein.

They had dinner in the living room and talked, although about what, she could scarcely recall. He cleaned up the dishes. She excused herself to the ladies room, ran a rake through her hair, brushed her teeth, and the next thing she knew they were making out on the couch. He was all over her and she was doing her best to reciprocate. Her mind was saying *no, no, no,* but her body, that was an entirely different story.

"Fee . . . this wasn't . . . it wasn't my intention when I stopped by."

They were both coming up for air. Her mouth was bruised from his kisses, aching, tingling. Every nerve in her body had become hypersensitive. Her panties, super damp. She wanted Glen in a way that she hadn't wanted a man in a very long time, human or vampire, and the thought of blood barely crossed her mind.

"Not your intention?" she panted, pushing hair

away from her face so that she could look into his brown, speckled-with-gold, heavy-with-lust eyes. "Yeah, right."

"No, I'm serious." He tightened his arm around her shoulder. "I came because I wanted to see you. Couldn't wait until Monday to see you."

Fia knew they were just words. She'd been betrayed by, lied to, cheated on by men often enough to know better than to believe any man's words. But he just seemed so damned sincere. And sweet. And he was a law-enforcement officer. They couldn't lie, could they?

"You don't have to say these things." She leaned toward him, offering her lips again.

"No, I do. I mean . . . I know I don't but, Fia. I really . . ."

She was trying to listen to what he was saying, but he was doing this little stroking, massaging thing on her collar bone with his fingertips that was amazingly distracting.

". . . Like you and . . ." He exhaled and started again. "I don't want to screw it up. Not here. Not at work. I knew I was taking a chance, agreeing to the transfer."

"From what I hear, you volunteered."

She could have sworn he blushed.

"Okay, so you don't want to screw things up." She shrugged. "So far, everything here is good." She leaned toward him.

He kissed her, but it was a quick peck and then he pulled back again. "I'm serious, Fia."

Since when did a man want to talk instead of have sex?

"And I want you to be, too," he went on. "At least just for a minute."

She stroked his cheek, drawing her finger along his jawline. He had a very nice jawline, sharp, but not too sharp, and taut skin that was just slightly rough with the day's beard growth. "I know you're serious. And so am I. Why do you think I'm cracking jokes? It scares the hell out of me, that's why."

"What does?"

She looked down, then forced herself to look up again. She'd faced some of the world's most terrifying killers, alone, in the dark, and she honestly thought this was harder. More terrifying. "It scares me to think that you and I . . . that I . . ."

"That you have a thing for me?" His voice was deep, sexy. Just a hint of tease to it. He was trying to make it easier for her.

"Yeah."

"Because?"

He was doing it again. That stroking thing. Fia could feel what little fight she had left in her melting away. Whatever idea she'd had of stopping short of actually doing the dirty deed was nonexistent, though it hadn't started out that way. The first time he'd kissed her, she'd told herself she'd just kissed him back out of curiosity. Same for the second kiss. The third. The breast caress. But now she was hot and bothered all over, her panties were damp, and she knew very well they were headed for the bedroom. The living-room floor if they didn't get moving soon.

She knew she shouldn't have sex with Glen and knew all the reasons why, the fact that he was a human and a colleague only two of the top ten. But she also knew that she was going to have sex with him. And she could accept that. She could accept that she would have to feel properly regretful later. She'd been Catholic for four hundred years; she was good with guilt. But what she was having a hard time accepting was the tumble of feelings that seemed to be attached to this tumble. Fia wasn't just sexually attracted to Glen. She . . . liked him.

"Tell me why this scares you," Glen said softly.

He was still doing that thing with his thumb, only he had slid his hand over her shoulder so that his fingertips were resting lightly on her breast. Sending shockwaves through her that hardened her nipples and made her so uncomfortable below the belt that she wanted to squirm.

She was having a difficult time concentrating on the question.

"I don't want you to be scared, Fee."

"Of this?" She made a weak attempt at a chuckle. "Please, Glen, don't tell me you think I'm a virgin."

He didn't grin back. "I'm serious about being serious. This, between me and you, doesn't have anything to do with breaking my engagement. It has everything to do with you. I think I fell for you that day in the post office with your uncle standing beside me and the stink of Bobby McCathal's burnt flesh in my nose."

She could feel herself crumbling inside. To most women, what he'd said wouldn't have sounded very romantic. But for a woman who had had her share of romance with no substance behind it, his words were sweet nothings to her ear.

"And I think," he went on, "that you knew there was something there, too."

"Okay, so you got that off your chest. Will you kiss me again now?"

He brushed the tip of her nose with his and she

tried to reach his mouth, but he moved away from her.

"You have to say it," he whispered.

"Say what? That I thought you were hot?"

"Of course you thought I was hot." He drew his lips along her cheekbone. "But I want you to say that you liked me from day one," he whispered in her ear. "I want you to say you wanted to get me into the sack the first time those blue eyes of yours saw me."

She giggled. He was making her hotter by the second. "What, are we in the third grade?"

"No, but close. FBI."

She giggled again. Felt stupid. And yet so good deep down inside. Inside where she was dancing. Singing. *He likes me! He likes me!*

He brought his hand up under her breast and squeezed gently.

She was unable to stifle a moan.

"Say it."

His mouth, magical, magnetic, pulled at hers. She slid her hand over his waist, over his abs that were still minus a love handle, over his hip, to the rise in his chinos.

"Say it." It was almost guttural this time.

"I like you," she whispered.

"Say it again," he taunted as he pushed her back on the couch, crawling over her, hovering, his mouth only centimeters from hers.

She looked up into his eyes and shared one of those moments she knew, only too sadly, rarely took place in a man's or a woman's lifetime. For a moment, for the briefest moment, both of them lowered their guards. In his eyes, she saw the pain of his breakup with Stacy, his fear of letting Fia see who he truly was.

"I like you," she whispered.

He rewarded her with a kiss that took her breath from deep in her chest and left her panting, aching, a thin sheen of perspiration on her forehead.

Fia allowed Glen to remove her T-shirt and toss it on the living-room floor. Next came her sweatpants. She started to wiggle out of her pale blue thong panties, but he rested his hand on the feminine mound between her thighs.

"Not yet," he breathed in her ear, sliding his finger into the crease of the sleek silk.

She moaned and brushed her lips across his neck. Nibbled, but did not bite. She could feel the blood pumping through the thick carotid artery; hot, sweet, pungent blood. But she did not bite . . . would not.

Fia lifted her hips against his hand and wrapped both arms around his neck, opening her mouth to his. He thrust his tongue and finger at the same time. She moaned.

"Bedroom?" he whispered in her ear.

"I don't need a bed, Romeo." She tugged at the buckle of his belt.

"Sure you do." He rose off the couch, taking her hand in his. "You going to show me which way or did you want me to carry you?"

"You wouldn't."

He leaned over the couch, arms open as if he was going to lift her and she jumped up off the couch and led him down the dark hall, wearing nothing but her panties. A soft glow of light came from the bathroom, but her bedroom was dark. At the bed, he kissed her, long and hard, the way she liked to be kissed, and then they fell onto the bed.

She found herself laughing, although why, she didn't know. She didn't remember sex ever being this much fun.

Again, her hand found his belt buckle and this time he let her have her way with him. Pants, shirt, socks off. Nothing left but the boxer briefs that were straining under the pressure of his erection.

Fia rolled on top of him, rotating her hips, pleasuring herself and him at the same time. They kissed again and then he rolled her over so that he was on top. Somehow, in the process, he lost the briefs.

"Oh, so you're one of those."

He held himself up with one arm and tenderly brushed hair off her cheek. "One of those?"

She lifted her hips to press them against his. "One of those men who always needs to be on top."

He kissed her lightly on the lips. "You one of those *women* who always needs to be on top?"

He made her smile. "No . . ." Then she had to laugh when she thought about it. "Okay, I guess maybe sometimes I am."

His hips were moving against hers rhythmically, making it hard for her to think about what she was saying.

"But I'm doing okay . . . at least for now? Me on top."

She closed her eyes, letting the waves of pleasure wash over her. "Okay for now," she agreed.

He reached down with his hand and she instinctively parted her legs, lifting upward to meet his first thrust.

Fia didn't know how long they made love. Ten minutes? An hour? Time became elastic. No past. No future. Just the now. Glen was incredible. Stamina. The right balance of tenderness and pure lust. She had three orgasms and fell asleep in his arms.

It was the first time she had slept with a man through the night in more than a hundred years.

A week later, Fia and Glen wound up at the same pub they had met in the day he came to town. One drink and she was ready to go home and hit the sack with him. But he insisted on dinner and conversation.

"My idea of foreplay," Glen whispered in her ear as they were shown to a table under the windows.

She gave his jacket a tug.

At the table, he ordered the house pale ale; she ordered her tonic and lime. She had no intentions of letting anything get between her and the orgasms she intended to have tonight. Glen was an amazing lover. Nothing like the man she knew in an investigation. Once between the sheets, his calm, calculating demeanor was gone. He was spontaneous, adventurous, eager to please, all the things she wanted in a lover. And the funny thing was, the sex, the closeness afterwards, was enough for her. She didn't need his blood. Didn't really want it.

While they waited for their drinks, he slid his hand across the table, taking hers. He was so cute. It was like a real date, only better because she knew they were going to end up in her bed later and it would be good.

She couldn't stop smiling. She felt like a dunce. As if she was fourteen again and just awakening to her sexuality. She thought about him when she was in the shower, driving to work, at work. Her obsession had fallen just short of doodling their names in the margins of her notes with a big heart around them. This week had been a real reminder of what Kaleigh and the other teens in Clare Point had to be going through right now.

The waiter brought their drinks, took their order. Glen wanted chicken Monterey, she, a steak, rare. The minute the waiter was gone, he reached for her hand again.

"You don't have to do this," she said.

"Do what?" He squeezed her hand.

"This. Dinner. Buying me drinks. Dessert. Holding my hand. I'm already having sex with you. I don't need to be bribed."

"So maybe I need it. Maybe *I* need to be wined and dined before I have sex with you."

She frowned, not sure how serious he was being.

Still holding her hand, he leaned forward. "You already know about my previous failed attempt to find love and happiness, but I don't know anything about yours. Good looking, hot six-footer like yourself, you can't tell me you haven't been in any relationships."

She looked away. They were sitting at a window that opened onto the street, but it was already dark out. All she could see were the flares of headlights as cars passed on the busy street.

"You don't want to hear my sad tale."

He leaned over the table bringing her hand to his lips. It was so silly. So 1940s-romance-movie. So stinking cute.

"I do want to hear your sad tale. I want to know why you're so cautious."

"It's the way we FBI agents keep from getting our heads blown off," she quipped.

"I mean, with your heart," he said quietly.

So he was serious. He really did want something out of her besides sex. She glanced out the window again and shrugged. "I told you before. Ian. Remember? Not that complicated a story. I fell in love. He said he loved me. I believed him." But as she spoke, the car headlights on the street turned to burning torches and she closed her eyes for just an instant.

Ian had asked her to marry him. She had told him the truth about what she was, but he had said it didn't matter. She had been meeting him in the forest, always careful not to allow him to know which tiny village she came from, where the others lived. But that night. The night the vampire slayers came on horseback, bearing their torches, Fia had been waiting for him. They were running away to get married. He had promised to come for her, to take her away, to marry her and to live with her until he grew old and died. He said he didn't care that she was only nineteen at the time, that she would always have to hunt, that blood was what sustained her. He told her that he didn't care that she could not bear children. All he cared about, he said, was loving her.

It had been a trap all along. From the first day he had met her in the meadow, he had intended to use her to seek out the sept. She realized it the moment she heard the pounding hoofbeats, saw the first torches, smelled the first peat roofs set ablaze. He had seen her hunting in that forest, seen her take blood, known that she was a vampire, and then he used his good looks and charm to win her over.

That night he had said he was coming for her to take her away, to marry her, but he had come to murder her. He was a vampire slayer, and with him he had brought a dozen men on horseback wielding swords to behead her loved ones. To behead her.

The only reason Fia had not died that night was because Mahon had forced her into that root cellar and locked her inside. The men and women of the Kahill sept had fought fiercely, eventually driving off the slayers, but not before they had beheaded more than a dozen. Before dawn the next day, the sept had left their village and the bodies of their loved ones behind, and gone into hiding. It had been the beginning of the end for them in Ireland and it had all been Fia's fault. All her fault because she had fallen in love. Because she had trusted a man she should not have trusted.

"Fee?"

She heard her name being called as if from far in the distance. Ian's voice?

No. Not Ian's.

Fia's gaze came back into focus and she turned toward Glen, her eyes embarrassingly wet. "Sorry," she mumbled.

"I didn't mean to pry." He watched her intently. "I just want to know you better."

"Fia!" Joseph sauntered up to the table.

It was like a bad dream. He was a bad penny.

Glen let go of her hand, stood like a gentleman and offered his.

Joseph pumped it. He was wearing a gray flannel suit with a lavender tie and matching silk handkerchief in his pocket. The suit probably cost three times what Glen's did, but standing next to each other, Fia was surprised to find that Glen far outclassed Joseph. There was just something about

Joseph that no amount of money or education could . . . make clean.

"Dr. Joseph Pineiro," Joseph introduced himself.

"Glen Duncan."

"Ah . . . Fia's new partner." Joseph nodded, smiled, all-knowing.

Glen glanced at Fia as he sat down, seeming to sense her discomfort.

"So you two are dating." It was more a statement than a question.

Fia didn't know what to say. She didn't know how Joseph knew anything about Glen, but he was making her more uncomfortable by the minute. Had he been snooping around her apartment building? Work? He had ways of finding out things. Always had. He had a knack for charming information out of just about anyone.

"We dated, you know." Joseph gestured to Fia, then himself. He was still smiling, but his voice had taken a dangerous edge.

"Did you?" Glen glanced at her across the table, then back at Joseph.

"She broke my heart." He clasped his hands, bringing them to his chest. "Captured my soul. Literally, eh, Fia?"

She tensed, but met his gaze. She wasn't afraid of Joseph. She was more powerful than he was and she had the whole sept to back her up. Surely he knew better than to threaten her. Surely he knew that if he pushed her, she'd make her confession to the sept and allow them to do what they saw fit with him.

"I think you should go, Joseph," she said under her breath.

"Go? Why would I go? Your new boyfriend and I

are just getting acquainted. We have a lot to talk about." Joseph slipped his surgeon's hands into his pants pockets. "I'm sure Special Agent Duncan is interested in hearing about your likes and dislikes. Your little *fetishes*, Fee?" He chuckled.

Glen half-rose from his chair, suddenly looking threatening, his hands tightened at his sides, his face hard.

Great, Fia thought. *I'm going to have a bar fight on my hands in a second.*

"I think you better go." Glen didn't raise his voice, but it was steely.

The man had more balls than she realized.

"Go? Why should I go when—"

Glen took one step toward him and Joseph backed up. Backed down. He'd always been a coward. Always preferred to prey on the weak. On the sick. On the bound and gagged.

"Well, you two kids have a nice evening. I've already taken care of your bill with the hostess." Joseph walked away. "Be talking with you, Fee."

Glen waited until Joseph was gone before he sat down across from Fia again.

"I'm sorry," she apologized, reaching for her drink. "Another ex. He's a real ass."

"He is that." She reached for her bag on the chair beside her. "If you'll excuse me."

"You okay?"

"I'm fine. I'm just going to the ladies' room. I'll be right back. Swear it."

Trembling with anger, Fia walked down the hall to the bathroom. Inside a stall, she fished her cell phone from her bag and punched in Joseph's number. She didn't even give him a chance to speak when he picked up.

"I'll go to *one* appointment with Dr. Kettleman with you. Then you leave Philadelphia of your own free will, or I make a call to my brothers. You know my brothers, Joseph. They won't wait for a decision from the sept to determine whether or not you're a danger. You know what they'll do. You don't want me to make that call."

She hung up. Peed. Washed her hands. Put a little lip gloss on her lips and went back into the dining room to finish her date. To go on with her life.

Shannon glanced over her shoulder as she walked up the dark driveway. Something or someone was giving her the creeps. She eyed the shadows in search of a tiger or a lion, thinking maybe Arlan was playing one of his practical jokes on her. Nothing stirred. Not the browning grass on the lawn or the crisp leaves that were beginning to fall from the trees.

She walked a little faster. She rented an apartment over Mr. and Mrs. Hill's garage at the end of the driveway. It wasn't that late, just after eleven maybe, but the street was empty. The streetlamps were on, but seemed to glow dimly in the hazy darkness. It had begun to rain when she was in the forest, hunting. Not a heavy rain, but the kind that slowly soaked through your clothes to the skin.

She knew the council had advised against hunting alone, but she had been doing it for so long that the idea of taking blood with someone else watching seemed repulsive. Maybe she just hadn't been doing it long enough, yet. But she hadn't stayed long because something had made her uncomfortable in the dark woods, even though she'd been hunting there for hundreds of years. There was something evil out there. Something that frightened her.

The discomfort had followed Shannon all the way home. But she was only steps from her door, and there was nothing there. No killer lurking behind Mrs. Hill's rhododendron bushes.

Shannon took the flight of creaky wooden stairs, thankful for the light that glowed at the top. Once inside, she'd lock her door, something people rarely did in Clare Point. She'd be fine.

The door hinges creaked as she opened it. Needed some WD-40. Inside, she flipped on the light switch. Light flooded the living room, kitchen, dining-room area. There were no killers lurking here, either. She twisted the lock on the door and turned around to face the open room. She still felt weird. On edge. She knew she was alone, but somehow the dark bedroom and bathroom down the short hall suddenly seemed scary places.

She shivered as she kicked off her shoes on the throw rug at the doorway. Her clothes were wet and she was cold. She should jump in the shower and get into some dry clothes. But that would mean going down the hall, into the dark.

Pretty funny for a vampire to be afraid of the dark.

On impulse, Shannon pulled her cell phone out of her jeans pocket and searched for Fia's number. Shannon had been meaning to get back to her. It had been nice of Fia to call her just to say hi after last weekend. The phone rang on the other end. Four rings and then Fia's voice. A recording.

Shannon glanced toward the dark hallway. "Hey. It's Shannon. Just called to say hi." She pushed a chair in under her dining table. "Martinis at my place next time. I'm thinking chocolate. Hope you're busy with the hot FBI guy. Talk to you later."

Hanging up, she eyed the dark end of the house.

"Oh, this is ridiculous," she muttered. "What would Fia Kahill do?"

March right back there. Prove to herself she was alone and safe, of course. Fia had been her hero for as long as she'd known her.

Shannon marched.

Chapter 19

Fia stood over Shannon's body. Shannon's cell phone was a smoldering cinder in her pocket. This morning, while waiting for Glen to finish in the shower, before going out for Saturday morning breakfast, she'd checked her voice mail and discovered that Shannon had left a message at eleven twenty-five the previous night. Just about the time Fia and Glen had been on round two. The call from Sedowski at the office came in at nine-forty, as Fia and Glen were walking into a diner.

Dr. Caldwell had taken Shannon's liver temp when he arrived at the scene. He put the time of death between 11 P.M. and midnight. Nothing Shannon had said in her phone message indicated there was anything wrong. She doubted it would have made a difference if she had taken the call, but Fia felt guilty just the same.

She stared at Shannon's body, then at her head, obviously posed by the killer. Sour bile rose in Fia's throat.

The murderer had decapitated Shannon just inside the bedroom door. Blood patterns, spray and pools, made that obvious. She was probably taken by surprise as there was no sign of struggle.

Her body had then been dragged to the bed, her breasts viciously cut off. The breasts were gone, but this time the head was left behind and displayed. As per the MO, there had been an attempt to burn the body, or at least a symbolic attempt. Shannon's bed linens had been set on fire, only the killer hadn't stuck around long enough to see his deed to completion. The bedspread, treated with some fire-retardant chemical, had prevented the mattress from going up in flames and the fire had eventually put itself out. The fire had done very little damage to Shannon's body, though it had burned off her clothes, leaving her naked in the bed.

The sick bastard.

Fia didn't think she had ever witnessed such a vicious crime scene in all her years with the FBI. Not even mob killings were this bad. What kind of hatred did a man have to have inside him to kill, to maim this way? It didn't matter that Fia knew Shannon's heart had ceased beating before her breasts had been sliced off. No one, alive or dead, human or vampire, should have been disrespected in such a way.

Her hand on her pocket, cradling the cell phone that would be her last communication ever with Shannon, Fia allowed her gaze to drift to the head propped upright against two flowered pillows. Shannon's beautiful blond hair, slightly singed, flowed over the pillows. Her blue eyes were half closed, her skin waxen. But what drew Fia's attention was her mouth. Shannon still had cherry lip gloss on her pouty lips; Fia could smell it. The sweet scent almost made her gag.

Sweet Mary, Mother of God, Fia thought. *How could the lip gloss survive this carnage?* Then a shadow inside Shannon's mouth drew her attention. "Gloves," she hollered, sticking her hand out behind her.

When she'd arrived at the scene, she'd insisted everyone get out of Shannon's small, purple-and-green bedroom, which appeared to be more a teenager's room than an adult woman's. Fia wanted to see Shannon alone. Be with her alone.

A pair of purple gloves appeared in her hand. Fia never saw which EMT handed them to her. She continued to stare at Shannon's pursed lips. "You have a tongue depressor?"

Behind her, she heard someone digging in a metal box, moving items wrapped in crackly plastic. A wooden tongue depressor appeared in her outstretched hand.

"You got something in there?" Glen asked from the hallway. He had been interviewing one of Uncle Sean's cops, the first person on the scene after Mrs. Hill had called it in. Mrs. Hill had gotten worried when Shannon hadn't brought Mr. Hill his morning paper from the driveway. Mrs. Hill said the door was unlocked, as always, and when Shannon hadn't answered her phone or a knock at the door, she had known something was wrong and had come in.

"Special Agent Kahill?" Glen asked from the doorway in his best FBI voice.

"Just a sec," she said. She approached the bed, trying to ignore the smell of singed hair and flesh that mixed with the sweet scent of the lip gloss. She ignored Shannon's half-lidded, empty gaze.

Something was in her mouth.

Touching the top of Shannon's head just gently

enough to prevent moving it, Fia pushed the tongue depressor into her mouth and poked at the object. It popped out and would have hit the bed had Fia not released the top of Shannon's head and caught it.

"Fee, what is it?" Glen's voice had gone from tough-guy special agent's to concerned boyfriend's.

She was barely able to choke the word out as she stared at her gloved hand. "Garlic."

"What?" He stepped into the room.

A wave of dizziness washed over Fia. For a moment, she thought she might faint or be sick. Maybe both.

Slowly, it passed.

"Garlic," she repeated, her voice stronger this time. She held up the cloves for him to see.

"Why the hell—"

Fia squatted and took a small evidence bag from the kit just inside the door, not really hearing what Glen was saying. She didn't have to ask why there was garlic in Shannon's mouth or what it meant.

"I don't understand why you have to go." Glen lay on his side in the bed with its ruffly blue linens and blue fish stenciled on the headboard. He was covered to the waist with a sheet, but as he grabbed her hand to stop her from climbing out of bed, it shifted, giving her a nice view of his dark nest of hair and dangling participles.

The man had fine participles, she'd give him that.

She made herself look away and think of something other than his rising hard-on. Something she disliked. Getting her teeth cleaned. Scraping the floor drain in her shower. "I have to go because this is the Blue Gill room and my room is the Starfish room."

He wouldn't let go of her hand and she sat back down on the edge of the bed. She tried to reach for her T-shirt so she wouldn't have to have this conversation stark naked, but he refused to give her enough line to reach it.

"Please don't tell me you don't want your parents to know you're sleeping with me."

"It's not the sleeping part I'm trying to keep from them."

"Fee. Once again, I'm trying to be serious, and you're not."

She groaned and flopped back down on the bed, head on the pillow beside him, taking care not to brush her hand against that which dangled. She didn't want to start anything she didn't have time to finish. She needed to get out of the room so that Glen would go to sleep, so she could make the council meeting. This was not a night to be late.

"Please." She turned her head to look at him. "I know where you're going with this and I don't think I can deal with this conversation tonight."

He was quiet for minute. "Okay."

"Okay?" That had been entirely too easy. Twice in the last week he'd attempted to talk about "their relationship" and both times she'd managed to sidestep the conversation nicely.

"Okay for tonight. I understand you've had a crappy day. Back in Clare Point again. Shannon this time." He drew his hand across her cheek. "But you're not going to keep putting me off. I know we're moving awfully fast, but you're trying to pretend we're not moving at all."

She stared at the ceiling, watching the fan turn. Painted blue, of course. "Glen—"

"This is not a conversation, which means you don't have to speak. I just want to say that when you're ready to have it, I am. I just want to say that even though this is early on and it's sudden and all that, I want to make it work. I'm not an impulsive guy, you know that, Fee. But *this* . . . it just *feels* right."

She turned her head. He was looking into her eyes. She was melting.

"*You* feel right," he whispered.

Fia sat up, grabbing the pillow, using it as a barrier between her naked body and his. Her heart and his.

He was a human. She couldn't do this. She knew she couldn't do it. Not again. It had been a mistake. She'd been wrong to think she could handle it. She'd been wrong to think that she could just make the relationship about sex.

"I really do need to get back to my own room," she said carefully. "And you need to get some sleep." She leaned down and kissed him, pulling the sheet up to cover him at the same time.

"What's the matter," he teased. "You don't want another *piece a dis?*"

She laughed, trying to keep her voice down. "Good night, Glen. See you in the morning."

"See you in the morning, *sweet britches.*"

She threw the pillow at him.

At 1:15 A.M. Fia stepped out onto the sidewalk in front of her parents' B and B. At 1:17 a black panther joined her on the sidewalk. The creature was sleek and massive. It had to go two hundred, two hundred and twenty pounds. As it walked beside her, its tail twitched. Golden, glowing eyes watched her.

"Can you do a bear?" she asked. "A hedgehog? This big cat thing is getting tiresome."

It's not safe for you to walk alone, Arlan said. Actually, he didn't speak, but Fia heard him clearly in her head.

"You don't have to worry about me." She spoke aloud, preferring the noise of her own voice to the stark absence of sound in the frightened town. Tonight, no cars purred down the streets. No doors opened and closed. Dogs didn't even bark. Did their domesticated companions fear for the lives of the sept, too? "I can take care of myself."

That's what Shannon thought, too.

"She was killed inside her apartment, not on the street."

Arlan walked beside her, light-footed, fangs bared, long black tail swishing back and forth in a grand arc. *So what does that mean, Fee, that none of us are safe now, anywhere?*

"Sweet Mary and Joseph, he cut off her breasts, Arlan." Fia's voice cracked with emotion as tears suddenly stung the backs of her eyelids. She covered her mouth with her hand.

She'd held it together all day but all of a sudden she felt lost. Defeated. "How could anyone do that? He cut them off and he took them with him in a garbage bag from a box under her own sink. He set her head on the bed and stuffed her mouth with garlic."

"You know what that means."

"Good news, I suppose." She reached over her

shoulder, trying to rub the knot that ached in the center of her back. "It's not one of us. Only humans believe that we give a shit about garlic."

"Thanks to our buddy, Bram Stoker." Arlan went from four legs to two in a split second. One moment he was sporting a tail, the next he was walking beside her in human form, kneading her tired shoulder muscles with his hand. "But not just him. There were others, too. I'm actually pretty up to date on my vampire-in-the-media trivia."

"Good to know. Should I get on one of those game shows and have to call my lifeline for the answer to a question pertaining to vampires in the media, you're my man, Arlan."

"Do you have to be sarcastic about everything?" He lowered his hand. "Shannon is dead. So are Mahon and Bobby. We have to do something, Fee."

She whipped around, stopping on the sidewalk. "You think I don't know that!"

He was quiet for a minute. They started to walk again. They passed under a streetlamp. A block ahead, an elderly woman, bundled in a hat and coat though it was sixty degrees, hustled across the street, headed for the museum.

"I think you're taking this too personally," he said. "No one cares if *you* find the killer, or if one of us does. It's not going to make us think any less of you, Fee, if you're not the one who stops him. It won't mean you're not a good FBI agent or you don't deserve to be on the high council."

She pressed her lips together. "The garlic is the best lead I've gotten on the cases, so far. I know now that it's a human and not one of us, thank God. But it's a human who knows how to kill us."

"Which means one of us had to tell one of them," he offered.

"Exactly."

They made the turn up the freshly blacktopped driveway to the parking lot behind the museum. Neither spoke, both lost in their thoughts, but Fia found it comforting to have Arlan beside her. It would make it easier to walk into the council meeting.

They entered the building by the dark rear hallway and made their way into the main room of the museum where chairs had been set up in a circle. Tonight there was no snack table. Not even a pot of coffee; no smell of aromatic coffee this evening, just the clear, strong scent of fear.

They were among the last to arrive so most of the seats were occupied; she took a chair close to the door. Arlan gave her shoulder a quick squeeze as he walked past her, taking a seat on the opposite side of the circle.

Peigi Ross cleared her throat, tapped her pen on her clipboard. Fia noticed that the board that usually listed a dozen items for the agenda was blank. Tonight they would only discuss one topic, and Peigi didn't need to remind herself what it was.

"Looks like just about everyone's here," Peigi said, "So let's get started. "This is the way we're going to do it tonight. I'm gonna talk and then I'm going to call on a few of you—"

"I don't know who you think you are, Peigi Ross," Bobby's wife said, gesturing grandly. "We all have a right to speak on this council. I have a right to speak."

Peigi whipped around to face the red-eyed

Mary McCathal. "You do have a right to speak, but we don't have time for arguin', Mary, and arguing is just what you're good at. All of us are. But I'm the chief of this council and that gives me the right to say how things are gonna be done." She shook her clipboard at Mary, at all of them. "Tonight, we're not all jabberin'. We're not making accusations, pointing fingers, or picking fights. We're going to figure out what we're going to do about this mess we've got here. And then we're going to do something about it." Sitting in her folding chair, she slid her clipboard underneath and folded her arms over her middle-aged breasts.

"Fia," Peigi said, settling her gaze on her. "There're plenty of rumors bouncing around Clare Point. Why don't you tell us exactly what we know and what we don't know and give us your assessment of the situation. Not just from an FBI standpoint, but as a member of this sept."

Fia debated whether to sit or stand but decided to stand, thinking it would give her more authority. "This is what we know. Shannon worked until nine at the Hill, and was out until sometime between 11:15 and 11:20 P.M. Liz Lilk, across the street, saw her walking up her driveway. Where she was between clocking out from work and arriving at home, I haven't been able to find out yet. Shannon placed a personal phone call to me at 11:25 and sometime between then and midnight, she was murdered."

Fia heard whispers, but no one spoke up. All gazes were fixed on her.

"The killer could have followed her in, but it's more likely he was waiting for her. Probably hiding in the bedroom. He decapitated her . . ." Fia kept her voice steady. "He placed her on the bed, he removed her breasts, put garlic in her mouth, and set the bed on fire."

"Her breasts," someone whispered. "Bobby's feet, Mahon's hands. Now Shannon's breasts."

Fia looked in the direction the voice had come from and the room was silent again.

"I don't yet know why the killer is taking body parts, but all of us in this room understand the beheading and the burning. The head is separated from the body, the body is burned, to prevent the body from regenerating and the soul reentering the body. What's different about Shannon is the garlic in her mouth. A few weeks ago we were looking at each other, wondering if one of our neighbors, our family members, could have been committing these heinous crimes. Now we know it's not one of us."

"How do we know?" Jim Hill piped up.

She turned to him. "Because only humans believe in the repelling quality of garlic among vampires. You put garlic in your marinara sauce, Uncle Jim."

He lowered his head, nodding in agreement.

Fia took the moment to look at each member of the council, slowly turning so that she could look into each of their faces. "So, the good news is that it's not one of us." She hesitated. "The bad news is that it's one of them, which means we've been found."

"What does the FBI think about all this? Beheadings. Now the garlic." Peigi asked.

"Fortunately for us, the FBI doesn't believe in vampires. The assumption is being made that the killer is just another one of the crazies we're all trying to rid the world of. The FBI is serious about this investigation and we believe we're getting closer to the killer." The words sounded hollow in Fia's ears. "What the FBI is doing right now, what I and my partner are doing, is trying to put all the evidence we have from the three murders together and figure out what it means."

"I can tell you what it means. It means one of us ran our mouths," Mary Hill blurted out, staring at Mary McCathal. "Means one of us got too friendly with the tourists. Too friendly with the Federal Express man."

"I never told anyone about us," Mary McCathal hissed at Mary Hill. "You're the one always gossipin', Mary Hill. You're the one runnin' around with people's husbands."

Mary Hill's mouth popped wide open, but before she could say another word, Peigi stood. "Ladies! This is just what I'm talkin' about. What I won't have." She glared at the two Marys. "Go on, Fia." She sat down again.

Fia opened her arms, then brought her hands together. "The good news is, as I said before, we're closer to the killer, closer to finding out who did this and protecting each other. The bad news is that now we have to decide how to figure out what the humans know about us."

"How we supposed to do that?" someone asked. "If I told the checker at the grocery store in Dover about me being a vampire, I certainly wouldn't admit it to anyone else!"

Everyone started to talk at once and the noise rose until it reached a crescendo. Fia let them talk for a moment or two more and then raised both hands. "Ladies, gentlemen, please."

Everyone quieted.

"Before we start accusing each other, thinking the worst of each other, let's consider this. Maybe no one told anyone anything. Maybe a human has learned of our existence by accident. Maybe someone saw something, heard something he shouldn't have. Think about all the humans that come and go in this town every day, especially in the summer—tourists, delivery men, college kids seeking employment."

"I don't understand." Rob Hail rubbed his balding head. "Why would someone seek us out and murder us? We've been living peaceably here for three centuries."

Fia shrugged. "Why have we been persecuted for fourteen hundred years? It's all part of the *mallachd*, Rob. We've just forgotten because we *have* lived so peacefully on these shores for so long."

Again, there were whispers, but people were listening now. They wanted to hear what she had to say.

"So what are you proposing?" Peigi asked.

"I think I should interview everyone in this town, find out what humans we each have contact with and try to cross-reference the names. See which humans are coming in and out of town regularly." As time-consuming as the idea seemed to her, Fia really thought that this was the best way to tackle it. It would be tricky with Glen in town, but she could manage it. Maybe once their official investigation was complete, she'd make some excuse to remain in Clare Point for a few days. Without Glen watching over her shoulder, she thought she could make her way through the townspeople pretty quickly.

"Interview every sept member? You know how long that will take?" Mary Hill demanded. "We'll all be dead before you get anywhere. I say we round up a posse the way we used to do it—"

"And what? Ride through the nearby human towns on horseback, or maybe in our pickups, in the middle of the night, setting houses on fire?" It was Fin who had spoken up. "Is that what you want, Uncle Jim? You want to go back to those days? Innocent people dragged from their homes, left to die in puddles of their own blood?"

A thick, frightened silence fell over the circle of council members.

"No. That's not what we want," Fin said, quietly but firmly. "We're here on these shores because we have been given a second chance to redeem ourselves before God. We're here to protect innocent humans, not kill them. So we'll do this the right way. We'll do it Fia's way." His gaze met hers across the room. "Because Fia will find him. Fia will stop him. I know she will. I would bet my life on it. I would bet hers . . ."

Chapter 20

The dining room of the B and B, which had become Fia's and Glen's makeshift office, was blessedly quiet as Fia logged on to her laptop to check her e-mail. It was the first week of October, and while her mother still had a few guests on weekends, the place was dead on a Wednesday afternoon. Pun unintended.

Fia could hear Glen chatting with Mary Kay in the kitchen. Somehow, over the weekend, they had become best buddies. Glen was complimenting Mary Kay's children, her cooking, and her choice of décor, and Fia's mother was baking cookies, brownies, and muffins left and right. If Glen continued to eat the home cooking the Seahorse advertised in trade and travel magazines, he'd need a double membership to the local gym when he returned to Philadelphia.

As Fia waited on the slow wireless Internet connection one of her younger brothers had rigged, her cell phone rang. Recognizing the number, she snatched the phone off the dining room table, knocking a stack of manila folders off the table onto the polished hardwood floor in the process.

"Shit," she muttered. Then into the phone, "What

do you want? I'm at work." She had no intention of telling Joseph where she was. If he showed up in Clare Point right now, she had a feeling there would be a lynching and it would be her own neck in the noose. Her family members couldn't kill her by stringing her up, but they could certainly make her uncomfortable for a couple of weeks.

As she got out of the chair, squatting to retrieve the mess she made, she glanced in the direction of the kitchen. She could still hear her mother talking.

"You're always so pleasant, Fee," Joseph said in her ear. "Always such a pleasure to talk with."

"What do you want?"

In the kitchen, Glen clasped the tray Mary Kay had made up and, for a moment, he thought he'd have to engage in a tug-of-war with her. He was just trying to be nice. Trying to get Fia a cup of tea and a couple of cookies, or a muffin or something. He hadn't intended to stand here and shoot the breeze with her mother for half an hour.

He was worried about Fia. She wasn't eating. Wasn't sleeping. She was leaving her room late at night to go God knew where and she was acting oddly, even for Fia. There was something going on in this creepy town of hers besides the obvious, but he couldn't put his finger on what it was or how she was involved. And he was beginning to wonder if his attraction to her was clouding his judgment.

The whole case was just weird. From the fact that Senator Malley's office had assigned her to the case, despite her relationship to the town and lack of jurisdiction, to the fact that the people of the town didn't really seem that upset that someone was beheading their friends and neighbors. Glen had been interviewing cops, and neighbors and friends of Shannon's for days, and everyone was cooperative and pleasant. Too cooperative. Too pleasant. Their interviews almost seemed . . . rehearsed.

What was also interesting, actually amazing, was that no one in the town would speak to the press. Not a word. Usually, especially in small towns like Clare Point, citizens were fighting for their one minute of fame. Typically in these cases, old school photos of the victims were plastered in newspapers and on the evening news. Everyone wanted to talk about what a good man or woman the victim had been or what good grades he or she had gotten in spelling in the third grade. But Clare Point had been so tight-lipped after the previous murders that local TV stations hadn't even bothered to send a crew when Shannon was killed. There had been nothing more than an inch of column space in the state's largest paper.

And the good citizens of Clare Point weren't the only ones keeping their mouths shut. Fia was remaining very closemouthed about how her interviews were going. She was the one making the calls in the case, deciding each day who would interview which people. He couldn't help getting the idea that she was trying to keep him away from certain members of the town; her uncle the police chief, an old codger named Victor Simpson, and Jim Kahill, her father, of all people.

"Thanks for the tea and brownies." Glen smiled at Mary Kay as he made a beeline for the swinging kitchen door, captured tray in his hands. As he entered the dining room, he spotted Fia on the floor scooping up papers. She had her cell phone to her ear.

"Because I can't say for sure I can make it," she said curtly. "Next week would be better."

Glen set the tray on the end of the dining room table and went around the other side to help Fia collect her notes on the floor. She shook her head at him, but he ignored her.

"I really can't talk right now." On all fours, she glanced at Glen. "See what you can do for next week."

"Who was that?" he asked when she hung up. They were both still collecting the papers scattered on the floor.

"Um . . . hair appointment." She gave a little laugh, not looking up. "Standing appointment. Forgot all about it."

She wasn't a very good liar. Why would she lie about the call?

Glen watched her out of the corner of his eye.

"You don't have to do this," she said. "I'm such a klutz."

He got to his feet, two folders stuffed with notes in his hands. "Fee, what's going on?"

"Going on?" She frowned. "Nothing's going on. That's the problem. I've been going over my interviews and not a single person seems to have seen Shannon after she left work. Not until she was walking up the driveway to her house before she was murdered."

"You think she was *with* someone?" Glen didn't want to make accusations and certainly didn't care who the waitress did or didn't sleep with, but she'd come on pretty strong with him a couple of times. Surely it had crossed Fia's mind that she was probably having sex with *someone*, a pretty girl her age. Maybe more than one guy. Maybe it was someone's husband or boyfriend. "Someone who doesn't want to admit to it?"

"It's possible. But that kind of stuff usually comes out pretty quickly in small towns like this."

There was no small town like this one, except in a Stephen King novel, Glen wanted to say. But, following Fia's cue over the last couple of days, he kept his mouth shut.

"I brought you some tea. Brownies. I know how you are with your chocolate. Want me to pour you some?" He set the folders on the edge of the table, resisting the impulse to glance at her handwritten notes. She wasn't really sharing much of what she'd learned from her interviews with him. But his notes were half the volume, no, *a third* of hers. He wasn't getting much more than name, rank, and serial numbers from the men and women he'd been talking to, the people who had been at the pub the night Shannon died.

So what was Fia writing down? And what were the lists of names he'd seen her stuff into one of the file folders?

"Tea? Ah, Glen, that was nice of you." She picked up her cell phone, glancing at the screen. "But I have to run. I'm meeting Kaleigh and her friends for breakfast at the diner."

"Breakfast? It's almost noon."

She grabbed the folders and stuffed them into the side pocket of her laptop bag. "But breakfast time for teenagers. I imagine the girls are just now dragging themselves out of bed."

"No school?" He grabbed a brownie. Someone had to eat them.

"In-service day or some such nonsense." She shut down her laptop.

She seemed eager to go. Way too eager to have fried eggs and hotcakes with a bunch of teenaged girls. He wondered who the phone call had been from. If Fia really was going to meet Kaleigh.

Then he felt guilty. What was making him so suspicious? Fia had done nothing that wasn't aboveboard. So maybe she was acting a little strangely. He would too, if he were investigating a murder on the block where he grew up.

He chewed on his brownie, not quite sure where to go from here. Fia was so different from Stacy. So much harder to get a fix on. So much more intense. "So you'll be back later?"

"Yeah. That cook is back in town. The guy from the Hill who went to his cousin's wedding in Connecticut. I'm going to talk to him after I see Kaleigh. Then . . . I don't know. I've got a couple of other things I want to do. Want to just meet me at the Hill tonight?"

"Tonight?"

"Like eight?"

That was a lot of time. What *things* did she have to do? "Sure. See you at the Hill at eight. I'm just going to go over my notes, make some phone calls. Maybe watch some soaps with Mary Kay."

"Catch you later."

Fia didn't smile, but what bothered him more was that he didn't either.

"That all you're going to eat?" Fia asked as the waitress walked away.

Kaleigh, dressed in sweatpants and a hoodie, looking as if she *had* just rolled out of bed, sipped her black coffee. She appeared hungover. Her eyes had dark circles beneath them and she looked haggard. Tired. Not her usual pretty self.

Fia wondered if she'd been out drinking with "the guys" last night, but decided this wasn't the time or the place to lecture Kaleigh on the dangers of vampires overindulging in alcohol.

"So neither Katy nor Maria could make it, huh?" Fia folded her hands on the table. Even though it was lunchtime, there were only a few patrons in the diner; all sept members. The hostess, Mary Ann, who was also the waitress this time of year, who was also the owner of the diner, had seated Fia and Kaleigh in a booth on the far side of the room. From their vantage point, it seemed as if they were the only ones there.

Kaleigh stared into the coffee mug she cupped between her hands. "They had stuff to do." She lifted a thin shoulder inside her sweatshirt. Let it fall.

Fia studied the teen across the table. "I guess you already know why I wanted to see you. Why I wanted to talk to all of you."

Kaleigh didn't respond.

Fia's phone vibrated. She pulled it out of her jacket pocket, looked at the ID screen and tucked it away. It was Joseph again. He just wasn't going to let it go, was he?

"You can answer your phone if you want," Kaleigh said. "I don't care."

"I'll take care of it later." Fia shifted on the bench, refocusing. "I'm interviewing all the sept members in the town, trying to create a database of humans we come directly in contact with."

"Must make things interesting. Your partner in the official investigation being a human."

Fia stared at the young girl for a moment. Kaleigh

was awfully perceptive for a teen who had not yet been able to develop her mental telepathy. Curious, Fia opened her mind and shot a thought in Kaleigh's direction, something that would surely get a fourteen-year-old's attention if she was *listening*.

You've got something stuck between your front teeth.

The teen lifted her cup and took another sip of coffee, not looking up. "What's his name?" she asked. "Special Agent Duncan, right? Glen. The other girls think he's hot. I think he's old."

No reaction to the telepathy. So maybe Fia was wrong. Some of the other sept members Kaleigh's age had already begun to cultivate their extrasensory abilities, but Kaleigh's development, or lack thereof, wasn't really unusual. Like humans going through puberty, it hit them at different ages. Over her last couple of life cycles Kaleigh *had* been a late bloomer.

"I guess Glen is kind of hot," Fia said, thinking she might try a different tack. Maybe Kaleigh would be more open to her if she just saw Fia as "one of the girls." "He's got a fine ass. I'll give him that."

"You sleeping with him?" Kaleigh looked up at her over the rim of her mug.

Fia frowned.

"Just asking. I mean, you could if you wanted to. You're freer to sleep with who you please than most of us are."

"He's a human, Kaleigh."

"So was Ian." Again, the look over the edge of the coffee cup.

"Ah, so you remember Ian now?"

"Not much." The same shrug. "Mostly just images. Gair says he'll fill in the gaps when I'm ready. But he says I'm not ready yet." Her last words were all teenager, full of sarcasm and resentment.

"So back to the reason why I wanted to talk to all three—"

"I told you." Kaleigh interrupted her resentfully as she sat back to allow the waitress to set down a plate with a toasted English muffin on it. "They had *stuff.*"

"I need you to tell me who your friends are at school." Fia pulled a legal pad and pen from her laptop bag. Mary Ann left a plate beside her with a turkey club, chips, and a pickle. "Tell me about your human friends at school."

Kaleigh rolled her eyes, sitting back on the booth's bench. "I don't have *friends.* You know what weirdos everyone thinks we are? There's just Maria and Katy."

"Okay, then. Tell me the names of your human *acquaintances.* I've already got Derek Neuman's name. And let's see—the two friends I've met are John Wright and . . . Michael Poors." Kaleigh remained silent so Fia went on. "I ran the boys' records. They've all been arrested. Once for a B and E. That's breaking and entering. And John Wright has a DWI on his record."

"So? The football team was messing with the soccer team so the soccer team got them back. It's not like they robbed banks or something."

Fia flipped the page back on the legal pad. Honestly, the charges didn't really mean anything in FBI terms. The B and E had involved stealing a chair from another student's house, some schoolkid prank, as Kaleigh had suggested. And the DWI was, unfortunately, a frequent event in a county with little for teens to do and no public transportation.

"Another interesting tidbit," Fia continued, "is that your boyfriend apparently lied to you. He *did* just have his birthday, but he's eighteen. Not sixteen. And according to the high school admin office, he dropped out last year. Only the other two boys are students. Which means *you* were telling a little fib, as well. You don't go to school with Derek."

Fia glanced up at Kaleigh. To her surprise, the teen's eyes were full of tears.

"We broke up," she blurted out. "He's not my boyfriend anymore."

Fia waited.

"I found out he was screwing this slut in my biology class and when I asked him about it, he said if I wasn't giving him any, he had a right to get it somewhere else." She sniffed and wiped her nose with the sleeve of her sweatshirt. "So I broke up with him. Last week."

Fia's heart went out to Kaleigh. Her first broken heart. At least the first she knew of. "I'm sorry," she said quietly.

"Are you?" Kaleigh looked up through teary eyes, then down again, into her coffee cup. "You wanted me to break up with him anyway. Everyone wanted us to break up. Now you have your way. I'm not seeing him anymore. Never. He's a jerk and an ass. Katy and Maria broke up with John and Mike, too. They were all jerks."

Fia wanted to smile, albeit sadly. "This probably isn't terribly comforting right now, but in a couple of years, Rob will—"

"Rob is like old and toothless."

This time Fia smiled. "I know. He is *now*. And I know you can't remember, but he won't be that way much longer. And after he dies, after he's reborn—"

"Are we done here?" Kaleigh pushed her untouched muffin toward the middle of the table. "Because if we are, I have geometry homework and a stupid project on Bosnia to do for social studies."

Fia looked down at her notes. "When did you say you broke up with Derek?"

"Last week." She stared at the table. "Like . . . more than a week ago."

"And before you broke up with him, I don't suppose you ever had any conversations . . . about the sept."

"You think I'm stupid?" Kaleigh snapped, rubbing her eyes with her sleeve.

"No, I don't think you're stupid. Just young." Fia inhaled. Exhaled. "So you don't care if I go by his house? Talk to him? Maybe his dad?"

"Could you arrest him, instead?" Kaleigh slid out of the booth. "I gotta go. You know where to find me if you need me. Like for the next million years. . . ."

Chapter 21

Fia had no intention of going to the appointment Joseph had set up with Dr. Kettleman. There was no way she could do it today, or even this week. By the time she got to Philly, went to the appointment, and drove back, she'd be lucky to make it to the Hill to meet Glen by eight. She was also concerned Glen would be suspicious if she didn't have anything to produce for the hours she supposedly had been interviewing. He was already acting suspicious.

But after another more heated phone conversation with Joseph, after she left the diner, she decided to go to the appointment, have it out with him, and be done with it. The last couple of days, between interviews, she'd been doing some research on the Internet and she'd found some interesting information she doubted Joseph would want her or anyone else to know about. It might just be the leverage she needed to get him out of her jurisdiction and her life.

After going to the police station, chatting with Uncle Sean, and then using the computers to access some information she couldn't reach with her laptop, Fia made a point of mentioning that she was going to interview some human teens who lived in the area. That way, if Glen happened to stop by the station and ask for her, the officers or Uncle Sean would provide a feasible alibi. Fia hated the idea of letting her personal life take precedent over her job, even for a few hours, but she wasn't putting anyone at risk by taking a few hours off. And if she didn't get rid of Joseph, it was entirely possible he *could* interfere with her job.

Fia was in Philly by five-fifteen. She ran by her apartment to check on her cat, who Betty was keeping an eye on. She stopped at Betty's to see if the elderly woman needed anything, and then went to Dr. Kettleman's, hoping she might be able to get a word in with the psychiatrist before Joseph arrived.

He beat her there and, because Dr. Kettleman's previous appointment had cancelled, Joseph was already seated on the cozy couch inside her office, chatting about some reality TV show about fashion designers they both watched.

"Fia." Joseph's face lit up as he rose to greet her, arms outstretched as if they were lovers, or at least old friends. She considered him neither.

The look on Dr. Kettleman's face told Fia that he already had her hoodwinked. She was at once disappointed in the doctor. So what if Joseph was charismatic? A psychiatrist should be able to see past the thousand-dollar suit and tooth veneers to the black rot of a man's soul.

"Joseph." Fia greeted him coolly, averting his embrace. "Dr. Kettleman." She nodded.

"Glad you could make the appointment after all," the psychiatrist said, crossing her legs. "I think this

is a step in the right direction. So let's get started."
She gestured to the couch.

Fia sat on the far end, as far from Joseph as she
could get.

Dr. Kettleman clasped her hands. "Now, Fia and
I have been discussing, over the last couple of weeks,
her concern about the two of you living in such
close proximity. How do you feel about that, Joseph?"

"I think Fia is making way too much out of this."
He raised his manicured hands innocently. "Years
have passed since our relationship ended. We've
both matured. We—"

"You promised you would go and never come
back, Joseph. You swore to me."

Dr. Kettleman looked from Fia to Joseph. "Did
you make that promise, Joseph?"

His smile grew taut. "I did, but that was a long
time ago. I had no idea I'd become a plastic surgeon of such renown. No idea my partner and I
would feel the need to expand beyond California."

"You can't stay here," Fia said.

Joseph whipped around. "And why not!" he
shouted. "Why not?"

Fia was so astounded that he had dropped his
cool facade that it took her a moment to recover.
This was the Joseph she knew. Not a Joseph she
feared, but one she knew well enough to fear for
others. "Because of my job. Because I know you
and I know your habits."

He scowled.

Fia lifted her chin in the psychiatrist's direction.
"Tell Dr. Kettleman why you're leaving California."

"I'm opening a new office."

"The truth." She stared at him.

He stared back and she was relieved to find that she no longer felt even a hint of desire for him. She hated him. She hated herself for what he was. What she had made him.

Fia looked at Dr. Kettleman. "It seems that Joseph has a little problem with picking up women in bars. He gets them drunk, convinces them to take him home, and then nearly kills them with his greed." As the words came out of her mouth, she got a chill down her spine. It was like some weird flash of déjà vu.

"So what I'm hearing is that your bloodletting with humans has possibly gotten out of hand, Joseph?" Dr. Kettleman asked calmly.

Joseph looked at Fia in confusion.

"You don't really think I would see a human psychiatrist," Fia said, deadpan. "She's one of us. A second cousin."

Joseph looked at Dr. Kettleman more closely.

The psychiatrist waggled a finger as if he were a naughty boy. "I'm sorry; we don't use telepathy in this office, Joseph. It's not conducive to good sessions. Here, we have to say what we want. We have to exercise our ability to share our feelings verbally."

Fia was still pondering the previous subject. "Joseph," she said softly. "You asked me a couple of weeks ago about the Casey Mulvine case. Why did you ask me about her?"

"I told you. I read about it in the paper." He looked at Dr. Kettleman as if Fia's question was ridiculous.

"When did you get here?"

"What?" He turned back to her. The smile he had worn into the office was gone.

"When did you arrive in the Philadelphia area?"

He turned his attention to the psychiatrist. "I don't see what this has to do with why we're here, Dr. Kettleman."

"Did you do it?" Fia's voice quavered. "I know you were questioned multiple times for the attempted murders of at least nine young women in southern California. They had all had blood drained from their bodies, and they all suffered from erotic asphyxia. They were picked up in bars, just like Casey Mulvine. Did you kill her?"

"Fia, how could you ask me such a thing?" He met her gaze, his cool voice suddenly full of emotion. "How could you jump to such wild conclusions? Of course I didn't kill anyone. How . . . how could you believe me capable of such things?" His eyes grew moist. "You and I, we once loved each other. No matter what's happened between us, how could you think that someone you loved could do such a thing?"

Fia exhaled. He sounded genuinely hurt and guilt washed over her. Maybe he was right, maybe she *was* jumping to conclusions. He hadn't denied the girls in California. And there, he hadn't really done anything more than she had done, although after all these years, after all her experience, she knew how much blood loss a body could sustain, depending on the height and weight of a victim. Joseph hadn't had that advantage of time yet.

Dr. Kettleman looked to Fia. Waited.

"I'm sorry, Joseph," Fia said quietly.

"You're sorry?" he asked.

"Sorry I accused you . . ." Against her will, her own eyes filled with tears and she fought a lump in her throat. "I'm sorry I accused you of being a murderer." She forced herself to look at him. "And I'm sorry for what I did to you. I'm sorry that I did this to your life . . . that I made you a vampire."

He slid his hand across the couch and covered Fia's, letting a moment pass before he spoke. "I just wanted to hear you say it, Fee." He squeezed her hand and let it go. "You never told me you were sorry. I just . . . I just needed to hear it from you." He picked up a box of Kleenex from the table beside the couch and offered it to her.

Fia took two.

"It's all I wanted to hear," Joseph said again, patting at his own eyes with a tissue. "I think that's why I came back. Not because I really wanted to move here, Dr. Kettleman." He looked across the coffee table to her. "But, because . . . because I needed closure. Does that make sense?"

"We all need closure to certain events in our lives, Joseph. Especially traumatic events such as the one you suffered. What Fia did was very wrong. And she knows that." She nodded to Fia. "And now, maybe through this apology, she can have some closure, too."

Fia felt like an idiot. For allowing Joseph to get her this worked up. For allowing herself to let her emotions get out of control. And there was a part of her still, deep inside, that didn't quite believe what he was saying.

"So, now that you have this "closure," can you go now, Joseph?" Fia looked to Dr. Kettleman. "This isn't just personal, Marie."

Fia made it a habit never to use Dr. Kettleman's first name in her office because it helped the doctor-patient relationship to flourish. But sometimes . . .

times like this, only another sept member could truly understand. So at this moment, Marie Kahill Kettleman wasn't just a psychiatrist, she was also Fia's second cousin on her father's side. "This is about my job," Fia continued. "Unsolved cases in the area cross my desk every day. If I saw a crime that I suspected Joseph had played a part in, I'd be placed in a very bad position. I would have to make the choice to either allow the humans to investigate him and put us all at risk, or take the matter to the sept." She shifted her gaze to Joseph. "And neither would be good for him."

"I don't have to put my office in Philadelphia." Joseph lifted his hands. Let them fall to his lap. "We're actually seriously considering Dallas and Las Vegas. I can simply tell my partner that the client base we're looking for isn't here."

"And that's it?" Fia asked him. "You'll just go?"

"I'm sorry, too, Fia, for doing this." He turned to her. "For all the trouble I've caused you the last couple of weeks. But I really do feel better." He slid his hand toward her on the couch. "Don't you?"

She pulled her hand away before he touched it. "So it's settled." She looked back at Dr. Kettleman. "Joseph's going to leave town and I'm going back to work."

"I'm sorry I was late. Sorry I missed dinner." Fia sat down on the edge of the bed, her back to Glen. She wasn't good at this. Not at apologizing. Certainly not at relationships. She didn't know what to say to him. How to say it. She felt as if she was making a mess of things . . . and things had barely gotten started. What had she been thinking when she even considered a relationship with a man, and with a human, no less? Maybe it just wasn't in her. Maybe she would never have anything more than glimpses of humanity in dark alleyways.

She'd left Philadelphia earlier than she'd thought she'd be able to, but then there was a serious accident on Route 1, and she sat with her engine off for nearly an hour. Then she had to stop for gas in Dover. She ended up not making it to the Hill until almost ten, about the time Glen was paying his tab and heading out the door. They'd walked back to the B and B in silence. Glen hadn't seemed angry with her. Just detached.

He laid stretched out, in his T-shirt and pants, shoes off, his arm tucked under his head. He was watching the ceiling fan slowly turn. "Not a big deal. Your Uncle Sean and his brother Mungo kept me entertained." He glanced at her. "How'd the interviews go with those boys? You get the impression they know anything about the murders?"

So, Glen had asked where she'd gone. Uncle Sean had come through for her. Good news. The bad, though, was that now she had to either confess that she'd gone back to Philly for personal reasons, or lie about the interviews. Neither was a good option.

Split-second decision. "The interviews ran longer than I thought they would. Actually, tracking down the boys took longer than I thought. Found out Derek's mother committed suicide when he was a kid. Father's a little distant, as far as his relationship with his son." All true. She just hadn't gotten the information directly through an interview. Fia's guilt gland swelled. She'd never lied to another agent about a case before.

"All three boys have a record," she continued, leaning over to remove her boots, avoiding making eye contact with Glen as long as she possibly could. "Nothing serious. Boys-will-be-boys stuff."

"Got a tidbit from the lab this afternoon. Preliminary, of course."

She turned, not just eager for information on Shannon's case, but relieved to shift the conversation. If she could just get out of this, she swore to herself, she'd never lie to Glen again. "What'd they come up with?"

"Soil on the shoes Shannon left inside the door matched the soil on scrapings from Mahon's shoes. She was in the woods within a few hours of leaving those shoes at the door. Lab says there's no way to know if the soil came specifically from the game preserve because it matches the soil in a pretty large area of the county, but I think the game preserve is worth revisiting."

Fia fought her disappointment. Of course Glen didn't know it, but everyone in the town had soil from that game preserve on their shoes.

But the soil was fresh. Had Shannon really been foolish enough to go hunting alone, even after the council had warned against it?

Or had she been there for another reason? Was there a connection to the game preserve Fia was overlooking? Like that old adage about not being able to see the forest for the trees?

She thought about the altar Shannon claimed she had seen. Had Shannon been hunting alone, or had she even more foolishly been out looking for the altar again? Shannon had seemed annoyed that no one had believed it was there, but as many people as they had traipsing through the forest after Mahon was killed, Fia would have thought they would have found it if it *was* still there.

Glen reached out and massaged her shoulder. "I think you and I need to go back to where Mahon was killed and have a look around," he said. "I can't shake the feeling this means something."

If she and Glen were going back into the forest tomorrow, she'd have to give everyone a heads-up. Sept members almost never hunted during daylight hours, but she couldn't take any chances if Glen was going to be knocking around out there.

"You okay?" he asked.

She rolled her shoulders, tipping her head back, closing her eyes. "Yeah, fine. Just beat." His fingers felt so good. The taut muscles in her neck and shoulders began to loosen up.

Glen sat up, wrapping his legs around her, and began to rub her shoulders in earnest.

She moaned. "That feels good."

He kissed the back of her neck.

"That too," she whispered, eyes still closed.

The pressure of his mouth against her neck sent shivers of anticipation through her. Tiny, electric pulses ignited nerve endings in every region of her body. It fascinated Fia that Glen could touch her ear lobe with the tip of his tongue and she could feel it in the crooks of her elbows, on her nipples, above her navel . . . lower.

As Glen kissed the nape of her neck, he teased at the hem of her silk T-shirt, his fingertips brushing against the sensitive skin of her abdomen. He slipped his hand under the shirt and brought it up to cup her breast. "Missed you today," he whispered.

"Mmmm." She leaned back against him.

He slipped his fingers beneath the underwire of her bra and she reached back and unfastened it. He cupped her breast with his hand and squeezed gently.

It felt good to be in Glen's arms. To feel the security of his entire body wrapped around hers.

He kissed his way along her jaw and she turned her head to meet his lips. Tonight he had the smoky taste of scotch on his breath. Uncle Mungo's influence, no doubt.

She kissed him hungrily, wanting to possess, be possessed at the same time.

Glen pulled her shirt over her head, tossed it to the floor with her bra. He drew his hand across her abdomen, his fingers lingering just below her navel. Teasing.

She lifted her arms above her head, caught the fabric of his white V-necked Hanes, and pulled it over his head, adding it to the growing pile on her mother's latch-hook rug. When she leaned against him again, the soft mat of dark hair between his pecs tickled her back. She rubbed harder, stimulating his nipples.

His husky groan in her ear sent her pulse up a notch. She caught his hand and drew it down over the fabric of her dress slacks, between her thighs.

"Here?" he whispered.

"Right there." Her words came out breathy.

Using both hands, his arms still around her waist, he unfastened the hook at her waistband. Eased down the zipper. He took his time, his fingers applying light pressure to her sensitive skin, skin that was becoming more sensitive by the moment.

When he slipped two fingers into her panties, her breath caught in her throat.

"And how about here?"

"There . . ." Past breathy now. Practically panting. "There's good, too," she whispered.

He kissed her cheek and she could feel him smiling.

Maybe she could handle this. Her thoughts floated somewhere above her. Maybe she could make it work. He was in no danger. Right now, blood was the furthest thing from her mind. She didn't want raw, hard, rip-your-clothes orgasms. She wanted his embrace. She wanted to feel loved.

Clasping her shoulders, Glen slipped out from behind her and knelt in front of the bed.

She rested her hands on his shoulders, feeling almost intoxicated by him, by his touch. By his warmth. Humans were always so warm. "You don't have to . . ." To her surprise, she felt her cheeks grow warm.

"Of course I don't have to." He tugged on her slacks, taking her thong panties down with them. "Relax," he whispered.

She gripped his shoulders, meaning to push him away. This . . . it was too intimate. But then his warm breath brushed between her thighs and she felt herself melting. She couldn't resist, even if she wanted to.

Threading her fingers through his golden hair, Fia tipped her head back, letting her eyes shut. Everything faded; the tick of the ceiling fan, the overwhelming blue of the Starfish room . . . even the *mallachd*, the curse that haunted her.

Fia leaned back until she rested on the bed, her

legs falling over the side, Glen between her knees. Waves of pleasure washed over her. First gentle, then stronger. His tongue . . . his fingers.

Fia moaned. Panted. Gasped.

"Let it go," Glen encouraged. "It's all right."

"No. No, it's not." She sat up, only opened her eyes halfway. Tonight, for the first time when they made love, she saw Glen and not Ian. "I need you," she admitted. "I need to feel you inside me."

Holding her gaze, he rose to his feet. She unhooked his belt and pushed his clothes down over his slender hips. Still half on the bed, half off, she lay back again, parting her legs for him. He placed his palms on hers and pushed down as he pushed in.

Fia gasped, lifted upward, taking him in. Wanting every part of him she could have for the brief moment.

"Fee . . ." he whispered.

Tears stung her eyes. He sounded so . . . sweet.

Fia turned her head away, squeezing her eyes shut, using her legs to pull him tighter to her. Deeper.

The moment of tenderness passed and he pushed into her.

Fia could hold back no longer. Glen came a moment later.

She vaguely recalled both of them crawling into the bed. Falling on the pillows, his arm comfortably around her. It seemed so natural to drift to sleep, naked limbs tangled.

The next thing Fia knew, the room was dark and the clock beside the bed was glaring red at her. It was 1:17 A.M.

"Sweet Mary, Mother of God!" she swore, easing

out from under Glen's arm and slipping out of bed, leaving him asleep on his stomach, his arms flung on either side of him. She grabbed her clothes and eased out the door. Tiptoed to her room, and hurried to get dressed.

Chapter 22

The council meeting. She was going to be late. Standing in her room in the dark, Fia hopped on one foot and then the other, pulling on a pair of jeans. She skipped the bra. Threw on a T-shirt and hooded sweatshirt to ward off the midnight chill. She was out the door and hurrying down the sidewalk in front of the B and B in less than five minutes.

As she reached the street, she got a weird feeling and turned back to look at the dark, sprawling Victorian house. It was a moonless night, heavy with cloud cover. In the distance, she could smell rain.

She threw back her shoulders, trying to physically shake off the chill.

No lights burned in the attic windows. No curtain shifted. No one was there, but she couldn't dismiss the feeling that something wasn't right.

Not enough sleep. Too many Alfred Hitchcock movies, she told herself.

She turned around and bumped into something thigh-high on the sidewalk. The thing hissed and Fia practically jumped out of her skin.

"Sweet Mary, Mother of God, Arlan! Do you have

to do that?" She glared at the sleek tiger staring up at her with giant yellow eyes and twitching whiskers.

Sheesh. You're jumpy tonight, he telepathed.

She stepped around the giant cat. "You would be, too, if you had a guy always creeping up behind you, looking like an animal that was about to eat you."

"Is that all I am to you?" He morphed into his human form. Tall, handsome, two-day-old beard. "I'm just a *guy*?"

"I'm late to council. You're late." She kept walking.

He followed. "Not going."

"Why not?"

"I got the watch."

She glanced at him impatiently. He was wearing a flannel shirt and goose-down vest. "What *watch*?"

"Human watch." He tilted his head in the direction of the house.

"Glen?" She walked on, her stride long, her footfalls heavy. "I didn't know anything about a watch."

Fia had thought that settling up with Joseph would make her feel better, but now she'd just moved on to a new set of worries. This really pissed her off, sept decisions being made without including her. After all, she was a member not only of the general council, but the high council, as well. "Why are you watching Glen?"

He stopped and glanced in the direction of the dark house. "I should get back on duty. You'll hear about it tonight."

"I don't want to hear it from them; I want to hear it from you, Arlan. What's going on?"

He exhaled, avoiding eye contact. "There're some people wondering if he has something to do with this. Him showing up when the senator had already requested you."

"That's ridiculous! Bobby was dead when Glen was called in."

"I know, Fee. Something about a plot. It doesn't make sense, but they're scared. Particularly of humans. At the very least, they're scared that with all his poking around, he'll see something he shouldn't and then decisions will have to be made."

Decisions will have to be made. There were various ways, over the years, that the sept had dealt with humans discovering the truth about the Kahills, or learning something that might lead to such a discovery—none of them pleasant.

Again, Fia felt uneasy. Something just wasn't right in the night air.

"That's ridiculous." She threw up her hand and then drew it over her hair, down the back of her head.

"It's all got to be sorted out. For now, there's no harm in watching him."

She exhaled, looking back at the house. Trying not to be too pissed. "I guess not."

"But they want him out of here. They're pretty set on that. They're going to talk about it tonight."

"Great. Perfect," she muttered and turned to go, again.

"Hey, Fee."

"Yeah?" She didn't look back.

"One more thing. Just so you know, going into it."

She moaned. Halted. "Yeah?"

"They're talking about sanctions."

"Against *me*?" She turned to him, touching her breast bone. "For what? I'm doing everything I can to find this killer. We're going back to the game preserve tomorrow. I think we might be onto something."

"It's not about the investigation. It's him." Arlan hooked his thumb in the direction of the house. At this distance, she could barely make out its outline. "You're fraternizing with a human."

"That a euphemism for screwing?" she demanded. "Why me? Don't tell me you haven't done it. Don't tell me everyone in this town hasn't done it at one point or another."

He just looked at her.

"Ah," she sighed, making no attempt to hide the bitterness in her voice. "This is still about Ian."

"Fee, you can't blame them for being—"

"Arlan, please." She held up her hand. "Don't make excuses for them." She walked away. "You better get back on watch. You don't want the human outsmarting you."

Fia felt Arlan's gaze on her back as she went down the street, but he didn't follow her. Eventually, she heard him walk back toward the B and B, remaining in human form.

She made a left at the stop sign, thinking she would take a shortcut through a yard. Just as she was opening a gate, she heard a twig snap and she turned in the direction of the sound.

Someone was sneaking through a yard across the street. Just passing through the opening between two ancient boxwood shrubs. Fia knew the silhouette. Tall, thin. Pink sweatshirt, hood pulled up and over her forehead to cover her acne-dotted face.

Kaleigh? What was she doing out in the middle of the night? Surely not meeting Derek. They'd broken up.

Or were they reconciling?

Fia felt a stab of bittersweet pain. First love. It was so hard. For a Kahill, even harder.

She stood at the gate in indecision. As a sept member, was it her duty to stop Kaleigh from making this mistake? There could, of course, be no future in the relationship. Even to consider it was dangerous, not just for the teenager, but for the whole sept.

So how was this different than what Fia was doing? How was her relationship with Glen any safer than Kaleigh's with Derek?

Kaleigh was still just a kid.

Fia had the benefit of past experience and Kaleigh didn't yet have that. Of course, one could make the argument that maturity was a good reason for Fia *not* to get involved with Glen. She, of all people, should have known better.

To Fia's surprise, tears stung her eyes. Was her relationship with Glen doomed? Were all her relationships doomed? Was that Ian's parting gift to her?

Fia saw Kaleigh stop, turn. The silhouettes of two more slender figures appeared in the darkness. Katy and Maria, no doubt.

Well, at least Kaleigh wasn't going out into the woods alone. At least she was traveling in a group. There was safety in numbers. Power in numbers.

Power in numbers.

The hair suddenly rose on the back of Fia's neck and she was instantly covered in gooseflesh.

Power in numbers.

Was it possible?

Against her will, memories of the past flashed through her head. Black-and-white images emblazoned in her mind burst suddenly into brilliant color. The flames. The blood that puddled in the grass. A sound script was added to the image in her mind. She heard the screams of those she loved. The clang of swords. The swoosh, the thud . . . the sound of a head rolling in the street.

Fia's tears gathered in the corners of her eyes as she opened them.

Power in numbers.

How had she missed it? She and Glen had been questioning how the killer was able to overpower his victims and so cleanly decapitate them. Fia, the entire town, had been trying to figure how one man could overpower a vampire, who had extraordinary strength. The answer was that it was not one killer.

And at that moment, Fia realized she had made a terrible decision a little over twelve hours ago when she made the decision to go to Philadelphia and meet Joseph. What she should have done was proceeded with the interviews. The interviews she lied to Glen about tonight.

Guilt washed over her. Heavy. Sour.

The girls moved up the street in a knot of quiet nervous energy.

Fia knew where they were going and a part of her wanted to call out to them. To warn them. It would be wrong to let them go. What if *she* was wrong?

She slipped her hand under her sweatshirt and unsnapped the leather strap that secured her firearm in its holster. She might be wrong.

But what if she was right?

Glen stepped into his wrinkled khaki pants and his belt buckle clacked so loudly that he thought for certain he had woken the entire house. He froze. Waited. He heard nothing but the usual night sounds of the old B and B. A ceiling fan clicking. A branch scraping an outside wall.

He glanced out the window beside his bed where the curtains had been left slightly parted. From there, he had just watched Fia disappear down the street. It was a dark night, no moon, and outside there was an eerie stillness. Though he had heard the branch and knew there had to be a slight breeze, nothing seemed to stir. Not the leaves on the silver maple tree outside the window, not a blade of grass.

Glen was not a touchy-feely guy. He didn't rely on *feelings*. On *hunches*. He had no rational reason to believe anything was wrong. Except that he could feel it deep in his gut.

The streetlamp cast feeble light across the front lawn and part of the driveway. There, between the darkness and the shadows, Glen saw him. Watched him.

It was the good-looking guy, Arlan. The one who had the thing for Fia.

Fia had obviously left Arlan to keep an eye on the B and B while she was out.

It pissed him off that she had sneaked out of the house again. Left his bed to go do God knew what. See God knew who. Go God knew where. And it worried him. No, he was more than worried. Worried wasn't a strong enough word for the fear he had carried in his chest these last couple of days.

All week, he'd told himself that Fia's odd behavior had nothing to do with the cases. That she had nothing to do with the murders, and knew no more than he did. But he had wondered if his at-

traction to her . . . his lust for her . . . was prevent-
ing him from clearly seeing what was going on
here. He knew Fia well enough to realize she had
nothing to do with the deaths, but what if she was
protecting someone who did? Anyone who could
look past the weirdness of Clare Point could see
how close these families were to each other. How
devoted they were. How they protected each other
and nurtured each other.

He pulled a T-shirt over his head, watching Arlan.

The man whose eyes seemed to glow in the weird
light watched the house. But he didn't see Glen.
Didn't know Glen was awake. That Glen was watching the watcher.

That would make getting out of the house un-
detected a hell of a lot easier.

Still in a quandary, Fia followed the teenagers
into the woods at the edge of the game preserve.
She'd immediately put up a mental wall to prevent
Maria or Katy from picking up any of her thoughts,
and therefore her presence. But it quickly became
evident that the girls wouldn't have noticed if an
entire pride of wild panthers were following them.
The girls were completely, sweetly, oblivious to their
surroundings. No one was thinking about Mahon,
who had been decapitated on the path they were
following. No one cared that Shannon had very
likely been followed out of the same forest. All that
mattered to them were the human boys they were
going to meet.

As Fia followed Kaleigh and her friends, she
caught snippets of their conversation and thoughts,
mixed with mental images. With the mental wall

raised to protect herself, Fia was unable to clearly read the girls' thoughts. Unfortunately, at least in Fia's case, the *wall* worked in both directions.

"So he called you?"

"Told you he was sorry he was an ass?"

You think he's really willing to wait to fuck you, or is that just another line he's feeding you?

"We're just going to talk. That's why I want you guys to come. To back me up."

Why the middle of the night? Why here?

"Our parents will kill us, they find out we're out here with that nut job wandering around hacking people's heads off."

My dad forbade me to see John again. Said he'd lock me in my room for the next century if he caught me sneaking out again.

The words and thoughts were jumbled. The girls and their feelings seemed so innocent. Their world so full of possibilities which they would all too soon realize were just dreams. Not realities. All too soon, they would realize the width and breadth of the *mallachd*. Cursed. Cursed for all of eternity.

"Now you guys have to stay here. He said come alone. He said I had to come by myself," Kaleigh whispered.

The girls had halted on the deer path, not far from where Fia, Shannon, Sorcha, and Eva had found the teens that night at the campfire.

Fia halted, remaining off the path, standing behind a stunted wild pecan tree. She could smell burning wood in the cool night air.

So Derek had a cozy little campfire going. How romantic. Maybe Fia was wrong. Maybe this really was just a teenage midnight rendezvous.

Then she smelled the faintest scent of gasoline and she tensed, at once.

Who started campfires with gasoline on a game preserve? Only idiots, or someone who intended to burn something more than firewood.

Chapter 23

It was easier to get out of the house, past Arlan, than Glen had expected it would be. A window over the washing machine in the laundry room off the kitchen, a sprint across the backyard, then over a picket fence and he was on the street that ran behind the B and B. He went up two blocks, cut across a lawn and walked in the direction Fia had gone.

The street, the whole town, was eerily quiet. There were no characteristic sights or sounds associated with a small town in the middle of the night. No dogs barked. No cats prowled, knocking lids off garbage cans. No heat pumps hummed. Not a car to be seen.

There was no sign of life except the glow of dim interior light he spotted behind the drawn blinds of the town's little rinky-dink museum, now closed for the season. And that was probably a light left on for security purposes. He hadn't visited the museum, but he guessed it was important to the townspeople that they protect the broken pieces of china and chipped arrowheads Fia told him were contained in glass cases in the building.

Other than the glow from the museum, not a

single window in the town shone with light. Not a single person was apparently in a bathroom, or watching late night TV. Even for this weird town, it was weird.

He kept walking. Hands in his pockets. Sidearm in the holster he wore under his jacket.

Glen didn't know where Fia had gone, only what direction, but he followed his instinct. Gave in to his gut.

As he walked, he thought about his father. Wondered if it was a night like this, if it had been *his* gut that had driven him to that street corner the night he was shot down.

Glen wondered if he was making a mistake.

But something was pulling him. Someone needed him. His gut told him it was Fia. Or it was going to be.

Later, when Fia would recall the chain of events that followed, she would remember them in painstaking detail, played out in slow motion. She would remember the odor of the gasoline fumes, the crunch of the leaves, and Kaleigh's muted cries. She would remember the overwhelming flood of guilt that washed over her, even as she flew through the forest, branches scraping her face, tearing at her hair.

But time seemed to speed up, almost to pass her, as the events actually unfolded.

Fia watched as Kaleigh left the path and her two friends behind. She saw the gangly young man in the hooded sweatshirt waiting beside the fire. Kaleigh threw herself into Derek's arms, making apologies. Declarations of love. He wrapped her in his embrace and their mouths met, the two of them seeming to Fia to be all elbows and angles and inexperienced at lovemaking.

It wasn't until the other two boys rushed out of the darkness and into the circle of firelight that Fia or Kaleigh realized something was wrong. It was a minute too late for both of them.

The hooded members of the high council stood around the ancient table, their daggers poised.

"These are unusual circumstances," Gair intoned gravely. "Not normal procedure. I am hesitant to call for an *aonta*."

"We can't wait," a young male, his face hidden by the hood of his robe, insisted.

"But Fia is not here. She should be included in such a—"

"She knew the general council was meeting tonight," he interrupted. "She knows a high council meeting can be called at any time, as part of the general council's decision. Once again, she's straying. Once again, she's not among us where she should be."

"You should call for a vote," an older woman argued softly. "He's right. She had her chance. Too many chances, if you ask me."

Gair studied the hooded figures around him. His lifetime task was to protect those around this table and those who slept in this town. He knew he could not show favoritism to any, not even to his dear granddaughter, who had always held a special place in his heart. It was also his responsibility to do what those who depended on him wanted him to do.

"Old man! Why do you hesitate?" the young man

demanded. "Call for the *aonta*. If it is not meant to be, the daggers will not fall."

"If it's not meant to be," chanted another. "It will not be."

"We must strike before it's too late. You heard our report. He knows more than he lets on. It's not safe!"

"Not safe," others echoed. "Not safe."

Their fear was sharp in their voices.

"An *aonta*!"

"An *aonta*," the council members demanded.

Gair lowered his head. Perhaps he was again getting too old to serve the sept as their chieftain. Too many years. Too much sadness. It was making him weak. "The *aonta*," he said softly.

The ten council members present lifted their daggers, and the ship's bell in the far corner of the room clanged angrily, seemingly of its own free will. At that moment, Gair knew he had made a mistake. He knew that he had allowed his people's fears to prevail in a room where logic and fairness had always come first. In calling for this *aonta*, he had set aside the sept's objective, which was to protect innocent humans.

But it was too late. He could not stop the daggers from falling. And at once, in unison, they all struck the scarred wooden table, tip down. Gair knew the count before he even gazed downward.

Unanimous. The human would have to die.

It happened sometimes. Not often, but sometimes it was the only way to protect the sept. In the end, they knew God would tally the hash marks on both sides, but for now, for tonight, it was so voted. It would be done.

"Now, when he has gone alone into the woods,"

Regan cried, throwing back his hood, yanking the knife from the tabletop. He bared his canines. "Friends, come! We strike now!"

"Stop! FBI!" Fia cried out, lunging forward. At the same instant, Kaleigh realized she was in danger, and that Derek and his friends were not what they appeared to be.

Maria and Katy screamed as the boys grabbed Kaleigh by her shoulders and dragged her backwards, pulling her to the ground.

"Run!" Fia shouted to Kaleigh's friends as she sprinted through the underbrush toward the clearing.

Fia couldn't have been more than two hundred feet from Kaleigh and the boys, but as she ran toward them, the distance stretched into two miles. Fia slid her Glock from its holster.

"Derek! What are you doing?" Kaleigh cried, her voice high-pitched and filled with terror.

As Fia ran past the other two girls, frozen on the path, she gave them a shove. "Run!" she insisted. "Don't stand there. Run!"

"But Kaleigh!" Katy protested as Fia shot into the darkness.

"I'll get her!" Fia called over her shoulder. As she turned back, she saw Derek raise a long, slender stick and throw the full force of his body into it as he lunged forward.

To Fia's disbelief, to her horror, the young man sank the stick into Kaleigh's abdomen, impaling her on the ground. The young girl's shriek rose up and rippled through the trees like the cry of a wounded animal.

"No! Stop!" Fia screamed, bursting into the clearing, her arms extended, her weapon drawn.

Derek turned to her, his fingers still wrapped around the stick. A pool cue. *It was a pool cue.*

"Back off, or I'll do it. I swear I will." He released his hold on the pool cue and drew an object from behind his back. The light of the fire reflected off the thin blade of the metal.

A sword? He had a damned sword?

"I'll cut her head off. I swear to God, I will," Derek threatened. "Put the gun down or I'll do it. You know I will."

Derek's two companions had released Kaleigh when Fia burst in on them; they were now standing, arms splayed, eyes round and blind with fear.

"Put the gun down," Derek repeated, drawing the sword over his head.

"Fee!" Kaleigh cried weakly. "Fee, please. Help me."

To give up her gun would put Fia at a serious disadvantage, but she knew in a split second that she had no other choice.

"Put it down," Derek repeated. "Guys. Get the gun. We might need it."

Fia separated her hands, showing him the pistol. "I'm putting it down." But instead of dropping it, she clicked on the safety and hurled it into the forest.

"What the hell! You crazy bitch. I told you I wanted that gun," Derek shouted, spittle flying.

Fia moved slowly toward them, her arms still outstretched. "You told me to put it down. I put it down. You don't think I'm handing you my sidearm so you can shoot me with it, do you? Then I really would be a crazy bitch."

"Shut up! Stop talking!" Derek ordered. "You *are* crazy. You're all crazy monsters." He still held the sword over his head, poised over Kaleigh.

Now that she was closer, Fia could make out the intricate details of the sword. It was some kind of decorative piece. *Sweet Mary, Mother of God, it was one of those damned Franklin Mint reproduction abominations.* But it was sharp. Someone had sharpened it. She could see that, even at a distance of twenty feet.

"Now you need to put that down," Fia said quietly. "And you need to step away, Derek. So far, nothing has happened here that can't be fixed. So far, you can get yourself out of this."

"Yeah, right. Like you wouldn't come after me in the middle of the night and suck my blood dry. Or . . . or send one of the other freaks from that freaky town of yours?"

"Derek? What are you talking about?" Fia slowly lowered her hands to her sides.

"Fia . . ." Kaleigh whimpered.

Fia made a split-second decision. If she could get the sword from Derek, she could take on all three of the boys without risking Kaleigh's life—

Fia leaped. At the same instant, Derek turned. Fia didn't know if he meant to stab her or if he just turned in startled reaction. The damned tip caught her in the shoulder and ripped her sweatshirt; pain blossomed as she tucked, fell, and rolled out of his reach.

Kaleigh screamed again.

As Fia spun in the leaves, trying to find the best position to gain her footing again, she heard the pounding of footsteps as Derek's friends took off.

"Hey, guys! Come on!" Derek shouted. "Mike.

John. Come back here. We're gonna finish them off. All of them!"

"Run, boys! Run while you can," Fia called, unable to stop herself.

"Shut up. Shut up, you hear me?" Derek turned back to Fia, brandishing the sword.

Out of the corner of her eyes, Fia could see Kaleigh struggling to pull the pool cue out of her own chest, but she was too weak. The tip was imbedded too far into the ground beneath her.

"Kaleigh, lie still," Fia called. "You'll just make the bleeding worse."

"You better shut up and start worrying about your own blood," Derek snarled, taking another step closer.

Fia pressed her hand to the wound in her shoulder. She was bleeding pretty badly. Her sweatshirt was soaked. She was dizzy. Slightly disoriented. *Think. Think*, she told herself.

Where were her supernatural powers now? This was ridiculous, to have allowed herself to be overpowered by a snotty-nosed teenage human with a toy sword.

"Derek . . . Derek listen to me," Fia started. *Negotiation. The FBI was all about the power of negotiation.* "We need to talk about this. About what's going on here."

"Nothing to talk about. I've been waiting my whole life to do this. To get you back."

"Get me back? Get me back for what? Derek, you don't know me."

"Not just you. All of them. All of them, for what they did to my mother!" He held the sword in one hand and wiped at his eyes with the other.

Getting him to talk . . . it was working. "What

about your mother? What did I . . . what did we do to your mother? Derek . . . your mother committed suicide."

"That's what they said, but it was a lie! They all lied!" Tears ran down his cheeks, but he placed his other hand on the sword again.

As Fia spoke, she shifted her hands behind her, trying to figure out how she could get to her feet, but stay out of his way. If she could get to Kaleigh, if she could get the pool cue, she could defend herself and Kaleigh.

"What wasn't true, Derek? She didn't commit suicide?"

"No. She didn't, I knew she didn't. My father. The police. They all said she slit her own throat, but it wasn't true. It was one of you. It was a vampire that killed her." His voice wavered. "They attacked her and they drained her blood. They just made it look like a suicide. I always knew it was vampires."

Fia looked quickly at Kaleigh, but the girl's eyes were closed. She was drifting out of consciousness.

"Kaleigh. Kaleigh, stay awake, hon," Fia called.

Kaleigh's body jerked. She opened her eyes.

Fia looked back at Derek. "Derek. Derek, listen to what you're saying. There's no such thing as vampires."

"Liar! I know it's true. I always knew it was a were-wolf or a zombie or a vampire that got her. Then I meet Kaleigh and she tells me there's a whole nest of 'em living one town over. Then I knew it was a vampire who killed her. I knew my mother wouldn't have killed herself. I knew she would never have left me like that. Let me find her that way."

Kaleigh whimpered.

Fia realized there was no sense asking the girl what she had said. Or asking Derek exactly what she had told him. It didn't matter. What mattered was that this young man was obviously mentally unstable. Meeting Kaleigh had sent him off the deep end.

What were the chances such a coincidence could have taken place? Kaleigh actually found the one young man in the state who believed in vampires and then admitted she was one. It would have been funny, had the circumstances not been so grave.

Fia shifted her gaze. Okay, so the kid believed in vampires. She could go in that direction. "Derek, think about it. It doesn't make sense. A vampire wouldn't kill your mother. He . . . he wouldn't waste the blood in a tub of bathwater," she said gently. "Vampires never waste human blood."

"Shut up!" Derek took another step closer and Fia had to lean back as he swung the sword in front of her nose, cutting the air with sharp swishes. "I know all about you. I read all about you on the Internet. You think I'm stupid, but I'm not. I'm smart. I read how to kill you. It's all on the Internet, you know. You just have to know where to find it."

"So . . . you killed the postmaster?"

A strange smile lifted the corners of the young man's mouth. "He was so easy, the fat bastard. Never saw it coming. That cop, he was a little harder. He fought, but the three of us took him down. You should have seen the look on his face when I pulled out Excalibur Three." He demonstrated by cutting the air with the sword tip again.

Fia drew her head back. *Nuts. He was fucking nuts.*

"We waited for the blond slut," Derek went on.

"Waited in her apartment. Ate her chips while we were waiting."

"And . . . and you chose people . . . randomly?"

The young man shrugged, pushing his hood back off his head. He was sweating profusely. His hands were shaking. He was scared. Getting more scared by the minute. Becoming less predictable. "The first one, yeah. The cop, he was snoopin' around in the woods. Found where we killed some rabbits. Gave up their souls to the Horned One."

Fia blinked, trying to absorb what the kid was saying. Realizing he was certainly no kid, and nothing he said was going to make sense. "Derek—"

"Don't say my name! Don't you dare speak my name!"

Derek took a swipe at Fia's head. She rolled, face down, grunting as he sank the toe of his boot into her side. Her body jerked involuntarily as hot, blunt pain shot through her body and she tried to continue to roll through the leaves, out of his reach.

But Derek caught the hem of Fia's sweatshirt with the heel of his boot and she looked up to see the young man, wild-eyed, lift the sword over his head.

Her neck was exposed. If his aim fell true, Fia's head would be severed from her body and she would die a vampire's death. She would be lost in everlasting purgatory. Dead but not dead. Living but not living.

Unforgiven.

Chapter 24

Glen heard the screams in the distance and drew his sidearm. It was so damned dark. Why didn't he think to bring a flashlight?

Because he hadn't expected Fia to be going into the woods alone. He hadn't thought she'd be this stupid.

Someone crashed through the underbrush toward him.

"FBI," he called out, halting as he lifted his weapon. "Stop where you are!"

"Don't shoot us!" a young woman cried as the branches of a bush parted.

Two shaking teenage girls peered through the tree at him, hands up, their faces white and stained with tears. "They have them. Derek and the guys. They have Kaleigh," the dark-haired one sobbed. "And Fia."

Glen's heart had been pounding in his chest. Now it seemed as if it were burstnig through his sides. *Fia was in danger.* Glen eased past them. "How many?"

"Three. Derek, Mike, and John. They hurt Kaleigh. We heard her scream," she managed through another wave of tears.

The boys Fia had interviewed this afternoon.

He tensed his jaw. Damn it! Why the hell hadn't she trusted him enough to tell him something was going on? Why would she have come into the woods to meet them alone? What the hell was she thinking?

"I want you to get back to town. Can you do that, alone?" Glen asked, already moving in the direction of Fia's voice. He could hear her speaking, though he couldn't make out what she was saying. What was obvious was that she had a *situation*. He could hear the graveness in her voice, interspersed with the staccato shouts of a young man. "Go to the police station. Have them send police here. And call for an ambulance in case anyone is hurt. Can you do that, girls?"

He hated to send them alone through the woods, but he thought they would be safer running for town than waiting in the dark for him.

"The police. We'll get the police."

"Good. Run," he called over his shoulder.

Hearing the girls' footfalls, Glen turned his full attention to the sound of Fia's voice. As he approached in the dark, he caught bits and pieces of the conversation. He only heard Fia and the one male voice. Derek, he guessed. The teenage boy sounded frenzied. Unstable.

Glen was nearly blind in the darkness. He followed the voices, staying on the path because it was easier than cutting through the underbrush, the way the girls had come. Finally, he spotted a flicker of firelight. There was a clearing with a campfire. He heard Fia call out from where she lay sprawled on the ground and saw the silhouette of a figure, illuminated by the glow of the fire, raise something over his head.

Holy hell. *He had a sword.*

Images of the decapitated victims in the town flashed through Glen's head like stills from a slide projector. But in his mind they were in living color, heavy with horror and the scent of freshly spilled blood.

"Stop. FBI!" Glen barked.

The young man heard him. Glen knew he heard him, but Derek didn't turn. Derek raised the sword high as if preparing to strike. Fia yelped. Rolled.

"Halt or I'll shoot," Glen warned, breaking into a run. "FBI."

It all happened so quickly that it would be days later before Glen and Fia were able to figure out exactly what happened. She rolled to get out of Derek's way and sprang up with inhuman strength. Derek missed, raised the sword again. Swung again, this time dead on, and hit Fia with the sword. Fia fell. Tumbled silent into a heap in the crackling leaves.

Glen called out in warning once more. It was the first time in eighteen years on the job that he had to make the decision whether to pull the trigger or not.

The young man ignored his warning and raised the sword again over Fia.

It was easier than Glen thought it would be to squeeze the trigger. He wondered, in that split second before Derek went down, if his father hadn't hesitated on that street corner, would he still be alive today?

Derek fell forward under the impact, his arms flying out in front of his body, the sword falling from his hands. He went down over Fia's body and Glen ran toward them, prepared to fire again if the teenager moved.

The gunfire echoed in Kaleigh's head and she felt her body convulse. Was she dying?

She smelled her own fresh blood, sweet and pungent, and the aroma teased her into awareness. The pool cue was still there, securing her bleeding body to the ground, but the excruciating pain had eased. Kaleigh could smell the grass. The wood burning in the campfire. She felt surrounded by the presence of the sept. Men and women who were individuals and yet moved as one.

Was this what it was for a vampire to die?

But Kaleigh knew she couldn't be dying. She could feel the life pulsing inside her. Her body, on a cellular level, was already rejuvenating.

She raised one hand slowly to touch the place in the side of her abdomen where Derek had impaled her to the ground. Tears filled her eyes and she gulped. How could she have been so stupid? So blind? How could she have risked the lives of those she loved in this town for a boy like Derek?

"Someone out there?" Kaleigh whispered, choking on her tears. All she wanted was to go home. To be home with her parents. With the sept. With those who had loved her all these centuries.

Where were they? She could still feel their presence.

Her eyes were open, but she saw no sept members. All she could see when she turned her head was Agent Duncan rolling Derek's body over onto his back and checking for a pulse.

Derek was dead. She knew he was dead. She could feel death's cold, spiny fingers in the air. She could smell Derek's blood, spilled into the leaves on the ground.

Get him.

Take him now.

The thoughts of sept members surrounding them in the woods hit Kaleigh hard. They really were here. *Sweet Mary, what was happening?* She wanted to call out. But the human was right there.

She could feel the sept members closing in. Eight or nine of them, creeping through the darkness.

Kaleigh squeezed her eyes shut hard and tried to listen, the way Maria and Katy said it was done. For weeks, Kaleigh had been catching pieces of other sept members' thoughts, but she'd been fighting it. She wasn't ready. Didn't want the gift that had somehow seemed more of a curse to her. At least until this moment.

But she was getting nothing! Just jumbles of words and thoughts and the overwhelming feeling that something terrible, even more terrible than this, was about to happen. . . .

Kill him. Kill the human FBI agent.

That thought came through so clearly that Kaleigh's eyes flew open. "No!" she shouted.

"It's okay, Kaleigh, I'm coming," the agent called from across the clearing. "Just try to stay still. Stay calm."

No, Kaleigh thought. *They can't kill him. I can't let them.* "Fia!" she cried out. Fia would stop the black-cloaked sept members approaching in the darkness, their daggers gleaming.

"Kaleigh," the human called to her. "Fia's not dead. She's hurt, but I think she's going to be okay.

She's breathing normally. Starting to come around.
I'm coming. Just hang on!"

Kill him. Kill him now.

He knows too much. He will be the death of us all.

The voices were suddenly so loud in Kaleigh's
head that there was no denying them. Misinterpret-
ing them. *Stop,* she warned them telepathically. *Stop
now. He saved us. He saved our lives, mine and Fia's. It
was Derek. Derek killed them. You can't harm the human.*

Kaleigh? A voice probed in her head. *It's Mary.
Are you all right?*

Now. We must strike now, one of the men in the
forest insisted.

Stop them, Mary, Kaleigh telepathed. *Stop them.
Special Agent Duncan saved our lives. He doesn't know
about us. Don't let them do this.*

Stop.

Stop.

More voices echoed in Kaleigh's head. It was the
oddest sensation. Not only could she hear the sept
members' words in her head, but lying on the cold
ground, she could *feel* their words.

Everyone was listening to her. They knew her
voice in their heads. There was only one dissenter.

No. He must die. It's the only way to protect the sept.

It was Fia's brother Regan.

Kaleigh remembered now why she had never
liked him in previous lives. She remembered that
she could never quite trust him.

*I said STOP NOW. Stop now, Regan Kahill, or you'll
stand before the council and defend your actions!*

"Kaleigh." Special Agent Duncan sprinted toward
her. He fell to his knees, looking down on her,
brushing her hair from her forehead. He looked
scared. He thought she was going to die.

She almost laughed. "It's okay," she whispered. "It's not as bad as it looks."

Around her, Kaleigh could feel the sept members backing up. Someone was arguing with Regan, putting strong hands on him. Leading him away. The others were quietly withdrawing . . . disappearing into the darkness.

"There's help coming," the FBI agent assured her, taking her hand in his. "Just hang in there."

"Kaleigh? Kaleigh, are you all right?" Fia stumbled toward the girl still sprawled on the ground. Still impaled. Fia was dizzy. Disoriented. Her head hurt like hell.

Glen was on his knees leaning over Kaleigh, talking softly to her, holding her hand. He looked up when he heard Fia.

"You okay?" His voice cracked with emotion. He was scared for her, for Kaleigh, God bless him.

Fia could tell that he wanted to go to her, that he felt torn between Fia and the teenage girl.

"I'm okay." Fia rested her hand on his shoulder and eased to the ground on her knees, peering into Kaleigh's eyes.

"I was afraid you were . . ." Kaleigh said.

"No," Fia assured her. "Derek didn't know what he was doing. How to wield a sword."

"But I saw—"

"He clopped me a good one. But with the flat of the sword, not the blade. He turned his wrist," Fia said.

Just as Fia had been returning to consciousness, she had heard Kaleigh's silent shouts of warning. She hadn't understood exactly what had happened or how they had gotten to this point, but members of the high council had been prepared to kill Glen.

They had been there in the woods. She had felt them. Heard them.

You saved him, Kaleigh, Fia telepathed, fighting tears that threatened to spill and totally embarrass her. *Thank you. Thank you.*

Kaleigh smiled up at Fia, her eyelids growing heavy. *You're welcome,* she shot back.

Flooded with relief, still scared, her head pounding, her mind reeling with everything that had just happened, Fia lowered her aching forehead to Glen's shoulder. "I'm sorry," she whispered. "Thank you for coming. Thank you for knowing I needed you."

The following week, back in Philly, Glen wanted to take Fia out to celebrate solving the Clare Point murders, but she had more than dinner on her mind. She met Glen at her apartment door in one of her leather miniskirts, a T-shirt, and tights. With a little makeup, the bruise on her temple and cheekbone from Derek's sword was barely more than a shadow. Glen grabbed her, pulled her to him, and kissed her hard.

Fia tilted her head back, baring her throat to him. His touch. His kiss was enough. She didn't need his blood.

"Dinner's almost ready. You going to come in or are we just going to make out here in the hallway?" she asked.

"I brought stout." He produced one of the dark, quart-sized bottles used at the Hill to bottle their beer.

"You brought stout from Clare Point?" She laughed, taking the bottle from him.

He followed her to the kitchen. "I know you don't

drink wine and this is supposed to be a celebration. What are you making? Smells good." He stood in the kitchen doorway, inhaling the spicy aroma.

"One of the few things I *can* make. Fettuccine with clam sauce." She opened the refrigerator and tossed him a head of lettuce. "Salad detail. Knives there on the counter. You can use that cutting board." She grabbed a wooden spoon to stir her marinara clam sauce. "So any word from the boys' lawyers?"

Fia had left the office early that day for an appointment with Dr. Kettleman. Joseph really had left town, and Fia and the psychiatrist had a good session, talking about moving on. Talking about handling a relationship with a human.

"The boys are offering statements out the ying-yang. Apparently, once they came off their high, once their lawyer talked some sense into them, they recanted the whole vampire story." He tore off leaves of Bibb lettuce and rinsed them in the sink. "They're saying that Derek was the ringleader and they never actually killed anyone. Of course, we know now that he's had a history of mental illness since his mother's suicide when he was a kid. Apparently, Derek made his friends participate in the murders in Clare Point. Threatened the boys, their families. Having Derek dead is convenient, of course. They can say anything they want. Not sure we can prove any differently."

"Any explanation as to why Derek cut off the body parts or what he did with them?"

"Boys say they don't know. One thought he might have wanted them to use for some kind of demonic sacrifices, but he says Derek never really said. He thinks the kid buried them in the woods somewhere."

Fia hated the thought that parts of Bobby, Mahon, and Shannon would never be reunited with their bodies, but at least they were buried.

She tasted the sauce, touching the wooden spoon to the tip of her tongue.

By the morning after Derek's death, the boys already had a top-notch lawyer out of Baltimore willing to represent them, pro bono, of course. Jeremy Procino, Mary Hill's son, was making a name for himself in the newpapers already. He would see that the two young men's rights were the focus of the case, and not the little town of Clare Point. The Kahill sept was safe for now.

"You have something else for this salad besides lettuce?" Glen struck her lightly on the buttocks. "Mmmm, nice."

Fia laughed. Allowed him to push her up against the counter, and they kissed hungrily.

"Hey, I don't know if I like these heels you're wearing," he teased. "I think you're taller than I am."

"So?" She nipped him lightly on his chin. "That a problem for you, Special Agent Duncan?"

He reached around her and cut off the flame under her sauce. "Not a problem for me, Special Agent Kahill. That a problem for you?" He drew his hand up her thigh and under her skirt.

Fia let her eyes drift shut, and when she closed them, it was only Glen she saw. Ian was gone.

Fia didn't know how long this thing with Glen was going to last. If it could last. But today in Dr. Kettleman's office she had decided she wanted it enough to try to make it work. She wasn't sure if it was possible for a human and an immortal to love one another, but she realized over the last few days that she wanted to know the answer to that question.

Glen slid her skirt upward with both hands. "You want to retire to the bedroom?" he whispered in her ear. "Or are you a counter kind of girl?" He slapped the top of the kitchen counter.

"I don't know." She met his mouth hungrily. "I'm thinking I might be both . . ."

A week and a half after the death of Derek Neuman, Fia returned to Clare Point in the dead of night. In the rear of the little museum on the quiet street, she stripped naked and pulled the black cloak over her head. Her dagger in her hand, she followed the others silently into the velvet darkness of the room. To the scarred table that had become a representation of their lives' mission.

Above the table, the candles in the black oak chandelier sparked and hissed and the room, at once, glowed.

"*Caraidean,*" Gair intoned.

In the days following, the general council would meet to discuss what had transpired over the last few months in Clare Point. Where the mistakes had been made and how they could be corrected. But tonight . . . tonight this was not about the sept. It was not even about their survival. It was about the world, about God's humans.

The Kahill sept had vowed to make the world a safer place for the humans and tonight another name would be brought to the table. A pedophile's case would be discussed. A vote would be taken.

Fia flexed her fingers, tightening them around the hilt of the dagger she held in her hand. At times, she wondered if she was worthy of this monumental task. She wondered if she could live up to the expectations of her sept. Of mankind. Of God.

But tonight . . . tonight of all nights, with the taste of Glen still on her lips, she knew this was where she belonged and she knew what she must do.

"*A name,*" she whispered. "*Present a name.*"

"*A name,*" the others chanted.

Fia looked up to see the cloaked figures, their canines bared, and she knew that she was one of them. She knew that for all her shortcomings, she was loved.

She smiled to herself. Was there anything more a vampire could wish for?

The Kahill vampire clan has lived among humans for hundreds of years in Delaware's peaceful village of Clare Point. In Undying, *V.K. Forrest introduces readers to Arlan, a fierce member of the clan who must fight his desire for a love most forbidden . . .*

UNDYING

As part of the Kahill clan's special operations "kill team," Arlan is devoted to ridding the world of its most depraved human members. He's been asked by fellow clan member and FBI Agent Fia Kahill to assist in one of her investigations: the notorious Buried Alive Killer case. Arlan agrees to meet with one of Fia's key informants, Macy Smith, but he's completely unprepared for his response to the young woman. Blond, petite, and achingly beautiful, Macy is everything Arlan could want in a woman—and it's clear the attraction is mutual. Although Arlan once vowed he would never again let himself fall in love with a human being, he surrenders to his overpowering desire for Macy . . .

Soon, Arlan and Macy keep mysteriously crossing one another's paths, even in Clare Point. In Macy, Arlan can sense a loneliness that reminds him of his own and a vulnerability that tugs at his soul. But Macy is a drifter with a past far darker than even Arlan can imagine. And when the Buried Alive Killer strikes again, he learns that Macy has a deep connection to the case—one that will put her in the crosshairs of the killer if Arlan can't find a way to protect her . . .

Please turn the page for an exciting sneak peek of
UNDYING,
now on sale at bookstores everywhere!

Chapter 1

He stood beneath the lengthening shadows of the Acropolis, high on the hilltop over the city of Athens, and watched as the last rays of sunlight faded. With the coming of darkness, he could feel the evil of the night slither in on its belly, much like the quarry he sought tonight.

Arlan walked quickly through the Agora, keeping his head down, leaving behind the noisy tourists boarding their tour buses.

Two weeks ago, thousands of miles away in the little U.S. town of Clare Point, the vote had gone against a human by the name of Robert Romano. With the plunging of twelve daggers into an ancient oak table, the man's fate had been sealed. For more than a decade, the pedophile, a monster who dealt in the underground sale of child sex slaves, had been pursued across several continents by law enforcement. Robert Romano, known by multiple aliases, had recently made the FBI's most wanted list after the abduction of a five-year-old from a grocery store in the suburbs of Detroit. At the present time, the FBI did not know his whereabouts. Romano was careful, and he was clever.

Not clever enough.

In twenty minutes, forty-six-year-old Romano would be waiting at a designated spot on the southern end of the Agora, a spot that came to life after dark, both with ghosts of the past and the haunts of the present. The human would be there to accept a cash payment for the delivery of two male children, ages six and nine, who were currently being held in an apartment two blocks away. Delivery of the children was to be made once Romano received his cash in small currency euros. The unfortunate buyer would not receive his merchandise because Arlan would be waiting. A clean-up crew would rescue the children and see that the buyer was arrested by local police. Romano would no longer be the authorities' concern.

Now almost dark, the warm evening air had grown thick with the sounds and scents of the ancient city. It was funny how cities all smelled the same, sounded the same, when Arlan closed his eyes. This could have been any street in any city in the world in the last thousand years.

He inhaled deeply, lifting his chin, flaring his nostrils. Someone was roasting meat in one of the nearby restaurants that catered to the tourists . . . lamb. Elsewhere, sewage overflowed. He caught the hint of a woman's cheap perfume on the air, although he walked alone in the twilight. Embedded in the night air was also the sour scent of human body odor. The fetid bouquet of fleas feasting on rodents.

In the distance, beyond the ruins, Arlan heard doors opening and closing. Footsteps, both heavy and light, echoed through the gathering fog. Over time, the sputter of car and motorbike engines had replaced the rhythm of wooden cart and carriage wheels, but in his mind, they were still somehow the same.

These were the sounds and smells of humanity. For better. For worse. Despite the ugliness of much of it, Arlan longed to be a part of this world. He was jealous of the man roasting lamb for gyros on the street corner, the woman slamming the window to muffle the harsh words she flung at her cheating lover. Arlan would never know the mundane life of a mortal.

At the sound of shrill laughter, he tensed. Despite the cover of darkness, standing here in human form, he was vulnerable. He gazed intently in the direction of the noisier, busier Plaka, blocks away, where tourists flooded the streets eager to sample the moussaka and ouzo. Eager to buy their trinkets to mark their journey, they had no idea of the evil that lurked in the shadows or the salvation about to descend on two helpless children.

Arlan's partner was late. He checked his cell phone, noting the time. No call and Regan was twenty minutes late.

Arlan worked his jaw in indecision.

The plan had been for Regan, pretending to be the "customer," to meet Romano at the Areopagus. Arlan would serve as the lookout. Regan was to lure Romano into a secluded area amid the ruins and there, the execution would be carried out as ordered by the High Council. Arlan and Regan would carry it out together. Two daggers. Two were required by primordial sept law.

But Regan wasn't here and time was running out. If Romano slipped out of their hands, there was no way to say when the planets and moons would align again. There was no way to know when the opportunity to catch him would offer itself again, or how many more children would lose their innocence in the intervening time.

The coarse laughter of the woman grew louder, closer. Arlan heard a second woman's voice. They were speaking Greek. Both were drunk, or high, or both. He caught a flash of short skirt and long bare legs. Prostitutes. After dark, when the museums closed and tour groups were led to the safe streets of the Plaka, the Athens underworld came to life here. From the shadowy Areopagus situated beneath the lights of the Acropolis, one could see the whole city. In this place, one could buy drugs, sex . . . and even children.

Arlan made the decision. There was no time to call the council. No time to await further instructions. The sept had been watching this bastard for eighteen months. They couldn't afford to let him go. The Kahill sept's duty to God would not allow it.

One moment Arlan was a thirty-something guy in jeans and a black leather jacket and the next he transformed into a hundred-pound canine with a mangy spotted coat and yellow eyes. The physical morph came easily to him, like slipping on a worn leather glove.

The moment the morph was complete, Arlan felt the change in his psyche. Judgment grew hazier. In this animal body, he lived for the moment. Surrounded by the scent of dangers, he had to force his man-brain to remain in control of the beast. He could feel that control stretched taut, thin and tight as a wire.

Arlan slinked behind a rock and darted across

the footpath, behind the women, his tail brushing a skirt. One of the prostitutes cursed him, first in Greek, then Italian, but they continued walking. Hundreds of packs of wild dogs roamed the streets of Athens. The locals gave them no notice. Arlan knew he could blend in with the others.

Knowing he had a few minutes before Romano would appear, Arlan had time to assess the area and determine how he could fulfill the mission alone. He wondered if it would be safer to appear as a man or as he was now, a four-footed predator. He trotted lightly up a slight, rocky incline, skirting the silvery light cast from the Acropolis, blending into the shadows of the olive trees.

It was fully dark now and while Arlan was not a superstitious man, mentally, he crossed himself. At night, in ancient places like these, the haunts came out. A man or beast could do his best to ignore them, but there was no denying their presence. The coarse yellow hair along his spine bristled and he caught a whiff of something that was not living, but not quite dead. Out of the corner of one rheumy eye he saw a misty human form floating just above the pathway.

Some said ghosts held no real presence, that they were only impressions left from the past. Arlan didn't know what they were; he only knew that he did not like this feeling of being watched. He had experienced similar encounters in several places in recent months; the Coliseum in Rome, Stonehenge in England, and the blood-soaked battlefield of Culloden in the Highlands of Scotland.

Bypassing the wispy spook, Arlan kept his head down, letting his long tongue loll. His yellow eyes took in his surroundings. With his long muzzle and enhanced sense of smell, he observed as only God's four-footed creatures could observe.

Stones pinched the pads of his feet as he followed a path tread heavily by tourists in the daytime. The Agora had once been a marketplace, a public area that served as an integral part of the ancient Greek city-state. It had not only offered a place to trade, but it also served as a forum to its citizens. Here, men once gathered to buy and sell commodities and also to discuss business, politics, and current events. Here was where Greek democracy first came to light, setting an example to other great cities in the ancient world.

At the far end, the rocky hill overlooking the Agora was where Arlan would meet Romano. The area of the Agora known as the Areopagus had been the sacred meeting place of the Greek prime council, which had once combined judicial and legislative functions in the sixth and fifth centuries BC. Much later, the apostle Paul was said to have stood on the same rocky hill and preached to early Christians.

A holy place. A haunted place.

Arlan caught the scent of another dog on the night air and thrust out his muzzle. He twitched his black nose. Two dogs, three. More. A pack.

The muscles in Arlan's rear haunches tightened as the dogs approached. Arlan could become any of God's creatures, although he was better at some manifestations than others, and some were much more difficult to keep in check. Despite his experience, there was always a moment of panic when he encountered a creature of the species he'd manifested into. There was the chance they would know

him for the charlatan that he was and attack him.
It would be impossible for them to kill him because he had to be beheaded to die, but dog bites
could lay a man up for weeks.

A whine and then a growl halted him. Out of a
grove of stunted olive trees came three, four, five
dogs, all his size or larger. A big gray with the pelt of
a wolf led the pack of three females and a sullen
young male. Animals did not speak, but they communicated. Members of the Kahill clan had some
form of extrasensory perception; they could all, on
some level, communicate with each other without
speaking. Arlan's accompanying gift was the ability
to communicate with animals.

The dogs' thoughts floated around him. They
were simple. Primal.

Fear. Distrust. Hunger.

But there was also an inquisitiveness, particularly
from the young male who hung back, guarding
the rear.

The big gray parted from the pack, leaving the
others behind to wait for his command. If he so ordered it, they would all attack at once. Arlan would
not have the opportunity to morph back into a
man before he was seriously injured.

The gray approached.

Arlan's hackles rose. He froze, eyes downcast. His
breath came in short pants as he attempted to stifle the twinge of fear he felt deep in his canine bones.

One of the others, a black bitch with a torn ear,
whined. She seemed to be the first to understand
he meant them no harm. That he had no intention
of usurping the pack leader's authority or taking
his females.

The gray bared his teeth but made no sound.

He wondered what Arlan was doing there. He recognized the stranger as one of them . . . and yet not one of them.

Arlan communicated that the pack had nothing to fear from him. That he was merely a traveler. He attempted to seem casual although he wasn't quite sure how that translated in dog language.

The gray met Arlan muzzle to muzzle and sniffed. Arlan kept his gaze downcast. To look into the leader's eyes would be a direct challenge.

I mean no harm, Arlan communicated firmly. While he had to make it clear he had no intention of taking the gray's place, he could not cower. To cower would show weakness, and the way of God's creatures is to kill the weakest. A form of natural selection, he supposed. *I simply wish to pass.*

Our territory. Why are you here? What do you want? Barely enough food for us.

On a journey. A mission. Passing through. I do not take what is not mine.

The gray looked Arlan directly in the face. Arlan slowly lifted his gaze. The powerful male's nose twitched. He was still attempting to assess Arlan, but he seemed to sense that Arlan was no threat to his pack.

I only wish to pass, Arlan repeated, lifting his gaze slightly. He still wasn't making direct eye contact, but now he was studying the gray in the same way that the dog was studying him.

The alpha male continued to stare, reminding Arlan of a game he used to play with other boys in the sept during mass or at a particularly boring family dinner. A version of Chicken. They would stare at each other until someone broke the spell; the first to look away was the loser and would later be subjected to juvenile name-calling and a healthy dose of shoving.

Pass, but continue on your way, the gray warned. *I see you again and I'll rip your throat out. My bitches will eat your innards.*

Ouch. Arlan choked down the growl that rose in his throat and remained where he stood until the pack leader walked away. The other dogs slowly turned and loped after him.

Arlan exhaled heavily, his hot breath stinking in his nostrils. He could feel his heart pounding in his chest. He waited until he saw the last swish of tail disappear into the olive grove and then continued in the direction he had originally set out. His tongue lolled, testing the night air.

He only had time to circumnavigate the meeting place once before he had to get into place prior to Romano's arrival. As he peered over a rock, taking care with his footing, he silently cursed Regan. His partner had not been himself for the last year. This was not the first time he had not shown up at an appointed time and place on sept business. Arlan had been trying to cover for him longer than he knew he should because he was Fia's brother.

Thoughts of Fia made him smile. At least on the inside. He didn't think dogs could really smile.

Arlan loved Fia Kahill. He had been in love with her for at least a thousand years, but it was unrequited love. Or so she said. Right now she had a boyfriend. A *human* boyfriend. She told Arlan that although she and Arlan were occasionally lovers, she wasn't interested in a relationship with him. With any man in the sept. But Arlan was sure he was slowly working a chink in her iron resolve, had been for at least a century. Fia loved him. She just didn't know it yet.

So . . . to protect her, he protected her kid brother. As did Fia's other brother, Fin. As did other young men in the sept.

Arlan wondered now if he had been remiss in not calling Regan's shortcomings to the attention of the council. His irresponsible behavior was not only affecting him now, it was affecting others. It was affecting the sept's ability to do its job efficiently. They could not afford to have one of their own so far out of step.

Maybe it was time Arlan talked to the council, or at least Fia. It was time he stopped trying to talk to Regan. The warnings had obviously gone unheeded.

Arlan shifted his weight on his haunches and eyed the place where Romano would come for his money. It was a good spot for a man dealing in the human slave trade to make a transaction. The cover of darkness. No police around. Few people present and those who were would turn the other way if they saw anything suspicious. There would be no good citizens loitering in the shadows of the Areopagus, waiting to give their statement to the authorities.

Arlan smelled the human before he heard the footfalls. The stench of his evil flesh pierced the air even sharper than the intense, smoky aroma of his cigarette.

This was, indeed, an excellent place to commit a crime. But it was also a dangerous place for a man being hunted by a dog.

Or a vampire.

More by Bestselling Author
Fern Michaels

__About Face	0-8217-7020-9	$7.99US/$10.99CAN
__Wish List	0-8217-7363-1	$7.50US/$10.50CAN
__Picture Perfect	0-8217-7588-X	$7.99US/$10.99CAN
__Vegas Heat	0-8217-7668-1	$7.99US/$10.99CAN
__Finders Keepers	0-8217-7669-X	$7.99US/$10.99CAN
__Dear Emily	0-8217-7670-3	$7.99US/$10.99CAN
__Sara's Song	0-8217-7671-1	$7.99US/$10.99CAN
__Vegas Sunrise	0-8217-7672-X	$7.99US/$10.99CAN
__Yesterday	0-8217-7678-9	$7.99US/$10.99CAN
__Celebration	0-8217-7679-7	$7.99US/$10.99CAN
__Payback	0-8217-7876-5	$6.99US/$9.99CAN
__Vendetta	0-8217-7877-3	$6.99US/$9.99CAN
__The Jury	0-8217-7878-1	$6.99US/$9.99CAN
__Sweet Revenge	0-8217-7879-X	$6.99US/$9.99CAN
__Lethal Justice	0-8217-7880-3	$6.99US/$9.99CAN
__Free Fall	0-8217-7881-1	$6.99US/$9.99CAN
__Fool Me Once	0-8217-8071-9	$7.99US/$10.99CAN
__Vegas Rich	0-8217-8112-X	$7.99US/$10.99CAN
__Hide and Seek	1-4201-0184-6	$6.99US/$9.99CAN
__Hokus Pokus	1-4201-0185-4	$6.99US/$9.99CAN
__Fast Track	1-4201-0186-2	$6.99US/$9.99CAN
__Collateral Damage	1-4201-0187-0	$6.99US/$9.99CAN
__Final Justice	1-4201-0188-9	$6.99US/$9.99CAN

Available Wherever Books Are Sold!
Check out our website at **www.kensingtonbooks.com**

More by Bestselling Author

Lori Foster

Thrilling Suspense From
Wendy Corsi Staub